Mrs Alice Hamilton rose from her chair and stood in front of Randolph, her hands on his shoulders in a manner encouraging to his ardent nature. She was that day dressed in a blouse of white silk and a black satin skirt, her full round bubbies and her broad hips filling out her garments suggestively.

He reached underneath her long skirt, smiling at the touch of her stocking under his fingers. Above the knee lay the ribbon that served as a garter and when he slipped his hand higher yet, his fingers lighted on bare warm flesh.

'Oh!' he exclaimed, his mind reeling at this impossible discovery.

'Yes,' she said with a smile, 'your senses do not deceive you, Randolph — I am wearing no drawers!'

The Delights of Women

Anonymous

HEADLINE

Copyright © 1991 The Estate of A.McK.H.

First published in 1991
by HEADLINE BOOK PUBLISHING PLC

10 9 8 7 6 5 4 3 2 1

ISBN 0 7472 3688 7

Typeset by Medcalf Type Ltd, Bicester, Oxon

Printed and bound by
HarperCollins Manufacturing, Glasgow

HEADLINE BOOK PUBLISHING PLC
Headline House
79 Great Titchfield Street
London W1P 7FN

PUBLISHER'S NOTE

Although this novel was first published anonymously in the late 1870s, the initials A.McK.H. on the title page make it possible to identify its author as Alexander McKendrie Hamilton. He was a highly respected barrister of the Middle Temple, and a friend of Henry Spencer Ashbee, compiler of the best-known catalogue of Victorian erotica.

It is by means of Ashbee's lists that Hamilton was identified, several of his novels being therein mentioned. On the present work Ashbee's comment was:

'The substance of the story before us is of an idle young man's search for sensual pleasure, which leads him into licentious episodes among the highest and the lowest. It is needless to add that the foundation for these curious episodes lies in the author's own experience of every kind of debauchery.'

CHAPTER 1
A Young Gentleman About Town

Very little by way of apology will be required for putting into print the following narrative for the instruction, and perhaps also the edification, of the reading public. It concerns itself with the adventures of a young gentleman of birth and breeding and the recorder of these events is assured that every genuine student of human nature will derive much of interest therefrom.

The subject of these memoirs was one of the many handsome and well-to-do young men to be encountered about London in the year 1877. The Hon. Randolph Joynes, for so was he named and styled, was a tall and slender gentleman of twenty-five years, fair-haired and elegant of manner and of attire. In addition to all the usual advantages of birth, kindly Nature had endowed him with an unusual warmth of constitution that made him unable to resist the attractions of the female sex, in all their most seductive variety. Never a day did he allow to pass without partaking of the divine frenzy of the sensual spasm that unites the fleshly male and female parts in throbbing ecstasy.

One fine evening in May, soon after dinner, Randolph left the house in Cavendish Square where he resided with his parents, he being the youngest son of the Earl of Broadwater, and the only child remaining at home. The intention he had announced earlier of popping into his club for a game of billiards with friends, or a hand of cards, was false. Needless to say, he had no such mundane intention, for this was his almost nightly excuse to leave the house. He took a hansom cab to St James's and after he had paid off the driver, he turned his back on Boodles Club and sauntered towards Haymarket to choose a young whore.

Randolph was still in the unmarried state, from which it must necessarily follow that the women with whom he shared so freely his natural exuberance were well beneath his station and rank. It would have been unimaginable for any young gentlewoman to allow access to her physical charms to one to whom she was not joined in the bonds of lawful matrimony. The conventions demand that a well-bred female is brought up in the knowledge that she is to maintain her young pussy unfingered and unbroached, her hymen intact, her titties virginally unhandled.

By dint of this strict restraint placed on the warmer aspects of her nature, a carefully brought-up female is enabled, on her wedding night, to reap the reward of virtue. She lies fearful on her back, half-dreading and half-longing for what is to come next, with nightgown drawn up about her waist and her bare legs well parted. In this sacrificial attitude, she offers her *all*, as ladies are pleased to call it, to a panting new husband. He, well-experienced in rogering by his sorties to females who set a cash price on the use of their cunny, now forces his way into his bride's tight little pussy, the first man ever to tread her pathway to pleasure, and relieves her of her young maidenhead in a gush of the hot essence of manhood.

In Randolph's view, marriage set too high a value on

female flesh. In his short life to date, he had taken his pleasure in hundreds of pussies, and hoped to attain the impressive figure of 10,000 before his rogering days were ended. In few words, since he had no intention of terminating his pleasant bachelor mode of life by taking a wife, Randolph had recourse daily to maidservants and girls of the streets, whose useful commodities were on offer for a few shillings in most parts of London.

Respectable society frowns upon men who slake their lusts on the compliant bodies of harlots, strumpets, demireps, Cyprians, and other beauties of the night. To that Randolph paid no heed — his hot masculine nature was such that it required constant lascivious gratification, capricious perversions, secret sexual aberrations and shameful fancies. Why this should be so, he did not know, nor much care. He held to the view that men and women have a right to make full and regular use of their bodies in any manner they chose.

He dismissed out of hand all attempt to theorise why some men took a young wife and made faithful and legal use of her cunny night after night, except for when she had been made too big-bellied to accept him, and by way of contrast, why other men, himself pre-eminently, lusted after change and diversity. It made no odds — no experience in life could ever compare with the glorious sensation of a hard-thrusting shaft fetching off inside a wet and throbbing pussy, whether the same one all the time or a different one every time. Each to their own taste, as the old woman said when she kissed the cow, or as it is more elegantly put in the language of scholars, *de gustibus non est disputandum*.

Young and pretty females were wont to congregate in a number of well-known places about the West End, both

3

indoors and out. Most especially regarded as useful meeting points for lustful young men desiring the use of a cunny were the Argyll Rooms and Cremorne Gardens in Chelsea, and many a time had Randolph taken his way to either the one or the other. That notwithstanding, a fine evening seemed to require a stroll in the open air, and to that purpose the Haymarket, off Piccadilly, was a fine spot for the observation and selection of available doxies.

In his black tail-coat and white tie, a shiny top hat on his head at a rakish angle, and a silver-knobbed stick in his hand, Randolph was a fine sight. As he made his way uphill along Haymarket, past the theatre, towards Piccadilly, little groups of unescorted young women chatting together on the pavement separated. Each hopeful young trull displayed herself to best advantage in order to attract his attention. Randolph strolled on in good humour, smiling and touching the silver knob of his cane to his topper in salutation to the wenches he recognised − the many who had rented their pussies out to him in the past.

As he walked along, he twirled his opera stick dashingly, but with his left hand. His other hand was thrust nonchalantly into his trouser pocket, and through the thin material of the lining his fingertips caressed that part of his person he addressed by various names, in accordance with the whimsy of his mood.

At this moment he had in his mind bestowed on his up-rearing shaft the appellation of *Mr Percival Proud*, that being a useful description of the admirable firmness to which he had fingered it. A smile flitted across Randolph's face as he strummed on Mr Proud with a delicate touch, and was rewarded with tiny tremors of delight in return.

One girl who was bidding for his attention he remembered in particular as exceptionally talented − a tall thin girl in a green cloak and a straw bonnet. She had brought him off three or four times when he had her, though he was damned if he could remember her name. Here she came smiling towards him, and he smiled back pleasantly and nodded, half of a mind to take her and fill her slit with his spending.

Not only her hot slit, but her mouth too, for as he recalled the detail of their encounter a fortnight or more past, she had conducted him to an accommodation house in Orange Street, where he had paid five shillings for the use of a bedroom. No sooner had he removed his trousers than she was on her knees, her arm round his hip to reach his pompoms from behind, whilst with her other hand she held his fast-hardening shaft and drew the soft skin up and down before placing the purple head to her lips.

There was no time to say her nay, and precious little wish to do so, after she had taken almost half of his straining shaft into her mouth and sucked at it. On principle, Randolph gave no consent or approval to any course of action he had not himself initiated, and to have a thirty-shilling trull take charge of his person was, to say the least of it, a piece of impudence that in other circumstances he would have resented and stopped. Yet the girl had a way of using her mouth on his leaping part that almost reconciled him to her insolence.

Instead of drawing away, he twined a hand in her hair to hold her at his mercy, whilst he moved swiftly backward and forward, rogering the girl in her mouth. Now the tables were turned, and she would have pulled back if she could, but he gave no quarter and kept at it until his shaft jumped and throbbed and spurted its stream of sticky sap down her throat.

Afterwards, while she was red-faced and gasping,

5

Randolph put his hands under her armpits and threw her bodily on the bed. In a trice he had turned her skirts up above her waist and had three fingers up her pussy, ravishing it by main force till she shrieked out and came off. By then Mr Percival Proud was stiff once more, and without a pause, Randolph rammed him deep into the squirming girl and rogered her soundly.

The memory of the satisfactions of that evening very nearly persuaded him to hire her again, and make her repeat the entire process as before. But the urge for novelty was strong in him, a fresh bit of meat to whet his appetite, another pair of soft titties to feel, a different pussy to finger and come off in.

That being so, he shook his head at the advancing girl, still smiling at her, and said, *Another night, my dear*. She fell back crestfallen into the shadows, while Randolph walked on slowly. He shrugged his shoulders – the doxy's disappointment was none of his concern. His masculine pride and vanity informed him it was very probable that the girl would prefer to be poked by a handsome young gentleman like himself than some pot-bellied old businessman. But that was not the point. Randolph was the buyer and she was the seller. The laws of economics held sway here – he was in a buyer's market and his decision was not to shop at her stall that evening.

A girl who stood alone in a doorway caught his eye, and he halted in front of her for a better look. She wore no hat and her hair was yellow, drawn back loosely in a bun. Her face was round and her expression sulky. Randolph tipped his hat to her and bid her *Good evening*, allowing her time to assess his fine features and the quality of his clothes. Evidently she was much impressed by both, for though she gave no hint of a smile, she informed him that she charged two pounds for a short time, during which satisfaction was guaranteed.

'You set a high price on your cunny,' Randolph informed her. 'I've only once paid that much for a girl along here. Thirty shillings would buy you for a short time, if I were disposed to haggle. But low and demeaning usages of that sort are for the mercantile classes, not for a gentleman. To show my magnanimity of mind, I shall ask you this – what will you do for three pounds?'

Her face unsmiling, but with a sudden gleam in her eye, the girl replied that for three pounds he could roger her lying, standing and sitting, front and back, up, down, and however else he chose.

'I admire spirit in a girl, damned if I don't!' exclaimed Randolph, reaching out to touch her titties through her frock. 'What do they call you?'

'Polly,' said she, opening her shawl to permit his hands to roam over her body.

The feel of warm flesh through her frock and chemise aroused in him a burning and unquenchable fire of lustfulness, with the immediate result that Mr Percival Proud, already stiff as a rod of iron, began to quiver inside his trousers. He stepped closer to the girl, and she pushed her belly at him, as in invitation. Their legs were close together, and his shaft pressed against her thigh. He moved his hips in a slow circular motion, to rub Percival on her and rouse blissful sensations.

She let him excite himself on her leg, then her hand touched the front of his trousers, and her fingertips traced through the costly cloth the length and thickness of Mr Percival Proud.

'You've a cockstand like a broom handle,' said she, 'I'm sure you've heard the rhyme –

7

> *"My titties and my cunny*
> *Are yours to use for money,"*
> *A girl said to a gent along the Strand,*
> *"I've no cash with me," he cried,*
> *But a cockstand she espied,*
> *And felt it in his breeches with her hand.*
>
> *He said "All right. I'm willing,*
> *But only for five shilling,"*
> *His piteous state would melt a breast of snow;*
> *But the farthing-grudging gent,*
> *While she held his cockstand, spent*
> *And in his breeches freely shot his roe!'*

Randolph chuckled, and the girl said slyly:

'That's enough feeling me for now. Any more and you'll come off up your shirt-front and diddle me out of earning my money.'

'If I do,' said he, his knees trembling a little under him at the force of the sensations coursing upwards through his entire body from his excited shaft, 'then you shall have half a crown for your trouble, and I will move along in search of another.'

'Give me five shillings and I'll put my hand down the front of your trousers and bring you right off standing here,' said she pertly. 'But why should a fine gentleman like you be satisfied with fetching off in your underclothes, when you could do it up my cunny?'

'It's your far-from-virginal little cunny I mean to make use of for my poking business,' said he, taking a step back from the girl, with reluctance, but to relieve the pleasant pressure on Mr Percival, lest that over-zealous gentleman wasted his riches in linen rather than in warm female flesh.

'If it's a young virgin you want for your pleasure,' said the girl, 'you must go and see Mrs Williams in Drury Lane. For fifty pounds she'll find you a girl who's never been done before — but my understanding is that such things are for weary old men with drooping rods, not for upstanding young gentlemen like yourself. My pussy's been poked plenty of times, I won't say it hasn't. You won't hear me crying out when your prick slides up it, howsoever long and thick it is.'

'Damme if you're not the most honest-sounding little trull I ever did talk to!' Randolph exclaimed. 'You'll be a fine poke, if I'm not mistaken.'

'Try me and see,' the girl offered, sliding a hand between his thighs to feel his dangling pompoms. 'Will you really give me three pounds?'

'Willingly,' he answered, 'but on the conditions you set out — I am to have your full consent to do you however I like, and as many times as I choose. Is it agreed?'

'There's nothing you can think of I haven't had done to me,' she told him. 'You can use me as you wish for your three pounds. Come on, there's a place just round the corner we can go to.'

As Randolph expected, she led him into Jermyn Street, where a great many upper rooms over shops were let out to young whores to ply their trade. He had been in a dozen or more of these convenient rooms, and in some of them several times. The one to which Polly conducted him was above a dressmaker's shop, and not one he had seen before, so far as he could remember. Not that there was much to identify it or recall it from memory — when Polly turned up the gaslight the sole furnishings of the room were a wooden chair and a wide bed with an old patchwork quilt and a mahogany headboard in need of polishing.

Randolph gave the girl her three sovereigns, hung his top hat on a peg on the back of the door and sat on the chair.

'Remove your clothes, my dear,' he instructed her, 'show me your titties first. How old are you?'

'Seventeen,' she told him, her expression remaining as sulky as ever while she unbuttoned the bodice of her dark brown dress and pulled it over her head.

Randolph observed that she wore a white cotton petticoat tied round her waist and descending to her ankles, with a flounce of cheap lace round the hem. That came off to reveal a knee-length chemise, also of white cotton, tied over the shoulders with bows of coloured ribbon. She came closer to where Randolph sat and stared at him in silent petulance while she took off her chemise and threw it with her other clothes over the footboard of the bed.

Long and intimate contact with girls of the street had taught Randolph that these handy little creatures hardly ever removed all their clothing, even for a good rogering. He felt sure that Polly's clients were content to have her remove only her outer clothing, and make use of her pussy through the long slit of her drawers. In the yellow gaslight her flesh was pale of hue, and her titties, bared for his inspection, were neither large nor small, but of a middle size. For all her youth, they were a little slack already from the daily handling they received, but Randolph's hard-on shaft bounded at the sight of them.

'There's something you like about me,' said Polly, noting the sharp movement within his trousers. 'Let's have it out – I want to see this mighty shaft that's going to do me upside down and sideways!'

She sank to her knees, a small insinuating smile on her face at last, and she pushed his legs apart. Her hand darted between them, and Randolph emitted a gasp as she ripped wide open his trouser buttons. Mr Percival Proud was so swollen and frantic that he leaped out of his own accord, at which yellow-haired Polly chortled and administered a few deft manipulations of her hand. In this part of his body, as throughout, Randolph had been well endowed by Providence, and the throbbing shaft held in Polly's hand was long, thick and well-shaped, with a loose fleshy hood that slid back to reveal a head as plump and shiny purple as a large plum.

The pleasing aspect of Randolph's person in the form of his male organ was lost on the wench − to her it was no more than another man-tap, through which desire could be drained away, to earn her money. She had seen bigger, and she had seen smaller, and had accommodated all sizes and shapes in her slit.

'Half a dozen pulls and you'll be finished,' she commented, sliding her clasping hand briskly up and down the hard shaft, 'you'll shoot your tallow in my hand − do you always come off so easily, or do you fancy me that much?'

'You're an inquisitive little trollop,' said Randolph. 'What is it to you whether I come off slow or fast? You'll be paid the same, either way. And if it's not my way to plunge straight into a pussy and shoot off in the twinkling of an eye, of what concern can that be to you? You've contracted your person to me, and I shall make such use of it as pleases me best.'

'I do love a masterful man, who knows his mind,' Polly said with complete insincerity. 'Tell me your fancy for tonight and it's yours − shall I bring you off in my hand?'

Randolph grinned at her compliance and reached out to seize her soft titties, and lay Percival Proud between them.

'That's what you're after, is it?' she asked, sounding very

uninterested. 'You've a mind to roger my bubbies – and so you shall! No man's done them for ages – they're almost virgins.'

He squeezed the warm fleshiness together round his throbbing shaft and thrust strongly inside the soft pocket he had made. Polly knelt with her head on one side and grinned quizzically up at him. Her hands felt inside his gaping flies to take hold of his hairy pompoms and roll them between her fingers.

'I've been done between my titties, up my cunny, in my mouth, up my armpit, between my thighs, on my belly, in at the back door – there's no way of telling how a gentleman will fancy to come off,' said she. 'Some girls object, but I'm always ready to oblige a generous gentleman, howsoever his fancy takes him.'

Randolph panted as he squeezed her soft titties together to accommodate his long fast thrusts. Polly stared downward at the shiny purple head of Mr Percival Proud, popping out and then disappearing again between the cleft of her pale flesh.

'You've started to fetch off!' she exclaimed. 'Look there – the little eye's wide open!'

Randolph moaned in bliss, his swollen shaft slid fast against the girl's hot flesh, and his whole body shook to the release of a gushing torrent between her titties. She grinned briefly to see it and feel the wetness on her skin, evidently of a mind to believe he would require little more of her now beyond perhaps a slow poke lying on her back on the bed. In this she grossly underestimated Randolph's interest and stamina.

When he was again in possession of his faculties, he told her to remove her drawers and let him see the rest of her body, to judge whether her lower half could raise his shaft to a hard-on stand as efficiently as her titties had done. She stood up and complied with his wish, posturing for his delectation with her arms akimbo, hands on her hips and her stockinged feet well apart.

Randolph nodded in approval as he noted the pleasing points of her person. Her belly he deemed good — it was round and just slightly curved, with a button deep-sunk in the soft flesh. Her bush was profuse, yellowish rather than brown, and but a shade darker than the hair of her head. Her thighs had a round female plumpness, and he could well understand how a gentleman might take the notion of fetching off between them, well up above her stocking-tops.

In the meantime, while he was assessing her for his pleasure, Polly was appraising him. Mr Proud had been relieved of all his pride and lay limp in the wide opening of Randolph's evening trousers. Young as she was, Polly had more experience of the ways of men than any married lady of seven-and-thirty. Most usually her fee was bartered down to a pound by the men who wanted a use of her cunny, their desire being no more than to have her on her back with her drawers down for a few minutes and slide in and out of her split until they spent and were done for.

Sometimes an officer of the Foot Guard from nearby St James's Palace would seek her out and have her a couple of times on the trot before he was satisfied.

Only one customer had ever rogered her more than twice at a session — and he didn't want her on her back at all. He had her on the bed, but on her hands and knees, and did her from behind — like a pair of mongrel dogs at it in the street. But he was a jolly sort of man, and he'd paid the full two pounds she asked him for.

There was, Polly dimly recognised, something about the cheeks of a bare female behind that made men letch and want to unload their cargo. What it was, she couldn't think. She had seen more than enough men's backsides and found nothing interesting about them at all. Except once a fat gentleman had paid her to spank his bare bum with her hand, and that had entertained her.

As if to prove her point, Randolph reached out towards her to fondle her bare bottom and give the cheeks a good squeeze. He put his face against her belly, and she felt the touch of his wet tongue thrust into her belly-button. He drew her down to sit on his lap and lean against him, her head on his shoulder. Her right titty lay loosely against the starched white front of his dress shirt, and while his attention was distracted by handling her titties, her sly fingers imperceptibly delved into the pockets of his evening waistcoat. Gentlemen frequently kept golden sovereigns there, she knew.

There were two or three small coins in Randolph's pocket, but being naked she had nowhere to put them for the moment, and let them be, until a better opportunity served. When he'd finished with her pussy she could easily slip them inside, but that lay in the future – under her bare bottom she could feel his shaft hardening, and guessed he would want to broach her very soon.

Indeed, the long wet trickle of his first spending descended between her titties to her belly, and the sight caused Randolph to breathe faster and rub his finger over her reddish-brown teats, until he had made them stand up firm.

'What are you going to do with me now?' she asked curiously.

Before he replied to her question, Randolph dropped his hand down between her bare thighs, and tickled the pouting lips of her pussy. Before long, despite her lack of interest in him as anything other than a paymaster, he had made

the soft and hairy slit gape apart, and had a fingertip inside
to find her secret button and tease it.

'Open your legs wider,' he instructed her, and she obliged
by spreading them very wide apart. His fingers probed deep
inside and rubbed her button until he had made her pussy
wet.

'This is the source of women's pleasure and satisfaction,'
he said, as he fingered her deftly. 'Talk to me a little before
I have you again, Polly. I will not ask how many men roger
you in the course of a day, for that is unimportant – but
what arouses my interest is this – how often during the
space of a day does the female orgasm overtake you?'

'What do you mean?' she asked, not knowing or
understanding the word he had employed.

Randolph smiled to himself and continued to manipulate
with a fingertip her slippery button.

'I mean the sensual spasm,' he explained. 'How frequently
do you yield to it? Or to put the matter as simply as is
possible without coarseness, how many times a day do you
come off?'

'Why do you want to know that?' she sighed, her bare
thighs beginning to tremble as his finger raised her passions
towards their natural culmination.

'I am a student of sensual matters,' said he. 'In the course
of my research and investigation I have formulated a theory
of female sexuality which is astonishing and runs clean
counter to all accepted opinion. Your views will be most
useful, Polly.'

'Oh my Lord – I'm near to coming off!' she gasped in
a weak voice, spreading her legs even wider. The pull of her
muscles opened her cunny as if it were a book – the type
of salacious book Randolph bought now and then for his
amusement in a little shop he knew of in Greek Street, Soho.

Polly was by then shaking and sighing, her belly was heaving and her titties flopping. The one thing she desired most in the world at that moment was to be brought off. Her entire body and soul demanded the satisfaction of a long deep hard spasm, as her gentleman client had called it. Seeing the plight to which he had reduced her, Randolph deliberately slowed down his deft manipulation of her button, to extend her sensations up to the limit her nervous system could endure, and undermine her will.

'How many times a day do you come off, Polly?' he asked her, 'I want the truth now!'

'Not many!' she gasped. 'Bring me off!'

'As soon as you tell me what I want to know, not before.'

'Once, maybe. Twice if I'm lucky,' she panted out. 'Most men don't make me − they push it up me and shoot off as if they'd sneezed. Sometimes I'm with a man of middle years who takes his time about it and brings me off without meaning to. But mostly I have to fetch myself off with my fingers before I get up in the morning.'

'Good girl,' said Randolph, quite fascinated by what she said. 'The answer is once, then. You shall come off now.'

He joined three fingers together inside her pussy and flicked the tips expertly over her button. She gasped continuously and wriggled the soft bare cheeks of her bottom in his lap, rubbing her warm flesh on stiff Mr Percival Proud trapped beneath her.

'Don't stop now!' cried she. 'I'm fetching off!'

Randolph maintained his brisk manipulation of her wet parts, until in another moment she shrieked and her body jerked wildly to the spasms of her delight. The sight and sound of it aroused Randolph to a perfect frenzy of lust, and while she was still shaking and sobbing in her joy, he rose to his feet with her in his arms and sat her on the side

16

of the bed. She fell on to her back, her stockinged legs dangling loosely down over the side, and he was at once between her parted knees, his stiff shaft at the mark.

'You'll kill me!' she whispered, her dark blue eyes staring at the long thick shaft aimed at her belly like a sporting gun in the hand of an expert huntsman, cocked and ready to fire.

Randolph gazed in delight at her yellow-haired pussy — open and wet from his attentions, and as lascivious a sight as he could remember laying eyes on. The hairy mound seemed to thrust forward from between her thighs, the pink-fleshed lips pouted clear of her bush, ready to engulf his shaft when he brought it close enough. He stroked quickly up and down the insides of her pale thighs, then slid three fingers into her.

'Do me,' she begged, 'bring me off again!'

In an instant Randolph was poised over her, his hard-on shaft between her thighs, its swollen head butting at the voluptuous lips of her cunny. She slipped an eager hand between their bellies to grasp Percival Proud and steer him into the haven he sought. With a long push Randolph sank his length into her, and she bucked her belly up at him in a lively rhythm.

'Excellent!' he panted, jabbing into her with short hard strokes that raised his sensations swiftly towards the oncoming of the sexual spasm, 'you are to come off when I do, and not before — do you understand me, girl? Wait for my sap to spring and then come off — not a second before, or a second later!'

CHAPTER 2
Continuing Diversions
with a Doxy

In the room above a shop in Jermyn Street, to where he had been brought for the purpose of lustful pleasure, Randolph was close to the point of consummation of his sexual frenzy within Polly Bates's wet commodity. She lay on her back, naked but for white stockings, on the side of the bed, her legs hanging down toward the floor, and Randolph stood between her knees, ready to leap upon her as a ravening wild beast on its trembling prey.

He stared greedily at her yellow-haired pussy — open and wet from the diligence of his earlier attentions, and as lascivious a sight as he could remember laying eyes on. The soft and hairy mound seemed to thrust out forward from between her thighs, the pink-fleshed lips pouted clear of her bush, avid to engulf his shaft when he brought it closer, and swallow it down into the wench's hot belly.

The contrast between their appearances he had purposefully engineered aroused Randolph immoderately. He remained fully and elegantly clothed, in white tie and black tails, starched shirt and shiny, patent leather shoes, thus demonstrating his superior station over that of the girl stripped naked for his pleasure. He almost sobbed in his joyful lust as he threw himself on her and penetrated her with a hard push of Mr Percival Proud.

In his hands he grasped her slack titties, using them freely for his delectation, whilst he assaulted her belly with short sharp jabs that made her body jerk on the bed and caused her to pant to catch her breath. No more than a minute after lodging his throbbing shaft within her, he spent copiously, and short though the poking had been, she too gasped and came off.

'There, you've had me on my back at last,' said she, grinning up at him slyly from her flushed face, 'I thought you'd want me that way before you'd finished. Whatever antics foreigners and Frenchmen may get up to, to lie down belly to belly is the most natural way to poke.'

'Damn this lying on beds,' Randolph answered, feeling his wet and softening shaft slide out of her, 'that's only for married milksops rogering their simpering wives in the dark twice a week, to get children. Come with me.'

He rose, took her by the wrist and pulled her to her feet, to lead her back to the chair on which he had first toyed with her bodily assets. He sat down, fully clothed, his limp wet shaft hanging out of his open trousers, that being his whim, and took Polly on his lap again. She lay against him easily and meekly, awaiting his further pleasure.

When he made no move to do more than stroke her bare belly with his palm, it came into her mind that this might be a good moment to abstract the coins from his waistcoat pocket and secrete them in her pussy until she was alone. To distract him from what she purposed, she asked what was the theory he had mentioned, when he asked her about coming off.

'You shall be the first female to hear the present outcome of my researches,' he said. 'Hitherto only a few close chums have been advised of my findings, over a bottle or two of port after dinner. Not all of them are yet convinced of its truth, since I have established facts that go against all accepted opinion. As you shall hear now. It is universally believed amongst the educated classes that lust is a wholly masculine attribute, and never experienced by females, whether ladies or common women.'

'Whatever gave you that idea?' Polly asked in surprise.

'It is the general belief, not mine in particular,' said he. 'The reason given for this one-sided circumstance is that the female constitution is too frail and unstable to sustain the physical force of the sexual spasm without grave injury.'

Polly looked at him sideways and said nothing, her fingers in his waistcoat pocket.

'Nevertheless, between husbands and wives who have sufficient confidence in each other to exchange views most often remaining a deep and inviolate secret,' he went on, 'it is known by those interested in sexual matters that an admission is occasionally made that, in the conjugal act the female sometimes experiences a slight paroxysm of sensation which can only be described as a type of coming off.'

'What's the conjugal act?' asked Polly.

'Rogering between married people. But to continue, the slight spasms which some wives confess to experiencing in the act are discouraged by medical men, and it is strongly recommended that married women avoid these emotions, save when they occur wholly by the chance of a husband being over-vigorous. And even then, this female paroxysm must not be allowed to take place with any regularity, but only on infrequent occasions, lest the female's health be seriously impaired.'

'Then I'm safe enough,' said Polly, 'since once a day is

the most I ever seem to be brought off, and usually by accident.'

'By no means,' Randolph advised her. 'The celebrated Dr Acton will tell you, should you care to consult him, that your life is in imminent peril. He believes more than one or two spasms a year to be injurious to the female constitution, and should a woman, married or single, be so ill-advised as to permit sexual excitement to get a hold on her, it must necessarily terminate in nymphomania, which is a form of insanity, and brings about physical decline and early death.'

'This Dr Acton — has he ever poked a woman?' Polly asked.

'Of that I have no knowledge, but he has written books on the topic, and his views are very widely respected. Nevertheless, having been with not a few girls myself since attaining the age of puberty, my own observation is that females come off almost as easily as men, enjoy it as much, and are eager to repeat the pleasure. This, as I say, represents a complete reversal of all medical and religious opinion at the present time, and has been of great interest to me.'

'Poking is always interesting to a man,' said Polly, 'but for women it's usually a question of spreading her legs to keep a husband quiet, or of doing it to make a living, like me.'

'That is the way of things,' Randolph told her, 'men poke and women are poked. My present area of research is into how often the female can repeat the spasm without the total collapse of her physical constitution.'

'You mean, can she be poked to death?' Polly asked. 'I've not heard of it, and I know plenty of girls on the game.'

'And I've poked plenty of them,' Randolph informed her, 'from which I have ascertained that a normal healthy young woman like yourself is capable of coming off as many times within twenty-four hours as a man of the same age.'

Polly had no interest in his nonsense. She had succeeded in extracting the coins from his pocket and had them folded in the palm of her hand. By then the discourse on females in sexual spasm had aroused Randolph's lust once again, and he required her to turn round on his lap, to sit astride his thighs, facing away from him. His arms were about her waist, his hand thrust down between her parted thighs, tickling at the wet lips of her pussy with a bent middle finger.

'I see you like it awkward,' she commented, 'lying down on a bed's for married couples and too dull for you, you say.'

'Keep a civil tongue in your head,' he answered. 'You agreed to as often and however I chose. Lift your backside.'

She leaned forward and raised her bottom, to present to him an unimpeded view of her hairy slit from the rear. He dabbled a finger inside it, making her slippery again, then took her by the hips and pulled her down on his upright shaft, spitting her on it. She sighed to feel his long hard gristle slide up in her depths, and whether her sigh expressed the anticipation of pleasure or resignation to a tedious performance, only she knew — and she sighed again when Randolph reached round her to take hold of her slack titties and grip them tight, while he rogered her from behind and beneath.

'You have the privilege of entertaining Mr Percival Proud in your cunny,' he told her, 'I trust that you appreciate the very considerable honour bestowed on you in having a gentleman come off up your slit.'

'Proud is right,' she sighed, shaken by his vigorous thrusts.

'And with good reason,' he said, his voice tremulous as

his sensations grew delicious beyond compare. He was pinching her russet teats between thumb and forefinger and rolling them hard as he neared the climax.

'Now, Polly!' he exclaimed. 'I have used you better than any girl of the streets has a claim to be, and I have brought you off as diligently as if you were myself. Now you shall feel the force of my flood inside you!'

His words stopped, and he cried out incoherently when his sap squirted up into her. She, to her amazement, succumbed to the manipulation of her titties by his fingers, and came off again. Afterwards she leaned back limply against his shirt front, her head back on his shoulder, whilst he slumped trembling in the chair, his chest heaving and his mouth open in shallow breaths.

Five or six minutes passed with no change in their position, then a tap on the door aroused both.

'Who the devil's that?' Randolph demanded. 'If the bawd who keeps this fusty place thinks to hustle me out before I've done with you, I'll lay my walking cane across her behind!'

Polly rose from his lap and slipped her chemise over her head before going to the door. She did not open it, but stood close while she asked who was there. Randolph heard another female voice reply, and Polly turned to look at him and explain.

'It's only a friend of mine,' she said, 'she hasn't come to disturb us. But she's got a bad cold and will catch her death if she hangs round in the streets waiting for men.'

Randolph glared at the young doxy as if he would murder her. 'What the devil does she want here, then?' he asked coldly. 'Send her away at once and get your backside on my lap again.'

Polly was rummaging through her discarded clothes,

anxious to hide from him the coins taken from his pocket.

'She's earned no money today and she wants a few shillings to buy a bottle of grog to help her sleep and throw off her bad cold, that's all. I'll lend her enough, and she'll be gone.'

'How old is she, and what's her name?' he enquired.

'She's about my age, though she can't be certain. And she's called Meg.'

Randolph left his chair and strode to the door, flung it open and stared at the girl standing outside. She would have been thought pretty, save for her reddened and dripping nose and her pale cheeks, the signs of her feverishness. She wore a black bonnet tied with ribbons under her chin, and was wrapped close in a long cloak. She was surprised to see Randolph at the door, where she had expected her friend Polly, and then as her eyes fell and she caught sight of his limp shaft dangling out of his trousers, she smiled and sniffed.

'Sorry to disturb you, sir, when you're occupied with Poll,' said she, her voice hoarse.

'It's money you want, is it?' he said, a lewd thought coming into his head at the sight of her. 'You shall have a pound from me if you will step inside and amuse me for twenty minutes.'

Even as he spoke, he wondered why it was that after rogering a thousand women, another pussy was irresistible to him. Was it simply because it was new to him, an unknown plunge into sexual adventure? This friend of Polly's was not much different from the little trollop whose parts he had made use of already this evening, and meant to use again. Her pussy would be similar to Polly's, though with curls of a slightly different hue.

The feel of her wet love-flesh round Mr Percival Proud

25

would be much the same as if he were inside Polly, that he knew, and the delight it gave would not be at all different from that he had felt already tonight. Yet, although the owner of this new pussy was an ordinary-looking wench, the unseen female charm in between her legs was exercising its silent spell over him. He felt that he must have her, he must gaze upon her bare pussy, finger it, poke it, and squirt his hot sap into it.

'For your pound you shall have whatever you can get from me in twenty minutes,' said Meg, 'though I think it won't be all that much, seeing the state of your dangler. I reckon Polly's taken it right down, and it won't do much more tonight.'

'That's for me to decide,' said Randolph.

He took her by the wrist and pulled her into the room, then led her to the bed, where Polly sat naked with crossed legs, to await the outcome of the conversation at the door.

'One thing, though,' said Meg, pulling off her bonnet to show a wealth of mid-brown hair, 'I won't take my clothes off for you tonight, like Poll, for with this cold in my head, there's no telling what might happen.'

'As you wish,' Randolph conceded, 'but you shall take down your drawers, at least. Polly — relieve your friend of them!'

He seated himself on the chair to watch, whilst Meg took off her warm cloak, and Polly slipped off the bed and sank down to her bare knees before her friend. She lifted her skirts and her petticoats, smiling slyly at Randolph whilst she uncovered for his avid gaze Meg's knee-length white drawers with frills.

'Show me her cunny,' he ordered.

Obediently, she held Meg's clothes up with one hand, and with the other she opened the slit in her drawers to reveal a thatch of mouse-brown hair.

'Give it a feel for me,' he said, 'tell me what it's like.'

He saw Polly's hand slip inside her friend's drawers, and by the way it moved, he knew that the new girl's pussy was being treated to a good fingering. In a short time Meg grinned, and her face began to flush, though that might have been caused by her head cold as much as by what was being done to her.

'Well?' Randolph asked. 'Do you mean to bring her off before informing me what she feels like?'

'She has a soft warm cunny,' said Polly, 'ready to take in a shaft at all hours of the day or night, and unburden it of its splash of tallow. Will you poke it?'

'In a while,' said he, 'sit yourself on the side of the bed, Meg, and be comfortable while your drawers are removed.'

She did as he bid her, sitting with her clothes up about her hips, and Polly, kneeling before her, untied the string of her drawers and took them down. Meg's thighs parted, giving him an open view of her brown bush.

'A pretty sight!' he exclaimed. 'Lie back now and take your ease while I survey your pussy and reach a conclusion as to how it shall be best used.'

Meg lay on her back, affording him a fine sight of her mound and the long lips under the brown curls. Mr Percival Proud, so long asleep, twitched and began to grow longer and thicker. The whim seized upon Randolph to recite for the benefit of his two doxies some lines by Mr Leigh Hunt, the celebrated poet:

> *A female thing that bears a well-known name,*
> *But is in truth a warm and tender spot,*
> *It sets always my mind and heart aflame,*
> *And just to catch a glimpse will make me hot.*

It is the sweetest thing this world can show,
Therefore my praises ring out loud and long,
It sets my blood to rage and fervent glow,
And brings my aching shaft up firm and strong.

When pussy is uncovered, take my tip,
To be ignored or shunned it will not stand,
But throbbing must be kissed by tongue and lip,
And to its spasm caressed by loving hand.

He heard Polly chuckle at the poet's words, and saw how she wiggled her bare bottom at him, her wet and hairy pussy visible below the crack of her cheeks.

'Delay no further, Polly,' he instructed her, 'bring the minx off at once.'

With perfect obedience, Polly bowed her head and brought her tongue to bear on the pussy she had stimulated by the use of her hand. Randolph experienced a deep and delightful agitation to see Meg being licked in this voluptuous manner. The girls formed a spectacle he had rarely witnessed before, but which he vowed to arrange again as often as he might, he found it to be so intensely arousing – Polly's head down between her friend's bared thighs and her wet tongue flicking in her exposed slit!

Mr Percival Proud had grown so hard and long that he stood up from Randolph's gaping trousers to halfway up his waistcoat. To clasp him in a trembling hand was the only practical course of action, and to slide his fingers up and down, to enhance those sensations of bliss that Mr Percival emanated by the regularity of his involuntary throb.

'No more, Poll!' he heard Meg moaning. 'Don't bring me off, for I'm not well enough for it. Leave me alone now . . .'

But Polly had her orders, and seemed to be taking enjoyment and pride in her work. Soon Meg was panting at the force of the sensual thrills inflicted on her by the darting caresses of her friend's tongue. Her stockinged legs kicked up from the floor, signifying that the culminating point of her bodily paroxysm would speedily arrive.

Randolph could hardly breath for his excitement. He was all on fire with a delicious lustfulness at the action before him. His encircling hand slid up and down his shaft so gratifyingly that he knew he would not be able much longer to restrain his fetching off. In the nick of time, Meg gave a loud squeal and kicked her legs high in the air as she surrendered to the spasm and fell into a climactic convulsion.

'I've come off, Polly, you bitch!' she gasped, 'I told you not to make me!'

Her physical climax prompted Randolph to take a more active part before he spent in his own hand. He held his jerking shaft tightly whilst he sped to the bedside and pushed Polly to the side. She gave him a conspirator's grin, and yielded her place on the bed to him without demur. Randolph's shaft was as thick and hard as a rolling pin. He set a hand flat on the bed to support himself, then leaned over the prostrate girl and stared down at her wet pussy with a ravening glee.

Meg stared back up at him, her eyes red-rimmed and her nose a-drip from her head cold. Her mouth hung open in amazement and dismay, to find herself brought off so casually by her friend's tongue and now at the mercy of a man with a shaft standing up like a broom handle. She looked speechlessly at Randolph, maybe thinking to herself that this was a damned hard way to earn a pound. Polly was giggling, either at her friend's discomfiture, or at the sight of Randolph in evening clothes seized by an access of hot lust, holding his bared shaft in his hand.

His feverish eyes were fixed on the brown-haired pussy below him, and in his mind ran the thought that here was another soft female slit to plunge his shaft into and enjoy to the full — a slit he had never before seen or unloaded his lewdness into. Mr Percival jumped for joy when Randolph brought his shiny purple head to the wet lips before him, and burrowed him slowly in.

'Ah, so wet and soft!' Randolph gasped. 'So slippy she is!'

And well he might say so, for Polly's tongue had liberally wet Meg's parts, within and without, so that Mr Proud slipped in without let or hindrance, until Randolph's muff and Meg's touched and intertwined. At once he commenced a long and busy course of sliding in and out, using the entire length of his shaft, from head to root.

'Be quick about it,' Meg implored him, moving her legs as far apart as they would go, 'I can't stand much more — I don't feel at all well and I'm hot and sweating with fever.'

'That be damned for a tale,' Randolph grunted, 'you're here to be poked, my girl, and poked you shall be, hard and wide!'

He still resented her impertinence in interrupting him whilst in the throes of his earlier encounter with Polly, for some paltry excuse of wanting a few shillings. That a street slut dared to burst in upon a gentleman at his lustful devotions! It was lucky for her that he had taken a fancy to rogering her while yet she stood at the door, otherwise he would have sent her packing penniless, to die of pneumonia in the street, if so she chose. And even after taking his money, the wretched trull had made it a condition that she would not take her clothes off for his pleasure.

Revenge was sweet, and his time for it was here — she

was pinned to the bed beneath him, her legs spread, and his hard-on shaft deep inside her. Whether she felt well or ill, of what concern was that to him? Seeing her on her back being fetched off by Polly had thrown him into a state of frenzy, and he was going to use her to the limit. If she died underneath him, then so be it — he would walk away and leave her on the bed, thighs parted and clothes up round her waist, for the peelers to find. But not before he had shot his angry load into her pussy!

'No more, sir, please!' she cried. 'I can't put up with it! Poke Polly if you must, or let me bring you off with my hand . . .'

'Lord!' said Polly, at Randolph's side. She had taken a seat on the bed, to observe the poking from close up. 'I've known the time when she's had a dozen men roger her between lunch and suppertime — yet now she's complaining about her first poke of the day!'

'Her pussy is so hot!' Randolph gasped, tupping away. 'It is the fever of her cold, I believe! Oh, how delightful a feeling it is! In another few seconds I shall fill her up to the brim and her pussy will overflow!

The strongest and most intense thrills the human organism can ever bear possessed Randolph at that moment. With sighing and moaning, he rammed so forcefully into Meg's slit that he came to the very pinnacle of voluptuousness, and flooded her with spurting essence. She shrieked aloud, though for what reason none could tell, and her belly shook under him to the jerking of his coming off.

When his revenge was complete, he rose from her with a smirk of triumph and resumed his seat on the chair, telling her to remain as she was until he gave her leave to depart. In truth, she was trembling and half-swooning from the ordeal she had but now undergone, and lay lethargic, legs

31

apart and clothes still up to her belly-button. Randolph pulled his chair round to face the bed, and nearer to it, in order to survey with wondering eye the pussy he had just used so vigorously. The lips lay wet and slack, the curls plastered down to the flesh.

How strange a thing it is, Randolph pondered silently whilst he stared between Meg's thighs, how strange that even when I have rogered so many, I pine always for every young pussy that has not yet felt the force of my shaft! They say that there are ten thousand whores in London — I want to poke every one of them under the age of twenty-five and after that every pretty married woman in the Capital, and then every unmarried girl, gentle and common alike, above the age of sixteen!

'Can I go now, sir?' Meg asked weakly, raising her head from the bed to cast a pleading look in his direction.

Randolph picked up his shiny black walking cane and held it out at arm's length until with the silver knob he could gently prod her wet pussy. At the touch of the cold metal, she closed her thighs, but the stick lay between them, the knob bumping on her with little pushes, as if a monstrous long and thin shaft tried to get into her.

'Go?' said Randolph. 'Yes, you may go, for I've had all that I wanted of you, a poke up your cunny. Off you go, girl, for I fear you will be neither use nor ornament while I roger Polly again. Take your drawers and go this minute!'

She rose somewhat weakly from the bed and stood with her feet apart while she wiped between her legs with her chemise.

'Go,' Randolph repeated, 'off with you!'

Without a word, Meg snatched up her drawers from where Polly had dropped them on the floor, and fled from the room, carrying them in her hand. The door had scarce closed behind her before Randolph told Polly to sit on his lap again. From her place on the bed she came naked to him, and took up the position that he required. They sat thus for three or four minutes whilst he ran his palms over her titties and toyed with them, she naked and he dressed.

'I hope you've found out all you wanted for your theory about girls coming off,' said Polly. 'What would your Dr Acton say if he'd been sitting here on this chair and watching for the last hour? Would he tell us we shall be dead before morning?'

'I do believe he would,' said Randolph, 'for he holds that we ought to employ our vital energies in building up the physical frame, and in educational activities of the mind. He thinks it most injurious to allow sexual impressions or fancies to affect either mind or body. In men this is mighty difficult to achieve to a high degree, as he himself allows, for the nervous system has a tendency to produce erections of the male organ without the need for external stimulus.'

'We all know the ways to bring down a standing shaft,' Polly remarked, 'but what does he say about women?'

'The woman of a well-regulated life and well-ordered thoughts is not susceptible to casual sexual excitation, Dr Acton says. Had he been present tonight to observe our frolic, his censure would alight on me for indulging my lusts so freely on you and on Meg, but his greatest strictures would have fallen upon you, in that you have allowed your desires to be inflamed again and again, to the detriment of body and soul.'

'If ever I meet this Dr Acton of yours, I'll offer him a free poke and see if he turns me down,' said she with a lewd laugh. 'More than likely he'll have me on my back and his shaft up me before I can draw breath! Is he old or young?'

'I hardly know,' said Randolph, 'but I take him for a man of mature years – about sixty, perhaps.'

'Then he's past it, and so are you for now,' she said to him, with her artful smile. 'You'll learn no more about female lust tonight, but if you'd like to try again tomorrow with me, for the same price, I'm game. Set a time and I'll be waiting.'

'Ha!' he snorted, displeased that she, a common girl of the streets, should think herself capable of besting him. 'Do you suppose that because Percival's head lies low it will not rise again – is that what you think, slut?'

'Not tonight, it won't stand again,' she said slyly, 'take it from me, you haven't a poke left in you.'

To prove the truth of her words, she took his soft shaft in her hand and tugged at it, letting her titties lie against his shirt front and her cheek against his. Randolph sat calm and still, summoning up his last reserves of strength. Before long, blissful tremors ran through his belly and he felt his shaft begin to rise once more to its proud length and girth.

'No, it can't be true!' Polly gasped, realising too late now that she had put him in a mind to roger her pussy again.

Randolph reached down between them, to press his fingers into the opening of her hairy cunny and rub her button with slow and steady strokes. He had no true desire, but he was impelled by the assertiveness of his nature into making a demonstration of his superiority over any female.

'I mean to poke you once more,' he said. 'You shall tremble to the push of my hard-on length, and remember ever after how you were poked to a frazzle on this evening by a man with an iron cockstand.'

He made her change position, to sit astride his thighs, pussy open and accessible to him. She lifted her backside a little, whilst he held his hard-on shaft at the best angle, so that it was driven up into her when she sank down again on him.

'Place your hands on my shoulders and do nothing more,' said he, 'for I mean to roger you, not allow you to roger me.'

She obeyed, and lay motionless on him in her languor, her arms hooked over his shoulders, and her legs dangling outside his, making no effort to assist him further. He drew in a long deep breath, then initiated a feeble rogering of her. It came as no surprise to either that the action was long and slow, and although Polly wanted no more of Percival Proud's attentions to her pussy, she was compelled at last, against her will though it was, to experience certain pleasant sensations from his sliding over her sensitive button.

'You mean to poke me to death,' she sighed, 'I see that now, too late! And according to your Dr Acton, you will drop dead when you shoot your last drop of juice into me . . . well, why not? It beats dying of cold and hunger.'

She lay still and let him have his way with her, content to know that the gentleman had paid her a week's keep for the use of her slit for a couple of hours. That was apart from the coins she filched out of his pocket, and which were now safely concealed inside her rear entrance. They'd be no worse for that, after a scrub with soap and water.

Eventually, she felt his shaft grow harder still and stronger inside her, and knew he was nearing the end of his journey. Not that she expected him to die of rogering — that was her joke to please him — but he'd be wrung out like a dish rag by the time he'd fetched off one more time. In another twenty strokes he sighed and moaned, then within her wet pussy his shaft jerked fiercely and he spouted his last few drops into her.

Polly shrieked at the ecstatic pleasure that tore unexpected through her, so intense as to be almost painful. It made her twitch and squirm against Randolph's belly, spiked as she was on his throbbing length. His jerking faded to a faint trembling and she guessed that he was faint in the aftermath of his long rogering. She let herself collapse upon him and sink down into oblivion.

CHAPTER 3

Improprieties of a Mayfair Society Hostess

After leaving the premises in Jermyn Street in which he had so greatly indulged himself in illicit sexual pleasure with Polly and her sniffly-nosed friend, Meg, Randolph strolled up toward Piccadilly in search of a cab. In truth, he had to admit with a wry smile that his knees were somewhat shaky underneath him, an outcome not to be wondered at after so extended a bout with the two doxies, and spending so often in a short time. That apart, a feeling of general contentment suffused his being.

The theatres had come out, and Haymarket and Piccadilly were crowded with people. The common sort would return to their home by public omnibus, but the better people were looking for cabs, and that would reduce Randolph's chance of finding one to take him to Cavendish Square and his bed. The roadway was equally as crowded as the pavement, for a variety of hansom cabs, private carriages and other conveyances were jostling past each other, to the imprecations of coachmen, the rattle of hooves and the creak of springs.

He heard his name called, and turned, to see a four-wheeler at the kerb, halted there for a moment by the great throng of vehicles. The nearside window was down and a top-hatted head thrust out.

'Lorimer!' said Randolph, recognising by the street lights the luxuriant mutton-chop whiskers of a good friend. 'Have you room for me, for I am damnably tired of walking?'

'Jump in, my dear chap,' said Lorimer Mawby, and swung open the door for Randolph to get in, 'what have you been up to this evening? Were you at the club?'

'I've been . . . nothing in particular,' he answered, sinking into the vacant seat. He had been on the very edge of replying that the had been hard at it since dinnertime rogering a brace of young trollops and in the nick of time he had noted the presence of a lady in the vehicle. Lorimer introduced him to her, and to the man who sat beside her. She was Miss Dorothy Harker, and the other was her brother, Devlin Harker, a distant cousin of Lorimer's. They dwelt in the wilds of Warwickshire, it seemed, and were making a stay of some weeks in London.

The party of them had been to the opera at Covent Garden, to hear the celebrated Adelina Patti sing. In the interval, said Lorimer, he had visited the box of Mrs Alice Hamilton, taking his cousins with him, to pay his respects, for he was of that lady's acquaintance. She had invited him and his party to join her and other friends for refreshment at her house after the end of the performance.

'By Jove!' Randolph exclaimed 'I envy you your acquaintance with a society hostess of such renown. How did you come to know her, if I may ask?'

At that Lorimer laughed oddly and suggested he should go with them to Mrs Hamilton's house, where he was sure to be welcome. Then speaking in an undertone so that Miss Harker did not hear, he declared that Randolph would be of damned little use to Mrs Hamilton, since by his pallor it was evident that he had been on the poke all evening.

'But you're not bad-looking, and she might well take a fancy to you,' he added with a chuckle. 'She's a devoted admirer of chaps our age, Randolph, just as long as they are strong-backed and vigorous.'

'Is that the way of it?' Randolph asked.

'Take my word for it,' said Lorimer, keeping his voice down lest any hint of impropriety should reach and disturb the young lady sitting opposite him, 'she drained me completely dry on a Wednesday afternoon last year, between luncheon and tea time, when I paid a social call on her, expecting nothing beyond a cup of tea and perhaps a quick feel of her bubbies, if I were lucky. While we were chatting I took the liberty of touching her knee lightly, and damme if Alice didn't push me down flat on my back on a sofa and straddle me, with her clothes up round her waist. Imagine my surprise and confusion!'

'She's a lady I could easily become fond of,' said Randolph. 'What then, Lorimer?'

'What indeed! She had my shaft stiff as an iron bar and well up her without so much as a by-your-leave, and rogered me twice before she let me sit up! Now I like a nice poke as much as the next man, but she was too confounded strenuous about it for me. Since then I've remained friendly with her, but at arm's length − a week or two of her would drain a chap for ever and finish him off for life! After she'd done with him, he'd never be able to get another stand or poke a woman again. So beware, my dear fellow, if she offers to lie down for you.'

No possible words of Lorimer's could be better calculated to arouse Randolph's interest in the well-known Mrs Hamilton than this reference to an affair of the heart started and called off in the space of a single afternoon. To dignify so curtailed and scant a friendship as *of the heart* was to do Lorimer too much honour, Randolph decided. What had been commenced was an affair *of the parts*, and had no more significance than an hour or two with a paid whore.

As for Lorimer backing away from Mrs Hamilton's enthusiasm, in all probability the situation was reversed — more likely she had cooled off after finding him to be an unsatisfactory bed-partner. That was the way of it, in Randolph's view, for he had never heard of Lorimer accomplishing any noteworthy feat as a cocksman. On the occasion or two in the past they had together sought recreation in a house of ill-fame, by the time Randolph poked his trollop to a standstill, Lorimer had long since done with his and was gone. From which the only deduction to be made was that twice was Lorimer's limit.

Mrs Hamilton's house was in South Street, Mayfair, and there were several carriages at the door when Lorimer Mawby's party arrived. For as long as Randolph could remember there had been gossip about the lady, some of it unflattering if any truth in it was to be discerned. Her first husband when she was a girl had been a fashionable captain of the Horse Guard, who died and left her a widow at twenty.

The manner of his dying was unusual and unfortunate — he had been shot to death in a highly unlawful duel in Hyde Park early one morning. The cause of the fatal meeting was said by those in the know to be his wife's honour, which no doubt meant that the Captain had surprised her in bed with another man between her legs. Randolph thought it extraordinary that a man should take the risk of being shot at with a pistol to decide who had the use of a particular woman's commodity. In these modern times only the French went in for highflown nonsense of that sort. Be that as it might, the lively young widow had shortly after remarried – and to the gentleman who was said by rumour to have shot her first husband to death under the trees by Park Lane.

This was Mr Moncrief Hamilton, a wealthy connection of a most distinguished family, and for a time it appeared that illicit love had triumphed. The newly-weds honeymooned abroad in Italy, and then were seen everywhere about fashionable London, seeming marvellously devoted to each other. Lady Antrey informed her close friends that she had been astounded and shocked to near-swooning by seeing the Hamiltons in a box at the theatre one evening, he with his hand thrust up his wife's clothes, and this in the second act of the great Shakespeare's *Macbeth*!

As for Mrs Hamilton's hand, Lady Antrey refused outright to particularise its position, though to her very closest friends she confided that Mr Hamilton's trouser buttons were undone and his person was exposed and erect. From that they must draw what conclusion they could as to the whereabouts of Mrs Hamilton's hand, for to say more would be indecent in the extreme.

Yet love-birds do not always continue to bill and coo on the perch together. Less than a year of wedded bliss with Alice was in the event as much as Mr Hamilton could sustain. He had gone abroad, and there he remained, leaving her in possession of the house in Mayfair and an adequate income.

Perhaps Mr Hamilton had been another like Lorimer, unable to roger the lady into submission, thought Randolph, as he handed Miss Harker out of the four-wheeler and to the open front door. A footman showed them up to the drawing room, where twenty or so people stood in conversation, sipping at iced champagne. All the guests but three were men, Randolph noted.

In addition to Miss Harker, whom he now saw by the gaslight to be a very pretty girl, there was a yellow-haired Frenchwoman in pink, her dress cut so low that her titties were near to bare. She evidently was the mistress of the man who stood next to her and who smiled foolishly at her conversation. Randolph eyed her with interest, drained though he was, and thought that she'd be a damned fine poke, if a fellow got a chance with her. Everyone said that Frenchwomen were highly skilled in the art of taking a man's shaft in their mouth and that was a national accomplishment he would be interested to pursue further, should opportunity arise.

The third female guest in the drawing room was a plump white-skinned girl of sixteen or seventeen at most, who looked quite lost. No doubt she was someone's sister, who had been with him at the opera, when he was honoured with an invitation by Mrs Hamilton. The little innocent could have no thought that the men in the room, her brother included, were much like swarming male bees round a queen, Mrs Hamilton, each vying to be the one who got his shaft into her.

That notwithstanding, the girl had promise, in Randolph's view – for no female escaped his assessment of her usefulness on her back. Little Miss Sixteen was possessed of a plump and warm succulence, like a ripe peach ready to burst in the mouth. At another time, and in another place, he would be most pleased to relieve her of her maidenhead, if sweet words and kisses could persuade her to allow a hand in her drawers.

It was some time before Lorimer could break through the crush about their hostess to present Randolph. He, nothing loth, used the respite to down a glass or two of iced French champagne, to raise his spirits and put spring into his step.

He wished that it might also put lead into his pencil, but that was to hope for too much after his long indulgence with Polly and Meg in Jermyn Street.

Mrs Hamilton, he observed, was a well-fleshed lady of middle height, almost thirty years of age, and of a markedly healthy appearance. She was sturdy of form, almost buxom, as the common parlance has it, full-breasted and short-necked, with a great profusion of thick and shiny black hair dressed upwards and set with small pearls. Her face was open and pleasant rather than pretty, her eyes large and lively, her jaw firm and resolute.

In short, a woman designed by Nature for daily and vigorous rogering, Randolph concluded. In his imagination he strove to see through her fashionably low-cut evening gown, in order to envisage the broad warm belly which Lorimer had been shown one afternoon, and the soft pussy into which that ineffectual young man had been awarded the privilege of fetching off.

Hers would be a pussy of weight and substance, Randolph was utterly certain, adorned by a thicket of jet black hair, with plump pink lips a man could kiss until they parted to reveal a well-developed pleasure-button for his tongue to caress. Even to think in this way made poor, worn out, shrivelled Mr Percival twitch faintly in Randolph's trousers, but no more than that. He could be compared with a bare-fist fighter in the fortieth round of a boxing match, who had been knocked down one time too many, and could not rise to his feet again, however loud the crowd roared for him.

Mrs Hamilton had a throaty chuckle and an ease of conversation, he found when at last he was introduced and allowed to take her hand for a moment and press it. As they talked together, he was aware that her eyes were on him boldly, weighing him up, and he stood straight and smiled for her. How it came about, he had no conception, but she was skilled in the social graces and from being one of a group of young men around her, he found himself alone with her by the drawing-room windows, where stood a grand piano, and they were leafing through pages of music, her hand touching his arm lightly.

To his delight and chagrin, she was asking, without the least indication of false bashfulness, if perhaps he might stay on a moment or two after the other guests had gone, to give her his views on the relative merits of something or other to do with music. Randolph had precious little taste for music, apart from the sentimental ditties and the low catches of music hall and public house, but he was aware that music was not the topic she wished to discuss in private with him.

'Dear Mrs Hamilton,' he said, a touch of sorrow in his voice, 'nothing would, I assure you, give me greater pleasure than to declare my views to you, in particular on organ music, where I consider myself to be something of a connoisseur.'

'Organ music!' said she, her dark eyes alight with interest. 'And an expert — delectable thought! Who are your favourite composers, Mr Joynes?'

'Why, Bach and Handel are supreme for organ performances, in my experience,' he replied, with a smile.

'You say that with a degree of warmth that hints at more than you make plain — acquaint me with your meaning, if you please.'

'I shall be happy to oblige you,' he said, bowing slightly at the double-meaning. 'For I am sure that with you on your *back*, and my *handle* at the ready, together we could enjoy an organ recital of some virtuosity.'

'You have a naughty wit, I see. I feel that I must learn

more of your qualities before you leave, much more!'

'The problem is,' said he, sounding most rueful, which indeed he was, 'I must in confidence confess that earlier this evening I dined with the widow of an old friend, a clergyman of Ebury Street, who was taken by the apoplexy not a month ago.'

The lie was absolutely necessary – to admit he had paid a pair of young whores to let him have the use of their cunnies would result, he feared, in his dismissal from Mrs Hamilton's side instantly. His ruse worked, and she heard his story with her eyes on him and a look of amusement on her face.

'I felt it my duty to do all I could to console the lady's loneliness,' he went on. 'After a good dinner and a bottle of port wine, one thing followed on from another, as often it does on occasions of this type . . .'

'Say no more,' exclaimed Mrs Hamilton in disappointment. 'How very provoking! The trigger was pulled and the shot fired, now the pistol is uncocked.'

'The question was not merely one of a shot being fired,' said Randolph, 'a veritable fusillade was shot off, a *feu de joie*, as the French have it, until the ammunition locker was empty. I am grieved beyond reason at this particular, for I feel that you and I, were you to permit it, could become fast friends.'

'We shall see,' she answered, tapping his wrist with her fan, 'call on me tomorrow at five.'

With that, she was gone. Not half a minute later Randolph saw her in conversation with another man, one with a neatly trimmed red beard, her hand resting lightly on his sleeve as, no doubt, she enquired of him if he were minded to stay behind after the rest departed, to explain something or other to her.

With a shrug of his broad shoulders, Randolph made himself acquainted with one or two of the other guests, including the Frenchwoman in pink, Madame Du Rocqueville, she called herself, and she had a lascivious and rolling eye. Her almost uncovered titties were a delight to behold from close at hand, until her protector took her by the arm and led her away from Randolph's attentions.

He would have transferred his interest to the pretty Miss Harker, but Lorimer seemed unusually attached to her, keeping a conversation going uninterrupted. That being so, Randolph made his way to the plump young girl in white muslin, who seemed to have been deserted, and she was overwhelmed by the attentions of so elegant a gentleman.

Flattered by the girl's response and to prove that, even if he were drained dry of sap, he retained his charm for the fair sex, Randolph led young Adelia, for that was her name, into a corner of the drawing room where the long brocade curtains made a useful place of concealment. He praised her looks and figure, and she, being unused to the deceit of flattery, made no move to stop him when he touched her face, and then her neck. She stared up at him in surprise when his hand sank lower, but gave no sign of distress while he treated himself to a good feel of her plump titties down the front of her evening frock.

A line or two of verse he had read in a volume of Mr Thomas Hood came into his mind, apropos of what he was doing to her, and he recited them softly to Adelia:

> *When she was twelve, I slipped my hand*
> *Up in her dress behind,*
> *And stroked her bum, you understand,*
> *Much as I felt inclined.*

She giggled and she squirmed about,
But liked my daring rudeness;
She dragged my trouser buttons out,
Returning all my lewdness.

At his words, Adelia herself giggled, and he would have gone on a little further and treated himself to a feel of her maiden cunny. Before he could do so, her brother came across the room in haste, with a suspicious look in his eye, whereupon Randolph desisted and went home to his bed and sleep.

Punctually at five o'clock the next afternoon he presented himself at the front door of Mrs Hamilton's house and gave his name to a footman who opened it. He was shown straightway into a ground-floor room furnished as a library, and asked to wait. Some minutes passed before a smiling lady's maid appeared, to conduct him to Mrs Hamilton upstairs, in a pretty sitting room looking out over a small formal garden.

She shook hands and said she was glad to see him, and hoped that he had recovered his powers of discourse. He gave her his assurance that his natural abilities were fully restored, and a pleased smile spread over her face. Before there was time for the conversation to progress to an elaboration of the topic of sensuality that was in both their minds, the maid and a footman together brought in tea. Mrs Hamilton did the honours with the silver teapot and handed Randolph a cup.

Seeing that some conversation was required of him to preserve the social decencies for ten minutes, he enquired of his fair hostess if she were acquainted with the theories of Dr William Acton on the regulation of the sensual impulse.

'Acton?' said she, 'I've met Lord Acton a time or two
— is this one related? And how on earth does he propose
to regulate the strongest force in human nature?'

'The strongest force in masculine nature, you intend,' said
Randolph, setting out to chaff her a little, 'but not in female
nature. Dr Acton's opinion is that women are not much
troubled with sensual feelings of any kind. However, if in
exceptional circumstances such emotions become aroused,
then they are very moderate, compared with those of the
male, he believes.'

'What!' Mrs Hamilton exclaimed. 'The fellow is a fool!
I've yet to meet the man who could match my own nature
for strength of sensual impulse. Do you regard me as
abnormal for that?'

'Not I,' said Randolph, smiling at her indignation, 'but
the learned Dr Acton says in his book that frequent
indulgence in sexual excitement by women leads inevitably
to nymphomania, and early decline.'

'Pish!' said she.

'With that sentiment I agree,' said Randolph, 'for to my
way of thinking, Acton is mistaken. In my own family there
exists a useful example to the contrary — an aunt, a widowed
sister of my father's — a lady above forty years of age, with
an adequate income of her own. She some years ago ran
off to France with a drayman half her own age whom she
encountered in Cheapside. She lives there happy still, having
pensioned off her flagging drayman and exchanged him for
an even younger Frenchman.'

'I like the sound of this aunt,' said Mrs Hamilton. 'Long
may she live and be rogered! They say that Frenchmen are
skilled in bringing ladies off by the use of their tongue,
although I have not found one yet who was any good at it.'

At the open use of words that few ladies had heard of

and, if they did, they would blush scarlet bright and cover their ears, Randolph decided that the barriers were down. He leaned forward in his chair and placed a hand lightly on Mrs Hamilton's knee, smiling knowingly at her the while. This was what Lorimer said he had done, to start off her lewdness. Would she try to throw him on his back, as she had Lorimer, and bestride him?

'There's a surprise waiting for you,' said she, and before he could ask what it might be, she rose from her chair and stood before him, her hands on his shoulders in a manner encouraging to his ardent nature. She was that day dressed in a blouse of white silk and a black satin skirt, her full round bubbies and her broad hips filling out her garments in a manner suggestive of delights to come.

Randolph reached underneath her long skirt, smiling to feel her stocking under his fingers, then up her leg, as high as her knee. Above the knee lay the ribbon that served as garter and when he slipped his hand higher yet, his fingers lighted upon bare warm flesh.

'Oh!' he exclaimed, his mind reeling at this impossible and yet incontrovertible fact.

'Yes,' said she with a smile on her face, 'your senses do not deceive you, Randolph – I am wearing no drawers. Feel a little higher up my thigh, and assure yourself it is so.'

His hand lay flat between her fleshy thighs, and he sighed to feel it caught and pressed by them.

'How very delightful!' he said. 'And how truly surprising – do you often go without underwear, dear Alice?'

It was quite out of the question to continue to address her as Mrs Hamilton now that his palm was squeezed between her legs within an inch or two of her pussy.

'After luncheon was finished I went to my bedroom and removed my drawers, to be ready for your assault,' she replied. He wished to raise his hand higher and touch her pussy, but the clasp of her thighs held his hand immobile.

'Don't you believe me?' she asked, seeing his expression of mingled astonishment and delight. 'Then I'll show you.'

All pretence discarded, she raised a leg and rested her foot on the seat of his chair, then hitched up her skirts and lacy petticoats as high as her hips, to display her bare thighs. Between their soft creamy-skinned fullness was set a pouting black-haired pussy. Randolph stared, his breath catching in his throat, while Alice ran her fingers over her uncovered cunny and drew the lips apart. Contemplating that soft pink and hairy delight, he felt very near to fetching off in his trousers, for it seemed almost to have a life of its own, not waiting passive to be rogered, but palpating with vitality and appetite.

'Damme, but I must pay my respects!' he cried, and clasped Alice by the hips, to ease her back a step or two, so he could slide off his chair and down to his knees. She stood with her legs apart and her clothes held up high, while he pressed his lips feverishly to the nether mouth that invited his hot kisses.

Her bare thigh touched his ear in a casual caress that made his shaft leap boldly under his shirt. He dropped his hand down between his legs, to press the lively organ close to his belly and stifle its jerking, lest its friskiness brought him off prematurely.

Alice's voice reached him through his sensual confusion.

'I like your manners, Randolph − we shall become good friends if you continue to please me, as you have begun.'

He knew precisely what she intended by her words, and what she required of him as a gesture of goodwill, if he expected to be allowed to poke her in due course.

'Allow me to demonstrate to you that an Englishman can

beat a Frenchie hands down,' said Randolph. 'Damn all foreigners — our ways are better than theirs, on that you may rely!'

'Show me!' she cried, a tremor in her voice.

Obediently he thrust out his tongue and brought it to bear on her impatient pussy. Very quickly he attained a great agitation of mind, whilst he licked her voluptuously, and he soon became intensely aroused.

'Ah, that does feel very nice!' Alice exclaimed. 'No doubt but you've kissed a cunny or two before, Randolph! I'm glad of it — I do so hate the fumblings of beginners.'

Her hand rested on his head to encourage his administrations, and her smooth thigh pressed against his cheek. Before long he heard her gasping at the force of the sensual sensations she was enjoying, and he redoubled the flickering of his wet tongue in her. Down below in his trousers Mr Percival Proud had become so big and hard that Randolph had no choice but to force a hand down inside his waistband and take hold of his quivering shaft, to control its furious leaping.

He heard Alice panting loudly under the darting caresses of his tongue, and he knew that her supreme moment would not long be delayed. He himself could hardly draw breath for his raging excitation. His body was ablaze with passionate lust, delicious spasms racked him from top to toe. Under his shirt his firmly clasped hand slid up and down his shaft, and he knew he could not endure much longer. Then Alice gave a shriek and jibbed her belly at him, her legs shaking to the throb of her climactic pleasure.

'You've brought me off, Randolph!' she gasped out. 'It feels wonderful! Don't let me stop!'

Nor did he — his busy tongue impelled her through a long and intense paroxysm of pleasure, until she breathed out in a long sigh and stood with her hands resting heavily on his shoulders, to support her trembling frame. Her clothes slid down over his head, and concealed him in intimate darkness, whilst her warm thighs clasped his face between them in repose. It was too much for Randolph's nervous system to tolerate longer. He moaned in delight, his hand rubbed faster, and an instant later he spent copiously in his trousers, his open mouth pressed to Alice's darling pussy.

CHAPTER 4
Some Doubt Cast on a Medical Man's Theory

Upstairs in Mrs Hamilton's pretty little sitting room, Randolph knelt before her, with his head thrust up her skirts and his hot mouth pressed against her hairy pussy. Homage had been paid to her charms, and an emotion of pleasant lassitude suffused his limbs. Against his belly, his shirt was sticking warmly, by the copiousness of his fetching off.

'Darling boy,' he heard Alice say, 'that was extraordinarily pleasing — you may come out now.'

She raised her skirts and petticoats to uncover his head, and for yet a moment he gazed in admiration at the fullness of her creamy-skinned thighs and the pouting black-haired pussy that was set between them. She could hardly deny him the use of it now that he had pleasured her in the French fashion with his tongue. Her dark eyes stared down at him, shining with approval and respect for his skill — and with perhaps a glint of greedy anticipation of what he would do to her next.

Whilst she stood with her hands on his shoulders, leaning her weight a little on him, and in some measure recovering herself, Randolph took the opportunity to find the placket of her skirt and undo it. He untied the strings of her petticoats, so that all fell down to the floor. Without commenting on what he had done, she stepped out of her skirts, and he rose to his feet to unpin the carved jet brooch that closed her blouse at the neck, and unbutton it all the way down.

'I've a mighty desire to be rogered by a hard-on shaft,' said she, 'are you able to oblige me so soon, Randolph?'

'Without a doubt,' he replied, 'for my desire matches yours.'

'Will you have me on the sofa?' she enquired.

Before answering her question, he lifted her chemise with an eager hand, and assured himself again that Alice was wearing no drawers. He slid a bent middle finger between the wet pink lips of her pussy, and tickled her.

'Damn all this talk of lying down,' said he, attending to her black-haired pussy's delight with a skill that brought a smile to her face, 'that's for ninnies and mollycoddles. I'll have you on your back only when I've had you so many times my legs won't bear me up any longer.'

He rose to his feet and gazed quickly round the sitting room, making his choice.

'Put your hands on the chair arm and bend over,' said he.

Without any word of objection, Alice tucked her lace-trimmed chemise up about her waist, placed her hands on the padded arm of the nearest chair. She leaned well forward from the waist, supporting herself with straight arms, displaying to him her bare bottom, full and round-cheeked, white-skinned and soft as down-filled pillows. Randolph stood behind her and clapped his hands to her lower cheeks, to squeeze and stroke to his heart's content. Then with firm fingers he parted her magnificent orbs and with a deft finger tickled her knot-hole.

'There's more to be said for this standing up to it than I at first thought!' Alice opined. 'You may kiss my bottom, my own dearest man.'

From a woman of lower rank, the same words would have been an insult beyond bearing, but from the lips of Alice Hamilton they constituted an open invitation to sensual pleasure beyond the ordinary. Randolph went down on his knees behind her, to do her homage, his mind in a frenzy of delight. He kissed her rotund backside and nipped the soft flesh between his teeth, causing her to squirm and cry out in pleasure.

'Roger me!' she pleaded. 'I am on fire for it!'

He stood up and tore open his buttons — and out there sprang Mr Percival Proud, quivering in his eagerness to show off his mettle. His hands grasping Alice's hips to steady her, Randolph pressed Percival's uncovered purple head into the hot and wet slit that awaited him. The bliss of that moment was beyond all belief, as his shaft sank by slow inches into Alice's slippery cunny. It gripped him closely, though there was nothing of the virginal about it, nor had been for many a year, but it fitted him well. He made a deduction that regular daily penetration and use had accustomed Alice's pussy to accommodate and welcome any dimension of male shaft.

'Do me harder!' she cried out, as he began to roger briskly. 'Ravish me to death, Randolph!'

He thrust in to the very hilt, his belly up hard against the cheeks of her bottom, and poked her with short and savage tups that brought whimpers of joy from her. Together in harmony of mind and body, they drew near to the sensual climax, Randolph's hands feeling up underneath Alice's loose shift, to grasp hold of her plump titties and roll them in his palms. She shrieked in rapture, and jerked her bottom back against his loins at the moment he spilled his essence into her hot and clinging pussy.

So thrilling were the sensations of that moment that in his exultation Randolph thought he would never stop fetching off in her! His stiffly swollen shaft throbbed and bounded while it discharged into the palpitating pussy that clung about it as if it would never again release it. Alice's cries of *more, more* rang shrilly about the room, whilst the ecstatic shaking of her body rattled on the floor the legs of the chair she leaned on.

However intense the pleasure, it can last but seconds. Soon the sharp thrill grew less, faded in both of them, then ebbed away to mere memory. Alice was left trembling over the chair, and Randolph close up but motionless behind her, his softening shaft sliding from her wet parts. They smiled at each other in approbation, then sat down on the sofa, side by side, to regain their equanimity a little before going further with their play.

'Are you now convinced that your Dr Acton is ignorant of the strength of sexual feeling in women?' Alice asked, rubbing her titties where Randolph had sunk fiercely grasping fingers into their soft flesh.

'Why, no — quite the reverse!' he said with a sly smile, 'Dr Acton predicts a raging nymphomania as the fate of any female who allows herself to indulge in repeated sexual gratification. My observation is that he is correct, for I never met a finer example of nymphomania in a woman than now — for which I am appropriately grateful. Be warned, dear Alice, for I mean to take every advantage of this sexual madness of yours.'

'If this is madness, then it is most enjoyable,' she replied. 'You have my fullest permission to take every advantage of me that you can, whatever the hour of day or night.'

There was good reason why Mrs Hamilton's servants had strict orders never to enter any room where she entertained a visitor unless she rang the bell. Leader of society though she was, and a frequent dinner guest of the highest in the land, here in her own house in the full light of day she sat on a sofa clad only in a thin shift and stockings, and the shift drawn up about her waist to expose her plump white thighs most indecently, to say nothing of the black-haired delight between them — on which Randolph had laid a comforting hand.

He too was in no condition befitting a gentleman calling upon an acquaintance at tea time. His grey trousers gaped open from waistband to seam, revealing his shaft — limp, yet thick and powerful of appearance even in repose.

'Explain this to me,' said Alice, 'why is it that, according to your foolish Dr Acton, men are able to sustain the sexual paroxysm repeatedly without ill effect, but women must refrain on peril of moral and physical decline. Does this not seem to you grossly unfair?'

'What the devil has fairness to do with it?' Randolph asked. 'Physical circumstances are as they are for an excellent reason — Nature intended it so. Mr Charles Darwin explained all about that in his book. There are the strong and the weak, the rich and the poor, the English and foreigners, the rulers and the ruled, the clever and the slow, men and women — how else could it be in a rational scheme of things? Nature gives to men a long thick shaft, and to women a soft slit, so that the one may be plunged into the other, for the release of the male essence, for his pleasure and gratification. How can anyone take exception to so very sensible an arrangement?'

'That be jiggered for a tale,' said Mrs Hamilton, lapsing

in the heat of disagreement into coarseness of expression better suited to a drab in a public house.

She rose from the sofa and collected up her clothes from the floor where they had been thrown.

'Come with me, Randolph,' she ordered, 'and we'll change this foolish notion of yours for the better.'

He followed her from the small sitting room into an adjoining dressing room beyond which, he guessed, lay her bedroom.

'Off with your clothes, and be quick about it,' said she with an ambiguous smile.

In short order Randolph was stripped down to his long under-drawers and socks, all else bare and exposed. Now it was that he received his first inkling of the far reaches of depravity to which Alice Hamilton's imagination extended, and her abiding lust for strong sensation. But only by degrees did this dawn upon him — at first he watched with some amusement whilst Alice donned his discarded clothes.

'My word!' she exclaimed when she pulled his shirt over her head. 'How wet and sticky you have made your shirt front with your spending, Randolph — I trust that you have enough left in you to continue?'

'Have no fear on that score,' he assured her, 'I have ample and to spare, to satisfy you, Alice.'

'A bold boast! Well, we shall see.'

His trousers were too long for her legs, and the sleeves of his shirt too long for her arms, as also were the sleeves of his frock-coat, but she turned them back to fit as well as she could make them.

'Now,' said she, attired in male clothing, 'since you have so kindly explained to me how very dangerous is the sexual spasm to the female constitution, though it is not so to the male, I have decided to change sex for a few hours and make myself out a young gentleman. By this contrivance no ill effect shall come to me from repeated rogering.'

Randolph laughed and seated himself on a chair by the window.

'Until further notice,' said his volatile companion, 'I am Mr Charles Hamilton, and so you must address me. I am at home from school for the hols. I suppose you must be my Mama's lover, as I find you here in her dressing room.'

When she moved within his reach, Randolph slipped a bare arm about her waist and pulled her down on his lap.

'No, no, you must not touch me, sir!' she exclaimed at once, 'I have been warned about the sort of men who desire to take advantage of young gentleman like me . . .'

'Do not be alarmed, young sir,' Randolph, putting on a manner meant to soothe and allay misgivings, 'you may entrust yourself to my honour, without reservation.'

'Not so!' she replied. 'For your bearing indicates that you have wicked and unnatural designs on my person! Fie, sir, for shame! I am sure you have a cockstand, you horrid man.'

During this complaint, Randolph's hand had slowly and almost imperceptibly, unbuttoned her trousers, and insinuated itself most stealthily inside, to touch the flesh of her inner thighs, and stroke there with a touch as soft as a child.

'But this is monstrous!' said she. 'How dare you touch me!'

Randolph's fingers were at her hairy cunny, hardly moving at all, but the sensation was so very thrilling to her and to him alike that only an effort of will held Alice back from pushing her split against his hand, and a similar effort restrained him from sliding his middle finger into her wetness.

'You are a wicked man, to finger an innocent young gentleman, and an Etonian to boot, in this shameful manner!' Alice said shrilly, her face flushed bright pink with emotion.

'You mistake my intention, I do positively assert,' Randolph replied suavely. 'As one with more experience than yourself in the intimacies of the sensual emotions, I mean only to examine your parts, in hope to establish that there has been no manual misuse or premature manipulation.'

'You insult me, sir,' said she, breathing more quickly to the gentle stimulation of his hand. 'I vow I have no idea of what you can mean by these words.'

'Do not attempt to deceive me,' Randolph retorted, 'if you were as innocent as you claim, you would not have let me put my hand in your trousers. I suspect the truth of it is that like all young gentleman of sixteen or thereabouts you have fallen into the forbidden habit of self-abuse, and make sport with your shaft continually.'

Whilst he was speaking, the tip of Randolph's finger grazed delicately along the wet lips of Alice's pussy, and her body shook with tremors of bliss within the arm that held her.

'Please, sir,' she said faltering, 'I humbly beg you not to inform anyone that you have discovered my secret shame, or I shall be beaten on the bare bottom. I don't make myself fetch off too often, you may believe me, hardly ever more than twice or thrice a day.'

'A likely story!' Randolph retorted. 'You will not bamboozle me with your untruths – the prevalence of precocious sexual excitation in adolescent males has been carefully studied by expert medical men, and the symptoms described. The celebrated Dr Acton goes so far as to declare that early incontinence and self-abuse are undoubtedly the most vicious of all courses.'

Still playing her role of young gentleman, shaken though she was by the thrilling sensations caused by the regular movement of Randolph's fingers, tiny thrills that made her pussy pout in eagerness for more, Alice raised her voice in protest.

'No, you are not to do this to me,'she said. 'It is infamous to handle a young gentleman's private parts in this way! I beg you to desist before you cause me to come off.'

'The bringing on of the sensual spasm by manual titillation is to be avoided,' said Randolph, 'for Dr Acton has explained in detail how it leads inevitably to an unmanly condition of undeveloped muscles, a pale complexion, and a soft skin. If the evil habit is persisted in, it brings on degeneration of body and intellect. The misguided youth who indulges himself may end up a lifelong invalid, or even a drivelling idiot, if the case is an extreme one.'

Alice was rubbing her pussy against his fingers. The lips had parted to allow him to feel the slipperiness within, and by it to appreciate the warm invitation it was extending to him.

'From this melancholy circumstance,' Randolph continued, 'we may note that wanton self-gratification by young males is equally as pernicious as a deliberate indulgence by females in the spasm of sexual excitation, and for both sexes the habit must eventually lead to the same mournful fate.'

'Then you must advise me,' Alice gasped, her hot breath on his neck, 'how is a young person like myself to throw

61

off this habit and escape the perils attendant on persistent stimulation of the sexual organ?'

'I shall instruct you in the means of avoiding solitary abuse and its outcome,' said Randolph, 'only be patient and trust to me, however odd you think my course of action.'

He undid the buttons of her braces and pulled down her loose trousers round her knees, she lifting her bottom a little from his lap to assist him. Mr Percival Proud had been at the stand and poking upright out of the slit of Randolph's underdrawers for long enough. His abundant spend in Randolph's clothes, when Alice had been licked off to the spasm, had not at all impaired his capacity, and he vibrated gently, begging to be plunged into a hot and wet slit.

Randolph slipped a hand under Alice's thigh to adjust her position relative to his own, so that her legs were well apart and his shaft stood up hard-on between them.

'What a beauty,' Alice sighed, gazing down at its length and thickness, 'how handsome a fellow he is, with his thick shaft and engorged head. I vow that if he were mine I would take him in hand and bring him off ten times a day!'

'You must cease from such talk,' said Randolph sternly, 'in a minute or two you will understand how perverse impulses of that nature may be banished.'

With eager fingers he parted the plump lips beneath her curls of shiny black, and tickled her exposed button till she uttered little squeals of joy. Then, she seated sideways on his lap, he manoeuvred Mr Percival Proud's swollen head between the swollen lips of her cunny, and placed her hand over their joined parts. Without a pause, she seized upon his lewd intention, and jerked Mr Proud quickly up and down, making the soft head rub over her button.

'Why yes!' she panted. 'This is an excellent way to prevent a lapse into self-stimulation. By manipulating your parts to the sexual climax, I ensure my own pleasure, without the shame of having fingered myself for even a moment! Nor do I submit to being rogered as a woman, which too leads to debilitation, you have asserted. Your contrivance to avoid these dangers is well thought out – I am most obliged to you.'

'And I to you,' Randolph exclaimed, greatly enjoying the rub of Mr Percival's tender head on her slippery flesh, 'for I too am engaged in neither rogering nor digital manipulation of the parts, yet I shall surely fetch off in another minute!'

'You are most welcome,' sighed Alice, her hand sliding faster over their contingent and throbbing organs of delight.

'Oh!' said Randolph. 'Oh, my dearest Alice!'

Even as he spoke, his belly heaved strongly to the deep inner surge of his sap. An instant later it was expelled from his convulsing shaft in a creamy torrent, that spurted high over Alice's secret button, then out from between her parted pussy lips, and halfway up the front of the shirt she wore, causing her to emit sharp cries of delight as she too came off.

They rested content for a time, hardly speaking in the soft languor that eased their limbs, relaxed their minds, and calmed their emotions. But not for very long, both being uncommonly greedy of sensual pleasure. It was Alice, her fingers stroking along his limp and wet shaft, who commenced the conversation.

'In your examination of the doctrines of Dr Acton,' said she, 'have you established beyond doubt in which class of society he conducted the researches on which his views are based? I mean, he would at the expense of a few shillings have free access to the private parts of as many adolescent girls of the labouring classes as he wished. But to observe the condition of the same parts in young ladies of the upper classes would be impossible, even for a doctor, in any numbers that were meaningful.'

'There is some truth in what you say,' Randolph said, struck by the logic of her argument. 'I cannot answer your question at present. I shall tomorrow or the next day refer to his books to ascertain if the extent of his researches into the well-being of young ladies' pussies is made plain.'

'My deduction is this,' said Alice, 'your Acton's strictures on indulgence in sexual excitement applies only to the lower classes, who are not so healthily bred, or fed, as we are. For persons like ourselves, there is no risk attached to constant rogering, of that I am convinced, for we have the appetite to it, and the leisure for it, and comfortable homes in which we may take as much pleasure as we choose.'

So saying, she rose from his lap and held out her hand to him − and led him through a door into the next room, which was, as he had already deduced, her bedchamber. Whilst he removed his underdrawers and socks, his only garments, Alice threw off the frock coat and trousers she wore, and the wet-fronted shirt. At that, she stood naked and unashamed before him, her plump round titties and belly exposed to his ardent gaze.

'Since it seems you have an aversion to poking a woman on her back, I shall respect your preferences,' she said. 'Lie down.'

Randolph mounted the matrimonial bed and lay with his legs spread wide, whilst Mr Percival Proud performed his usual trick of growing twice as long and twice as thick as when at rest. Alice seated herself naked on the bed beside him, her shining eyes attracted unerringly to the stiff and strong-looking shaft that pointed upward toward her face.

She stroked Randolph's bare belly with one hand, whilst

with the other she took hold of Mr Percival and gave that gentleman a hand massage that made him quiver and jerk in expectation of more to come. Seeing how susceptible he was, she bent over him, her tongue flicked out and teased the purple head, which soon began to ooze tiny droplets of love juice. Randolph smiled and reached out to play with her soft dangling titties, whilst her little tongue flicked out to tease Mr Proud, before she sucked the shaft in between her lips.

She sucked vigorously at Randolph's throbbing muscle, until on the bedcover his bottom was squirming in blissful sensation, at which she transferred the seat of her attentions, lest she should inadvertently bring him off before she was prepared. She ran her tongue up and down his belly, brushing her soft cheek against his trembling shaft. Her hands moved over his body, to pluck at his flat teats and tear gasps of joy from his lips.

'I mean to have you again, Randolph,' she announced, 'three or four times, before I send you away. Conserve your strength, and let me arrange things to my own liking.'

At that, she slid herself on top of him, her mouth searching eagerly for his lips, and kissed him passionately, her bare thighs moving on his until their hairy muffs rubbed together. A hand felt between their hot bellies – her hand, shaking with emotion – and steered his straining shaft to the opening of her slippery-wet pussy. Then with a strong push, worthy of a man, she moved her hips forward, and cried out in delight to feel Mr Percival's swollen head forced deep into her.

'How many times can you fetch off before your shaft lies limp and useless?' she demanded of him. 'Four, five?'

'You must find that out for yourself!' he gasped.

'Then I shall roger you until you can no more,' she said

most firmly. 'I will send you home a nervous wreck in a cab, before dinner.'

Her plump belly plunged on his, rubbing her love-button up and down his embedded shaft, to bring on her own pleasurable thrills. Randolph moaned and rolled his head from side to side, as the climax of sensation came ever closer.

'Acton's warnings are for shopgirls and working-men's wives, not for people like you and me!' Alice panted. 'Rogering's the healthiest exercise in the world − I've known that since the very first time I came off as a girl!'

Randolph was unable to make any coherent reply to her daring statement, for sensation overwhelmed him just then and he shot spurt after spurt of hot essence up into her pussy. Her eyes opened wide as she felt him spend, and together they jerked and bounced in their paroxysm, each biting at the soft flesh of the other's shoulder. They both shrieked in their excitement, until all was done and they sank back, sated for the moment.

CHAPTER 5
A Halt is Called,
or Nearly So

In the days that followed his introduction to the enthusiastic Mrs Hamilton, Randolph acquired by intimate acquaintance with her desires some small knowledge of her character, and of the reach of perversity she was wont to enjoy with never a qualm or second thought. Had she been born a male, this would have been of no account at all, and certainly not a reproach — merely the sign of a good fellow, who enjoyed rogering in its many forms and variations.

In a woman, no such easy verdict could be given. Perhaps, to stretch a point, this degree of lubricity was acceptable in a young whore, seeking to gain her livelihood. Even then, such a trollop would have the sense to await her client's lead, before plunging into the wilder forms of sensual pleasure. Men are men — and are by no means pleased if their male right to choose the sport is undermined by female pushfulness.

More to the point yet, when found in a gentlewoman of style, these characteristics of demanding constant rogering were not wholly admirable. To speak frankly, Alice Hamilton's insatiable need for a shaft inside her was becoming tedious to Randolph. He had known her for a little less than a fortnight, in which period he had rogered her 32 times, if his reckoning was right, brought her off in the French way by the use of his tongue 17 times more, and fingered her cunny to climactic spasm another dozen times, in round figures.

In addition to fetching-off in her pussy 32 times in the 12½ days, he had shot his roe between her titties 4 times, besides in her mouth 7 times, and in her rear entrance twice more, she having an occasional fancy for the Turkish style of love, and between her thighs once, by accident. He said nothing of the times he had come off in his trousers, manipulated by her busy fingers in hansom cabs and carriages, in the theatre and once at dinner in the Cafe Royal, under cover of the tablecloth.

The fact had to be admitted that the superb and haughty Alice Hamilton, in the world's eyes so refined, so fastidious, and so lady-like, was in private the most lascivious of harlots. Even Randolph, experienced as he was in the ways of women, high and low, was astonished and almost daunted by the intensity of her passions and the never-ending requirement to be brought off.

Whenever she was alone with a likely young man, some devil of lechery seemed to take possession of the lady. Propriety and common decency meant nothing to her at such times – she ceased to restrain her sexual propensities and gave fullest vent to them. Like Eve herself in the Garden of Eden, Alice had tasted the forbidden fruit, and was determined to gorge herself on it to total repletion, let the consequences be what they might.

These displeasing thoughts passed through Randolph's mind one morning when he awoke in his own bed after an evening out with Alice that had drained him of every drop and fatigued him to the point where he had fallen asleep in the cab conveying him at midnight to his home in Cavendish Square.

He could see very well that, far from being Alice's lover, he was only the recipient of her lust and the handy instrument for her sensual satisfaction. He had heard tell of great ladies who used their footmen in this manner, summoning them to their side in idle moments, to pull open the buttons of their breeches and lift out the fleshy shaft, without so much as a word addressed to the menial who owned it.

Indeed, Randolph recalled reading more than one account of an exploitation of their servants by ladies of title and quality. These domestic secrets were not published in *The Times* or any respectable periodical, of course, but in books published most confidentially. They could be purchased from only a very few booksellers in the Strand and elsewhere in town, by gentlemen trusted by the vendors. One such that Randolph had bought for a couple of guineas recently, and perused with great attention, concerned a youngish countess, who dwelt in Belgrave Square.

It was made apparent by the relater of this curious account that her husband was somewhat older in years, and incapable of supplying her need more than once a day. From this particular there arose in the lady an untoward attention to the servants, the male ones, that is to say.

On an evening when, after dinner, the Earl of Caterham had departed to his Club, the Countess rang the bell in her drawing room for a servant. The scene Randolph had read still remained clear in his mind.

The Countess was seated on a chair by the fireplace, having cast aside a novel by Mr George Meredith as much too dull for her mood. Her summons on the bell pull was answered by Henry, the handsomest of the four liveried footmen kept by the family. He inclined his head and waited for his instructions from Her Ladyship, but she with a little gesture of her soft white hand made him stand closer.

A strange expression passed over the footman's face when the slender fingers of the Countess tugged open all his breeches' buttons and reached delicately within to find his thick though quiescent shaft. His eyes stared down respectfully at her face, which was as calm and gentle as a child's — no man, or woman either, unless a witness to the lewd movement of the Countess's hand inside her servant's breeches would dream that she whose face showed such tranquillity to the world could be capable of so grossly improper an act!

Not so Henry, for he had been fingered by the consort of his employer many a time before. He stood straight-backed and still while she pulled into view his lady's plaything, now long and stiff. The Countess was left-handed, and in her right she held the balloon glass from which she had been sipping her after-dinner brandy. She held the glass close to the uncovered head of Henry's shaft while her other hand moved on his hot flesh, which continued to expand under her manipulation.

Soon it could grow no more, but bucked in her hand, for the footman was almost fetched off. He expected she would collect his gushing cream in her brandy glass, and braced himself on sturdy legs for the spasm that he felt to be imminent. Why Her Ladyship was bringing him off did not concern him at all — his duty was to wait upon her, and if her whim was to play with his shaft, then so be it. It relieved him of the need to perform the same office for himself when he went to bed, for he had no access to the female servants.

The mood of the Countess changed when she saw Henry's great shaft leaping in the premonitory spasms of coming off. At once she relinquished the grasp of her slender fingers, and left him shaking, while she turned up the skirt of her evening gown and her petticoats, to uncover fully her lacy drawers. Henry stood quivering in a frenzy of sexual excitation, his massive out-thrust shaft nodding up and down.

Her Ladyship parted the slit of her white drawers to bare her brown-haired aristocratic pussy. She was watching Henry's eyes bulge from his head, and his mouth, which hung open.

'Ha!' said she. 'I'm sure you'd finger me if I let you, but you are to remember your place and keep control of your emotion — indeed, now I come to think of it, it's highly insolent for you to have sensual emotions when you look at me!'

Henry was staring desperately at the pink lips of her cunny, afraid that he was about to fetch off involuntarily, over Her Ladyship's drawers! No doubt she'd punish him if he subjected her to so gross an insult — stop his wages for half a year, or even perhaps dismiss him. She noted on his face his feeling of alarm, and at once took the opportunity to remind him of his lowly station in life — for his own good, naturally.

'Stare you may, till you turn black in the face,' said she, 'I possess the prettiest pussy you'll ever see. I've been told by more than one admirer how very pretty it is. But how could you possibly tell, in your position? The only ones you've had to do with are the common slits between housemaid's legs.'

'Yes, milady,' he gasped, scarce able to speak.

'You've a good big shaft, Henry,' she told him, her face as tranquil as if she were conversing with a vicar on good works and charity. 'Far too well-grown for a servant's need or use — it should stand between the thighs of a gentleman of breeding, who knows how to satisfy a lady with it.'

Henry said nothing more, only ravished with his eyes the soft and hairy pussy exposed to his view by the immodest Countess. He could hardly believe his ears when she ordered him to kneel down and put his shaft up her.

'Are you deaf?' she cried, when he hesitated, quite unable to trust himself to such luck. 'Do as you're told!'

Her graceful white fingers reached for the lips of her pussy to part them, while the footman sank to his knees between her legs. She moved them wide apart, abandoning her cunny to him, but turning her head to the side, lest he forget himself and try to kiss her mouth. She uttered a little sob of joy to feel his long thick shaft penetrate her deeply, then began to gasp to the thrust of his heavy body rogering her fast and hard.

The ecstatic spasm overtook her well before he came off. She cried out in bliss, her uncovered legs kicking in the air, her hands tugging at the hair above the footman's ears, to pull him closer to her. He groaned aloud, then his body heaved in great convulsions, while he spurted his creamy liquid into her.

The moment that her tremors of pleasure faded, she pushed at his shoulders with both hands, to indicate he should dismount. He scrambled to his feet, his shaft still hard and standing up, though slippery and spent.

'Thank you, Henry. You may go now,' said Her Ladyship.

A like position was his own, Randolph saw — Alice had turned him into a lackey, to bring her off whenever she felt the urge. Confound the woman, it was intolerable — good though the poking was. Randolph was no flunkey and would not permit himself to be used in so slighting a manner, not for all the poking in the Kingdom. Last night, for example, after they returned to her house in Mayfair after attending a performance of Mr Gilbert's and Mr Sullivan's operetta *Trial by Jury*, Alice had removed her clothes completely in her bedroom — keeping not even a chemise to preserve her modesty, and on her hands and knees had invited him to play stallion to her mare.

Naturally, he had obliged her, for the sight of bare lips and black curls was quite irresistible. Being in a generous mood, he obliged her twice without getting down, but that proved to be insufficient. She looked over her bare shoulder at him, her eyes glowing with lewd intention, and recited some lines which he recognised as forming part of *Don Leon*, a work by Lord Byron in favour of unnatural pleasure:

> *Oh, lovely woman, by her Maker's hand*
> *For man's delight and solace wisely planned.*
> *Thankless is she who Nature's bounty mocks,*
> *Nor gives Love entrance, whereso'er he knocks.*

Her meaning was plain enough to him — that she wished him to seek admittance at another, and less conventional, entrance. So with scarcely a pause to recover himself, Randolph placed his trembling hands on the full round orbs of her bottom and parted them. No warm saliva or other artificial aid was needed to ease the insertion of Mr Percival into where she would have him next lodged, for he was wet with the slipperiness of spending, and the dew of Alice's arousal. Randolph thrust him strongly into her back door, and pleasured her in the Levantine style.

So much for the past. Randolph's pride was bruised and broken beneath Alice Hamilton's despotic sway, for he was reduced to a slave, and less than a slave — a living dildo to gratify her in any manner she chose. He would have no more of it — he meant to put a complete stop to his mortification.

There being little if any hope that Alice's nature could be changed to conform with his preference, the single course of action open to him was the drastic one of not seeing her again.

This was the decision he had taken by the time an under-maid brought his morning tea to his bedside. Her name was Lizzie, a girl of seventeen or eighteen years, of pleasant aspect and fair-haired, not long in service at Cavendish Square. Without being fully aware of what he was doing, Randolph had been stroking his shaft in a consolatory manner during his train of thought concerning Alice and with the result that Mr Percival stood stiff as an iron bar.

'I have made a resolution,' Randolph told the maid, at which she stared at him puzzled.

'What might that be, sir?' she enquired.

He sat up in bed, arranging the pillows at his back to prop him in a comfortable position, the bedclothes about his waist.

'My resolve is to have no more truck with female tyrants, but to allow my nature full scope and resource for its expression,' said he, smiling at the girl.

'I'm sure you know best, sir,' she said, not understanding.

She set the tea tray down by the bedside, whereupon Randolph seized her wrist and dragged her hand under the bedclothes, and down his belly, to where Mr Percival reared stiffly hard-on. After one brief pass of her palm over the rearing shaft, Lizzie struggled to disengage her hand from his grasp, and looked most awfully abashed.

'Oh sir, what are you doing?' she cried, her eyes downcast.

'Damme, Lizzie, don't be so innocent,' said Randolph. 'I want your hand here, on my instrument of pleasure. Feel how hard and strong it is to the touch. Grasp it in your hand — it throbs with desire to be brought off.'

The girl's face was scarlet to the roots of her hair, but as if mesmerised by his words, she ceased from trying to pull away and let him rub her passive hand over his fleshy shaft.

'Why is your nightshirt up round your waist?' she asked, 'I think you must have being doing something very wicked, to make yourself as big and hard as this.'

'I had a strange dream,' he answered untruthfully, 'and when I awoke I was in this condition.'

That caught her attention and held it, for like all her kind she was prodigiously credulous and interested in tea leaves and other omens and the interpretation of dreams.

'What did you dream?' she asked, and made no resistance when Randolph pulled her down to sit beside him on the bed.

'In my dream I was alone in the morning room, and I rang the bell, but no one came. After a little time I went downstairs to the kitchen, to enquire further, and you were there alone, none of the other servants to be found. You stood at the sink, your sleeves turned back to your elbows, and you were washing a pair of drawers.'

He watched her face blush fiery red again at the mention of her underwear, and continued to make up his story.

'I asked you what you were doing, Lizzie, and you explained that my father's valet had caught hold of you on the stairs and touched you up, so that you came off. You were rinsing through your drawers to remove any sign of your spasm.'

'Good Lord!' she gasped. 'I swear he's hardly ever tried to touch me, sir. And then only up above the waist! I'd never let him do what you say to me, never!'

'Then you admit that John has felt your titties? Where did this take place – in the kitchen?'

'In the pantry,' she confessed, her voice trembling to her confusion and dismay at being questioned closely, 'he asked me to make him a cold beef sandwich, cook being in her room lying down, and he followed me in while I was spreading butter on bread for him, and put his arms round me and interfered with me.'

'I expect you thoroughly enjoyed it,' said Randolph, 'and I'm sure that you had his trousers undone in a jiffy and stiffened his shaft. Did you bring him off, standing up together?'

Crimson from hairline to throat, Lizzie insisted that she'd done no such thing, but had eluded the valet's grasp.

'Strange,' Randolph said musingly, 'for in my dream you made no effort to elude my grasp, when I pinned you against the sink and had a feel of your titties from behind. I vow my shaft was every bit as thick and hard as it is now — have you ever held a better one?'

The better to respond to his query, Lizzie clasped her hand around Mr Proud, who bounded nervously as her touch aroused in him lively sensations of pleasure. Randolph took advantage of the maid's perplexity by slipping a hand underneath her clothes and upward to where her black woollen stockings were gartered. She had neither the wit nor adroitness to prevent his fingers entering the slit of her drawers, until he had possession of her cunny. Nor was that the limit of his unwelcome attentions, for he inserted a skilful finger into the sensitive spot at the top of her hairy little pussy!

Lizzie trembled mightily and would have moaned, but Randolph ordered her to be silent. His active finger in her pussy tickled her hidden button into the moistness of arousal, causing Lizzie to blush yet again, to feel her person being abused and, worse, her emotions responding.

'You've had your fun, sir,' she stammered, 'let me go now.'

'Not I!' said he. 'For I have a great letch to do what I did to you in my dream, when you stood at the sink, your drawers in your hands, and I pressed close behind you. I raised your skirt behind and made you bend over while I pushed my shaft up your cunny, and did you until I spent.'

'Let me go, and I'll do anything else you wish,' she implored him, 'but not that.'

'Then use your hand to relieve me of my raging lust, Lizzie. I'm sure you know well enough how to.'

She took his words as a promise, started to rub firmly up and down the jerking shaft she held under the bedclothes. Randolph spread his thighs and leaned back at ease against his pillows, breathing faster to the raising of his lust. In his considered view, servant-girls were put on this earth for the use of the gentry, and it was an indication that all was well with the world that she was at work to pleasure him and he awaiting the moment of his fetching off in gentlemanly style.

'I can feel my shaft shaking like a leaf,' he gasped to the thrills coursing through his belly to the fast movement of her fingers, 'in another minute you'll have a sticky handful!'

Lizzie felt his loins rising up from the mattress, to push his throbbing shaft hard into her ministering hand. Then the sensations of fetching off coursed through him, and he writhed and squirmed to the gush of his thick white essence.

When no more squirted into her hand, she drew his nightshirt down to his knees and stood up from the bed, wiping her hand on her long white apron.

'Will there be anything else, sir?' she asked.

'That's all for now, Lizzie,' he replied.

He thought she would depart, but at the door she turned and came back to stand at his bedside, and stare down at him with a thoughtful expression on her face.

'Excuse me if I'm speaking out of turn, sir,' she said, 'but

I thought that you being a sporty sort of gentleman, you might want to see a contest that's being held tomorrow, in a public house not far from here.'

'A contest, Lizzie? Do you mean a prizefight?'

'In a manner of speaking, sir, you might call it that, for there is a prize for the one that beats the rest. But he's not allowed to use his fists.'

'What then? What manner of contest is it?'

'A poking match, sir. I'm sure you know what that is.'

'I've heard of such bouts but never seen one,' said Randolph in sudden interest.

Though he had only a moment or two ago finished fetching off, he looked at the maid with a rekindled interest. Yet again he wondered what it was in his Nature that drew him to unfamiliar pussies, as a steel bar is drawn to magnet. After his long stint with Alice Hamilton the previous evening, he had woken indifferent to women and poking, pussy and the use thereof. The prospect of fingering Lizzie's, a new one to him, had proved to be more than he could resist. Though it differed in no way from a thousand he had felt before, he had found the experience comforting, and he was pleased that she had made him spend.

Now, even before the wetness of his spending had dried on Mr Percival, the girl was arousing his raging curiosity again with talk of a poking contest. The name itself was enough to ensure his fervent interest – if he had been invited to dine with the Queen at Buckingham Palace that evening he would have refused for the sake of attending the lewd entertainment that Lizzie had mentioned.

'Will you go?' she asked. 'Several gentlemen will be there, by all accounts.'

'Damme, I wouldn't miss it for the world!' said he. 'Tell

me the name of the public house where it is to be held and I'll see you right, my girl.'

'The Ratcatcher's Arms in Marylebone,' she informed him. 'You will find it in Norton Street. Tip the landlord the wink and say Mrs Laycock asked you to drop by.'

'How do you come to be in possession of this information? An honest girl like you?'

'If you promise not to tell, sir, the coachman next door let on to me, when we met by chance on my afternoon off.'

Randolph took note that a coachman's rough fingers had parted the pussy-lips he had himself played with only a few minutes ago. Perhaps more than that even. Lizzie might have allowed the fellow's low-class shaft to penetrate her slit. And the valet — he was sure that sly one had done more to the girl than fumble with her titties in the pantry.

No doubt, Randolph's feverish imagination suggested to him, other servants have handled Lizzie's titties and fingered her pussy. In his experience of housemaids, those that were made use of by the master of the house got a taste for being poked, which they then indulged with their fellow menials in off-duty hours. A warm young pussy was too damned good for coachmen and lackies — it was for his disposal, and roger it he would!

Without a second thought, Randolph threw aside the bedclothes and swung his legs over the side of the bed, where he sat with his nightshirt pulled up about his waist, to show off Mr Proud to the best advantage.

He took the startled girl's hand, to pull her down beside him on the bed. He darted his hand up her clothes once again.

'Open your thighs, Lizzie,' he instructed her, 'Damme if you haven't given me another mighty cockstand. There's nothing for it this time but to have you.'

'No, you will hurt me!' she said.

'What!' cried he, his fingertip busy with her fleshy little button, for he had forced an entrance between the lips below. 'Do you take me for a fool, to pass yourself off as a virgin to me? I've spent in more girl's cunnies than you've had cooked meals — there's little or nothing I don't know about girls of your class, I'd wager of ten pounds you lost your maidenhead to some low class ragamuffin boy a long time ago.'

'Sir, you must not say such a wicked thing!' Lizzie gasped. 'And you shall not take away my honour.'

'What the devil have housemaids to do with honour?' Randolph exclaimed scornfully. 'Open your legs, girl, for I like better than anything else the touch of pussy flesh under my hand.'

'You will ruin me!' she exclaimed, scarlet of face.

'Fiddlesticks! Do not presume against good sense,' Randolph retorted. 'My shaft will not be the first up you, not by a long chalk. Would that it were — I'd gladly give you five sovereigns in gold if your cunny was virgin, and my sap the first to flood it. But my finger informs me that your maidenhead went years ago, and therefore you must be satisfied with a present of 10 shillings, when I've poked you.'

'No, none of that!' she said hastily, her hand clutching at his stiff shaft, to push it away from herself. 'I won't let you do that to me.'

'Then you'll be the loser,' he replied, 'for if you won't let me, I'll get one of the other maids to come in, and she shall have the money.'

'Lord! Have the other servants let you poke them, sir?' she asked, looking curiously into his face.

'For 10 shillings a time I've had everyone of them, with only the exception of the housekeeper,' said he, 'and she is too fat for my taste, and besides, she must be near forty years old, and I have a letch for young girls.'

He could see that she was hesitating at this information, and guessed she might be at the point of surrendering herself to him. He directed her attention to Mr Percival Proud.

'See the frisky fellow in your hand,' he said, 'he shows his pleasure by bobbing up and down. Rub him a little for me.'

'Seems to me he's been rubbed enough for one day,' she said, her former coyness beginning to be lost in wonder at Randolph's rapid recovery to full size. All this while his deft finger had been busy in her pussy, to good effect, for the wetness of her arousal imparted itself to his touch, and he judged her ripe for broaching. He put both hands on her shoulders to press her down on the bed, then turned up her clothes to her waist. She began to breathe more rapidly, and her uncovered legs shook.

'A girl like you with no education is unlikely to have heard the verses by Lord Macauley, the celebrated author and poet,' said Randolph, 'but they are apt to the moment:

> *Drawers and shirt both off together,*
> *Naked is our sweet embrace,*
> *Nothing is concealed by either,*
> *All as naked as your face!*

> *See, my eager wandering hands*
> *Fondle cunny, belly, tit,*
> *And my upright manhood stands*
> *To pierce your wet and open slit!*

'Oh sir, do you really mean to do me?' she murmured timidly.

Her eyes were fixed in apprehension on his face, as he leaned over her. Without deigning to reply, Randolph threw himself on top of her, his nightshirt about his waist to uncover his parts and behind. In an instant his hot belly was on hers, her thighs forced to spread wide by his own thighs between. With expert hand he slid the head of his straining shaft into the open slit of her drawers, and up against the hairy lips of her pussy. A strong push of his loins rammed Mr Percival right up her.

'Oh my Lord!' she moaned. 'It's too big for me — you'll tear me apart!'

She resigned herself to being rogered and ended her complaint when he began to slide in and out. Not that she made any move to assist him in the Rites of Love, for her sensuality was not engaged, and the first tremors of pleasure he had aroused by his finger vanished when his shaft entered her. She lay still, staring at the ceiling, while he had his way. Soon the short strokes were reached, and Randolph started to fetch off.

He had no reason to consider the housemaid's feelings, for she was to be paid for the use of her commodity, over and above her natural duty to make herself available to her betters. Randolph enjoyed himself fully, groaning and panting, while he inundated her cunny with spurting floods of hot lust. Then, his career on horseback finished, he dismounted from the saddle and rolled on his back to draw deep breaths of satisfaction.

He watched Lizzie get up from the bed and dry herself between the legs with her chemise. He told her to take 10 shillings from the tallboy, where the previous night he had deposited the contents of his pockets, whilst undressing for bed.

CHAPTER 6

A Sporting Contest in Deplorable Taste

When Randolph stepped down from a hansom cab at the corner of Norton Street, he saw it to be a collection of shabby buildings of the sort put up by a speculative builder half a century ago and now let out in rooms and in apartments. These were not the foul-smelling slums to be seen in the East End of London, but the dwellers in Norton Street were not likely to be the cream of society. Bankrupted shopkeepers, Randolph guessed, pimps and counterfeiters, small gentry down on their luck.

The Ratcatcher's Arms stood on the far corner, and he made his way at a genteel stroll over the broken and uneven pavement towards it, swinging his silver-knobbed stick, and whistling a jolly music hall catch. Gentlemen in full evening fig of topper and tails were a rare sight in this street. A five-shilling whore pressed forward from the shadows, and slunk back again at the curt shake of his head. Two ragamuffin lads who played bat and ball against the wall stared as he passed, and touched their peaked caps respectfully. Randolph felt in his pocket and threw a penny coin at them.

Inside the public house there was a great deal of noise and tobacco smoke, but only a few workmen. Behind a long counter of beer-stained wood, a bruiser with only one eye stared curiously at Randolph and asked his pleasure.

'A glass of your best brandy,' said he. 'Mrs Laycock informed me that there was entertainment to be had here, though I see no sign of it.'

The other filled a large glass with amber-coloured liquor and set it before Randolph, asking for four pence. Then with a nod of his head he indicated a fat man in shirtleeves standing by a door in the rear of the taproom.

'See Hankey if you're a friend of Mrs Laycock's,' he said.

Hankey proved to be the landlord of these dubious premises, and on seeing a gentleman approach him with the password, he grinned to show broken teeth and stood aside to let Randolph pass through the door.

'Up the stairs, sir,' said he, 'you'll find plenty of company there already. The match is just about to start – you're in the nick of time. That'll be a guinea, and well worth it, for the cunnies are in for a hard time tonight.'

Randolph paid his entrance money and passed through the door. Up a flight of unwept stairs lay a large room, where twenty or more well-dressed men stood in conversation. In the centre of the plank floor half a dozen straw-stuffed mattresses had been laid down side by side, forming a rough arena of sorts for the athletic contest shortly to take place.

By the wall was a long bench, on which sat five young women, gin glasses in their hands and blankets wrapped about them. The contestants, thought Randolph, eyeing them with keen interest, stripped and ready for action under their blanket, no doubt. He contemplated them while deciding which he would choose to poke, if given a free choice.

Before he had settled the issue between the two middle women, the landlord came upstairs, bowed to the company and took up a position in the centre of the room by the mattresses.

'My lords and gentlemen!' he bawled in a loud voice. 'Your silence, if you please! You are bid welcome to the celebrated Ratcatcher's Arms, Josiah Hankey at your service.'

That got him a round of applause from the crowd, which with a clumsy bow he acknowledged before continuing his announcement.

'Now, since I see you are all sporting gents here,' said he, 'and impatient for the first bout of the evening, with no more ado I shall call forward the first contestant to get us off to a good start. The contest is for a purse of two guineas, and here is a favourite of yours and mine, Miss Dolly Burkitt. The sweet little lady is barely twenty years of age, but she is endowed with the strength of Hercules.'

At his words a hardy young woman rose from the wooden bench and advanced to the centre of the arena, where she threw aside the blanket that served her as cloak, and stood revealed to the noisy crowd. Her yellowish hair was cut short as any man's, and she wore nothing whatsoever but a pair of white drawers, tied firmly about her waist and stretching to below her knees.

The crowd fell silent in awe to see her take up the classical pose of athletes, leaning forward on bent knees, with one fist raised to her forehead. The biceps of her arms were well grown and developed, and when she turned so that all around the room might inspect her broad bare back, the muscles there rippled in fine style, and stood out strongly.

'She has not much by way of titties,' Randolph commented to the man standing next to him, a gentleman of middle years with a face reddened by the constant and liberal imbibing of brandy and port wine and other delicious liquors.

Indeed, Miss Dolly's titties were set high on her chest, but they were ungrown and flattish, offering a man little to fondle and even less to take hold of.

'What you say is true,' Randolph's neighbour agreed, 'but for all that, she'll not prove an easy filly to mount and ride, you mark my words. There's a wild gleam in her eye, and a flare of the nostrils that bodes ill to the unwary. I'd want four strong fellows to take an arm and a leg each and hold her down, before I'd go near her with my shaft at the ready.'

The landlord resumed his laudatory introduction of the woman, a hard grin on his face.

'Miss Dolly will take on any male adversary in a poking bout, offering the pleasure of her cunny to whoever can pin her down and get into it. No punching or kicking, no biting or gouging is allowed, and we give no guarantee against broken bones or other accidental injuries.'

The woman in the drawers raised her arms high in the air and paraded herself around the arena, letting all see as much of her body as was bare. About the ring voices were raised by top-hatted gentlemen, making offers of a guinea or thirty shillings for the pleasure of rogering her without having to fight her to secure the prize. She stared at them scornfully, and declared that she set a higher price than that on the use of her cunny.

'We have a volunteer to go into the ring against the lovely Miss Dolly,' announced the landlord in his hoarse voice, 'your applause if you please for this young hero who will take on our Amazon, Mr Will Hocking, a market porter of this parish.'

The newcomer who pushed through the crowd to gain the arena where the mattresses waited was no sudden volunteer, Randolph guessed. The bouts and opponents had been arranged ahead of the match, as a sporting spectacle, and there could be little doubt that the female contenders would be available to be rogered for a price at the conclusion of the athletics.

Will the market porter was bare-legged and unclothed to his shirt, the male labouring classes having no thought of wearing underdrawers or socks. He was a strongly built young fellow of perhaps five-and-twenty, and Miss Dolly acknowledged his entry into the arena with a vigorous nod of her head. By way of reply he lifted up the front of his shirt and, as if threatening her, showed her his hard-on upright shaft. The crowd roared their appreciation, and he grinned foolishly and took it in his hand.

'Of average size,' said Randolph's neighbour, who had by now introduced himself as Hartley Bingham, MP, 'but he's a sturdy rogue and may just get the better of her.'

In the sight of all, Will was running his clasped hand up and down his shaft, stimulating it to grow stronger and harder. The expression on Miss Dolly's face as she observed her opponent's antics was one of derision.

'Call that a shaft?' she said loudly, for the whole room to hear. 'I've seen bigger on twelve-year-old boys pissing against a brick wall!'

'Is that right?' Will retorted. 'Well, take a good look at it, bitch, because it'll be up you before long, and you'll sing a different tune then!'

'Take your places,' the landlord ordered, gesturing the two together in the centre of the mattresses, 'no rounds, no breaks or rests. The bout ends when Miss Dolly is well and truly poked or when Will abandons his attack on her virtue.'

'I'll wager five guineas that fellow doesn't best her,' said Hartley Bingham to Randolph. 'Will you take it?'

Randolph stared thoughtfully at the contestants, now circling each other slowly on the mattresses, arms outstretched to make a sudden snatch at the other when the moment came.

'They're well matched, and no mistake,' said he, 'but surely the advantage must always lie with the male, for so Nature has decreed. I'll take your bet, Bingham. Five guineas says that he pokes her.'

Even as he spoke, Dolly feinted swiftly, then seized Will's wrist in a twisting grip that forced him to bend over sharply. She turned her hip into him and threw him down on the mattress, following him down smartly, to lock his head between her thighs and hold him helpless. He squirmed furiously, but she had him pinned firm, until his hands found her hips. Then like a shot, his hand was in through the slit of her drawers, and he crowed in triumph to have possession of her pussy.

Dolly released her leg hold and twisted away, rising to one knee above him, but he gripped her round the waist and thrust his head up under her. She let out a loud cry, and the cheering spectators saw that he had his face between her thighs and his tongue at her pussy. To break his hold, she reached far out to seize hold of his hard shaft, and run her hand rapidly up and down its length.

Whilst she was thus occupied in attempting to relieve him of his urge by manual abuse, Will had without her knowledge undone the string of her drawers. With a heave of his back, he rose to his knees, and dragged her undergarments down her legs. Long and loud and fervent were the plaudits of the crowd to gain at last a sight of the mouse-brown curls that adorned her cunny. Dolly struggled to rise to her feet and escape from her danger, but her movements were hampered by the drawers Will had pulled down about her ankles.

She was badly off her balance, crouching with one leg folded beneath her and the other stretched out, so that her heel only touched the mattress. She would have fallen over backwards but for her hold around Will's neck, and he, seizing his glorious opportunity, pushed his outthrust middle finger up her pussy. She screeched, and the crowd shouted their encouragement to Will as, in plain sight for their benefit, he slid his digit in and out of his struggling opponent.

'Damned if I didn't get it wrong!' exclaimed Hartley Bingham in dismay. 'He's got her now!'

It was no more than the truth. Before Dolly could devise a means of escaping the finger that was invading her pussy, Will threw her on her back and himself on top of her. Her legs waved in the air above him, and she shouted out, *No, no!* But he had a clear advantage of position now, and with a heave of his hips and a sharp push, he was into her, and tupping fast.

Dolly had missed her chance by trying to hold her opponent by his shaft too soon. If instead she had grasped him around the body and thrown him on his back, she could have pinned him with her legs while she used her hand to drain him of his juices and win the bout. As matters stood, it was she on her back, and his shaft well into her – and in another ten or a dozen strokes he cried out in victory and squirted his essence into her. At once she ceased to resist and lay still, recognising defeat.

The landlord parted them and helped Dolly to her feet. Will had already jumped up, to raise his arms and wave them in the winner's gesture. He lifted his shirt front and made a tour of the arena, proving his win by letting the spectators observe that his shaft was wet and sticky with his spending, and waning shorter and softer. He was cheered to the echo for his success and essayed a comic bow and scrape.

After that came Dolly, led round by the hand of the landlord, so that all might see her slippery pussy, and know that she had been truly poked and defeated, and had not tricked her opponent to bring him off between her legs or on her belly. She too was cheered, though derisively, the loudest acclamation saved for Will, when the landlord handed him his prize money.

Randolph too extended his hand, for Bingham to count out the five guineas in his palm.

'Better luck next time,' said Randolph, privately wishing him no such thing, for he saw a golden chance here to part his new acquaintance from as much money as he had with him, 'will you take a glass of brandy with me?'

'Why, gladly,' said the other, 'after which I shall look to win back my money, with interest.'

Randolph gave the order to a potman making the rounds of the crowd, and asked Bingham if he had witnessed a contest of this sort before, or was it his first time, as in his own case? The genial Member of Parliament freely avowed that he had seen many a titanic struggle between young men and women for the use of a pussy, or otherwise, according to the outcome of the bout. Most especially in public houses south of the Thames, he apprised an interested Randolph, in the area generally known to the local inhabitants as the Elephant and Castle.

Whilst they drank their brandy and awaited the next contest, he told Randolph of one bout especially he had seen, a year or two past. The opponents were so close-matched, said he, in each particular of height and size and weight, and possessed of such physical strength and endurance, that the bout had gone on for nigh half an hour! By then every stitch of clothing had been torn from both contestants, and they were wrestling stark naked down on the mattress, their bodies glistening with sweat.

Eventually, he said, the bout had ended in a win for the

man, but only because the woman had become bored with the struggle, and though she was by no means fatigued, she desisted from all further resistance. She turned on to her back, spread her legs wide, and let her panting opponent's shaft stab into her and roger her, till he spent and claimed the victory.

'I wish I had seen that bout,' said Randolph, 'it sounds to be most stirring.'

'It stirred me, I must confess,' said Bingham, 'for my shaft was at such a stand that I could do no other than give the girl a couple of sovereigns to let me stick it up her and add my sap to her brother's.'

'What?' Randolph exclaimed. 'Her brother?'

'So she told me, the opponent so much like her was indeed her brother, who rogers her regularly, she claims, at contests for money, and at home for pleasure.'

'My lords and gentlemen!' the landlord called. 'Your kind attention, if you please. The next contender of the evening for your entertainment, and for a purse of two guineas, is none other than the ever-popular Miss Phoebe High. Your applause, please.'

The woman who rose from the wooden bench by the wall and came to the centre of the room was hardly older than the first had been — Randolph put her at twenty-one or twenty-two — but she was in all other respects very different. She was, not to conceal the truth of it, excessively stout.

Her huge lax titties hung almost to her belly-button, which itself was nearly lost in a belly round as a beer barrel. She troubled with neither blanket about her shoulders nor drawers, so that her great columns of thighs were plain to see, and her massive behind was like a regimental drum.

The hair on her head was a light brown in colour, and tied in a short pigtail by a red ribbon. The hair between her thighs was very sparse, and did nothing at all to cover the long thick lips of her cunny. She stood solidly in the middle of the arena with her arms raised high, proudly showing off her naked body to all who wished to inspect it.

'Ah,' said Hartley Bingham, 'I'd love to give her a rogering. Just imagine to yourself the sensations of lying on that great fat belly and getting your shaft up her! And those titties — by George, I'd dearly love to get them into my hands and stuff one into my mouth!'

'I make no doubt you will be able to do that later on,' said Randolph. 'My own taste is for thinner wenches. But to our bet, sir — do you fancy Miss Phoebe to win or to lose?'

'To lose,' said Bingham, regarding her backside with his head tilted to one side, 'she cannot possibly have strength enough to move that heavy body about nimbly. When her opponent has her on the floor, she will be unable to rise, and she will be poked in no time.'

'I fear you may be right,' Randolph agreed, 'but what of it? Betting is all a matter of luck. The same stakes as before, but to give me some faint chance of success, will you set a time in which she must be rogered?'

'Your request is a reasonable one,' Bingham conceded. 'I bet five guineas she's done soundly within five minutes — does that satisfy you?'

'Accepted,' said Randolph.

In another noisy burst of information, the landlord told his patrons that the volunteer to take on Miss Phoebe was Ned Aker, a soldier of the Queen who had been discharged after service in the Ashanti War. Ned bounded into the arena in lively style, a burly man of two or three-and-twenty, with a back marked by old scars from a field punishment flogging for misconduct.

He stared at the expanse of Miss Phoebe's nakedness and

said loudly, *If that's the way of it, naked as savages, so be it*, and he peeled off his shirt, to stand in his nudity, as she did. In an instant exclamations of surprise rose from the spectators, who saw now that Ned's shaft hung limp between his thighs. Miss Phoebe pointed at it with an extended forefinger and mocked him.

'Pooh!' she cried. 'Do you think you'll ever get that weak little dangler into me? Say your prayers, Ned Aker, for you're a goner, my lad!'

'Don't count your chickens till they're hatched,' he retorted to her scorn. 'It'll stand up hard enough when I've got you on your back and your legs open. I've poked black women in Africa bigger than you, and they haven't forgotten me yet!'

'Stand ready,' the landlord ordered. 'Get set – fight!'

He moved well back out of the way as Ned took two short steps and hurled himself bodily at his opponent. His scheme evidently matched Bingham's assessment of the position – that as soon as Miss Phoebe was on her back, her bulk would render her helpless as an overturned turtle on a beach. To this end, his shoulder struck against her breastbone, between her fat titties, whilst he pushed at her wide hips to up-end her.

However, in this Ned had taken on more than he knew. Phoebe grunted hard as she received his charge, and stood fast on the firmly planted pillars of her legs. Before he could recover from his thwarted assault, she had his head clamped under her arm, and being shorter than he by half a foot, it was necessary for him to bend over forward. She held him thus trapped whilst she reached over his bent back and delivered a smart smack or two on the cheeks of his bottom. At this he howled and wiggled more than ever, to break loose from her hold.

Only when she had humiliated him enough did she release

his head from under her arm, and let him stagger away. He was game, whatever the odds, and after a second or two of deep breathing to recover himself, he dashed at her once more. He came in low this time, running his head at her fat belly, his hands groping for her meaty titties, to get a firm hold on her. She gasped to the escape of her breath from the impact of his head, but even so, Ned was unable to turn her off her feet.

He would have retreated to try again, but she had her hand on the nape of his neck and forced his head down lower, and lower yet, until his face was pressed to her pussy.

'By Jove!' said Randolph, 'She's going to make him lick her, I do believe!'

He was wrong in that. Phoebe got Ned's neck between her great thighs and squeezed until he fell onto his knees, held fast in a trap he could not open. She stood laughing, her hands juggled under her titties, to bounce them up and down for the delight of the crowd, who roared their encouragement.

'There's not a man here who can get into my cunny free,' she boasted, 'but if any gentleman offers me a couple of pounds, he shall have his will of it.'

'A bargain!' cried Hartley Bingham, MP, 'I'll pay you that, Miss Phoebe, as soon as you're at liberty, whether or not this fellow has you first.'

His was not the only voice raised to accept her offer, but he was the first. Phoebe smiled and waved her hand, from where she stood on the mattresses, with Ned's neck squeezed between her legs.

'What do you think?' Randolph asked. 'A drawn bout, I fancy, for he cannot overturn her, but she is too ungainly and slow to best him. Shall we cancel our bet?'

'Not a bit of it!' said Bingham, his face flushed red with

the thought that he might be rogering the stout Miss Phoebe ere long. 'Let the bet stand – never let it be said of me that I am not a sportsman!'

'But you've bet against her,' said Randolph, 'you've bet that she will lose the bout.'

'I regret to say that I am still of that opinion,' said his companion, his lips pursed, 'for she will sooner or later have to release him from Chancery, whereupon he will try again, till he in the end succeeds in getting her off her feet. On her back she will be easy meat.'

Even as he spoke, Miss Phoebe shuffled her bare feet apart to open her legs, and took a step back. Ned had evidently reached the identical conclusion to the sporting Member of Parliament, for, without rising from his knees, he seized Phoebe's ankles and tugged, whilst he butted his head into her belly. Her pudgy arms waved, but her balance was lost, and she sat down hard on her well-padded backside.

A roar arose from the spectators as Ned launched himself at her, rolling her flat on her back, with himself on top.

'I knew it!' Bingham exclaimed. 'She's as good as rogered!'

He spoke too soon, for Phoebe was an experienced contestant at poking matches. She used one arm and one leg to push hard on the mattress and roll herself over, bouncing Ned off her belly. Before he could get clear, she completed her turn and lay on top of him, pressing the breath out of his lungs by her weight of flesh.

Her movements were ponderous and slow, but Ned was not in the position to counter them, for he lay gasping on his back, half-dead from being overlaid. Phoebe sat astride his belly, facing his feet, her bulk pinning him immovably to the floor.

'Yes, Miss Phoebe!' Hartley Bingham called out to

encourage her. 'You have him now! Finish him and come to me to be poked, my Amazonian queen!'

She grinned at him from her sweating face, and her thumb and forefinger closed round Ned's soft shaft and jerked it briskly to shake some life into it. He squirmed and swore beneath her, furious at being bested. His fingers were at her bottom, hoping to get at her pussy and torment it until she released him, but she was too heavy for him to slide a hand under her, nor were his arms long enough to reach over her thighs and reach to her slit from that direction.

Meantime, her vigorous stimulation had brought his shaft up hard. Her hand clasped round it, and she rubbed swiftly along its length. Ned sustained his resistance to the very end, his legs thrashing on the mattress as he attempted to unseat her — but to no avail. She had beaten him fair and square, and he let out a wail of defeat as the creamy liquor of his defeat spurted high, almost up to her grinning face.

The crowd roared its approbation of her success and several gentlemen threw florins and half-crowns into the arena, to add to the prize money. Hankey the landlord took hold of her wrists and heaved strenuously, to help her rise from Ned and gain her feet. He led her round the edge of the crowd, showing her pussy unbroached and inviolate, before giving her her prize.

'Get a move on, damn your eyes!' Bingham called out to him. 'I'm standing here with a hard-on shaft like a rolling pin! If I can't poke Miss Phoebe soon, I'll come off in my trousers!'

The gentlemen spectators laughed at him for that, Hankey took the hint and pushed Phoebe towards him, before leading Ned on a tour of the arena, displaying his dwindled part. Bingham seized Phoebe by one hand and one titty, so eager was he to get into her. She grinned and led him through a door into the rear part of the public house, where,

Randolph presumed, a bed or two was available for the use of the contestants and the clients who wanted them.

Bingham had been too hot for Phoebe's pussy to remember that he owed Randolph another five guineas for his lost bet. Randolph nearly went after him, then thought better of it — it would be damnably poor taste to interrupt a chap while he was unloading his lust into a willing whore. Nor was he required to wait long for his money — the landlord was announcing the next bout, when the MP returned with a contented smile on his face.

He resumed his place alongside Randolph and removed his topper to wipe the perspiration from his brow.

'Was she up to scratch?' asked Randolph.

'A damned good two sovereigns worth,' said the other, 'I had so violent a letch for Phoebe's body that I came off twice in her for the price of one. Here is the five guineas I owe you. What say you to this match — will you bet on it?'

On the mattresses Miss Sal Roper was in contest with Lemmy Bly for her virtue — if she yet possessed any remnant of that elusive quality. She was a strongly built woman of nineteen or twenty, of a dark complexion and hair, with loose titties and sturdy hams. Her opponent was younger — not more than seventeen or eighteen at most, and his rolled-up shirt sleeves displayed impressive biceps.

'By his broken nose and thick ear he is an apprentice bare-fist boxer,' said Randolph, studying the man and woman locked together in a wrestler's hold, their bosoms pressed together, their fingers interlaced, as they fought for mastery, pushing and panting.

'What of that?' said Bingham. 'Punching is barred. His skill at boxing gives him no advantage. And the woman looks capable of heaving sacks of coal. She'll be no easy lay for him.'

At that moment the struggling contestants lost their footing on the mattresses and fell together. To Randolph's surprise, it was Sal who was the quickest witted — she was on Lemmy's back in a flash, her legs wound about his waist, an arm round his neck to pinion him. He flailed his arms about, but could secure no grip on her.

'Commonsense instructs me that a strong male must always have the advantage over a strong female,' said Randolph. 'The stiff shaft is mightier than the female slit, for Nature designed it in the shape of a weapon to stab between women's legs and wreak its lustful will. Men are constructed to ravish women, and not vice versa. Lemmy will overcome her and spend in her cunny — oh damnation, look at that! She's got a hold on his shaft!'

Sal had her opponent on his side, his face pressed hard into the mattress, his legs trapped in the grip of her encircling thighs, and her hand over his waist to flip up his shirt out of the way and massage his stiff shaft with rapid movements.

'She's got him!' said Bingham, grinning broadly. 'Where is your commonsense now, Mr Joynes?'

'You asked me to lay a bet,' said Randolph, 'and so I will — I'll wager 10 guineas that Sal wins.'

'But the flag's up and the runners are over halfway round the course!' Bingham protested.

'I took you to be a sportsman, sir,' said Randolph, 'not a confounded bookmaker.'

'Very well,' the MP grumbled, 'no one shall say I turned down a bet because I feared the odds. I'll take your wager.'

Randolph stared at the locked combatants, waiting eagerly for the moment when Lemmy's sap spurted out and Bingham's money was his. He reckoned without Lemmy's experience of the boxing ring as training for poking contests. How it happened was hard to say, for Lemmy moved very quickly when he chose to — but a gasp arose from the crowd as he, from being underdog, shook off the woman on his back, rolled her over with his bare foot in her belly, seized her by the hair, and dragged her up on her hands and knees, with himself behind her.

At once he brought his throbbing shaft up to the slit of her drawers and pushed into her pussy. She shrieked to feel him go in, then his belly was pressed to the backs of her thighs and he rogered her with a masterful stroke. She panted and groaned, to feel her sturdy body so used against her will, whilst Lemmy grinned and slowed down, now the tables were completely turned. The wondering spectators observed his engorged shaft gliding in and out of Sal's pussy, and raised a cheer for him.

'I've got you now, my girl!' he crowed, tupping at her. 'And for a thirty-shilling whore you're not a bad poke.'

Sal moaned and swore and tried to shake him off, but he held her head back by her hair and rammed against the round cheeks of her behind.

'You'll have the lot up you in another second,' he boasted, 'like a bitch in the street. Do you like being done backwards, Sal, or are you only comfortable on your back? Not that I give a tinker's damn what you want — you'll get what I give you!'

No doubt if he had the time to spare he would have said more about the pleasures of rearward rogering, but a sudden tremor passed visibly through his body, and with a loud cry of triumph he shot his sap into her pussy. Or nearly so, for at the first spurt of hot tallow, Sal made a supreme effort and pulled away, collapsing to her belly on the mattress. Lemmy howled in rage whilst his cream gushed over her fat bum.

'Devil take it!' Randolph exclaimed. 'Did he poke her or

did he not? I say yes, for he got his shaft into her, at least.'

'But can he be said to have rogered her when he is coming off over her backside?' Hartley Bingham countered. 'He's dribbling on her cheeks still. We must wait for the referee's decision to settle our bet.'

'Which must be in my favour,' said Randolph spiritedly, 'for had she been a virgin, he went far enough into her to take her maidenhead — will you concede that?'

'Women like Sal can't even remember having a maidenhead,' the MP replied with a shake of his head. 'But if she had — what of that? I define the act of poking as requiring an insertion and an emission in the pussy. Otherwise a man could claim he rogers twenty times a night, when in truth all he does is push his shaft into a pussy twenty separate times at ten-minute intervals and wait for it to go slack, but fetch off only on the last time.'

'There is some truth in your argument, I must allow,' said Randolph. 'But what of *coitus interruptus*, as medical men name it, when a man pulls out at the moment of spending, not to put the girl in the family way, and comes off on her belly? Surely you will agree that he has rogered her, though he has not spent inside her pussy.'

'These are complicated matters,' said Bingham. 'What do you say of the man who thrusts his shaft up a woman's rearward hole and spends there? Has he rogered her, even though he has come off in her body? Yet she may remain a virgin, however often he may do her in this way.'

'Complicated indeed,' said Randolph. 'It may be that a great specialist in rogering, such as the celebrated Dr William Acton himself, may be required to settle the finer points of the bout — but as he is not likely to lend us the benefit of his wisdom, let us agree to leave it to Hankey to decide.'

CHAPTER 7
Solace in
Mrs Jeffries' Household

Randolph's emotions were heated to a lustful glow by the poking bouts he witnessed at The Ratcatcher's Arms, yet he found that he had no great letch for any of the female contestants. All of them seemed to him too muscular, too sweaty, too coarse, or too damned something or other, for a gentleman of his taste and refinement. Accordingly, after the final match of the evening, he went straight by hansom cab to Chelsea.

There were many houses he knew where abatement of his passion could be pleasantly arranged, and all closer to hand than that he chose. However, by way of repulsion from the brawny women he had seen wrestling down on the floor to keep common shafts out of their cunnies, he had taken a fancy to having a ladylike and tender creature. He felt certain that Mrs Mary Jeffries, whose house in Church Street, Chelsea, catered to royalty and titled persons, would be well able to provide for his needs.

Money was no object, for he had ten guineas he had won in bets from Hartley Bingham, the affable Member of Parliament for some dismal Midlands manufacturing town. He would have had more, but after much consideration the landlord had declared the contest between Sal Roper and Lemmy drawn. All bets were called off, to the anguish of Randolph and those others who had wagered that Lemmy would roger the wench, and to the delight of that portion of the crowd that had fancied Sal to beat him.

Mrs Jeffries was a genteel sort of woman, for a bawd, above fifty years of age and neatly dressed in shiny black satin. It was said that she had been housekeeper to Lord Mountrosset for many years, and more than that to him, and that when he died he left her money enough to set up her place of business in a pleasant Chelsea street. She sent out printed cards, it was rumoured, to His Lordship's wide acquaintance, informing them where she was to be found, and the particular services her house offered.

Be that as it may, she greeted Randolph with a warm regard, though some weeks had passed since last he was there. Her way was to offer gentlemen a glass of wine in her sitting room, not to hurry them, and when she had ascertained to her satisfaction by discreet conversation the thrust of their desire, she would send for whichever of her fair throng she judged most suited to the alleviation of their letch.

Randolph drank a glass of port wine with her, and the matter of the drawn bout being still on his mind, he explained to her the circumstances and asked for her expert opinion. Had Lemmy well and truly rogered the wench, or had Sal brought off a feat of deception in the final moment, and kept herself unpoked?

Mrs Jeffries had no doubt at all.

'If he had it up her, then he poked her,' she declared, 'that is the rule of the house here.'

'Whether he comes off or no?' asked Randolph, to elucidate.

'Coming off has nothing whatsoever to do with it,' insisted Mrs Jeffries, 'for some gentlemen produce so little essence as not to be noticed, and some arrive too far gone in drink to be able to come off at all — and lucky to get it hard-on enough to put it in. But once in, the contract is complete.'

'Your approach is refreshing in its simplicity,' Randolph was compelled to reply. 'I declare you are a veritable Solomon, my dear Mrs Jeffries — I would you were with me earlier tonight in the public house, for then I would be twenty guineas better off.'

While they thus conversed politely, the woman summed Randolph up and sent the parlourmaid to ask Miss Jane to come down and take a glass of wine with a gentleman visitor of distinction.

'Miss Jane,' said Randolph thoughtfully, 'I do not believe I have had the pleasure of making her acquaintance before. Is she a newcomer to the house?'

'Tolerably so,' Mrs Jeffries replied, 'for she has been here but six weeks or two months, not a day longer. I take care to choose who she shall meet, for as you will see, she is a young woman of rare charm and beauty, and not to be pawed about and poked by persons of questionable breeding and background. In short, Mr Joynes, she is in reserve for gentlemen like yourself who truly appreciate the bloom of youth on a snowy bosom, milk-white thighs and other charms too superior to be spoken of in general conversation.'

'Damme, but the girl sounds a paragon!' Randolph exclaimed.

'You will be delighted by her, and you may have her all night and poke her thrice or more, to your heart's content,' said the smiling bawd.

'What fee do you ask for this young Venus?'

'Ten guineas,' said she, 'and worth every penny of it, I have been assured by several peers of the realm and a bishop.'

Randolph thought it damned steep, and would have said so, but he guessed the wench must be exceptional to command so elevated a price. He would take a close look at her, the size and shape of her titties, the state of her teeth, the colour of her hair, and the fullness of her backside, before deciding whether she was worth a poke or two by him, at that price. He had questions to ask of Mrs Jeffries, but the parlour door opened to admit the young charmer herself, and he rose politely to shake hands. She was eighteen or nineteen years of age, he saw, her tresses raven black and her large eyes so dark brown as to be almost jet. She wore a simple white gown, cut square on the bosom to reveal the upper slopes of plump titties, the skin white and smooth.

At Mrs Jeffries's invitation Miss Jane seated herself and took a glass of port with them. She had a soft voice, without a trace of lower-class accent that Randolph could detect, and her manner was affectionate without being forward or pert. In all, she could have been mistaken for a young lady by those not in the know.

Randolph decided that he must have her and conveyed this to his hostess. She smiled with toothy graciousness, and asked for the price to be paid to her. The transaction completed, and the golden guineas safe in Mrs Jeffries's clutch, Miss Jane rose and extended a hand toward Randolph, inviting him to accompany her to her room above, that she might make his better acquaintance.

It was a well-furnished bedroom to which she conducted

him, equipped with a four-poster bed with green plush curtains tied back, and a green counterpane. There was a fire burning in the fireplace, and over the mantle a large gilt mirror on the wall. There was a sofa and two chairs, and a cheval glass which could be placed to reflect the antics on the bed, for those who liked to watch themselves poking.

Miss Jane smiled at Randolph and drew her long white dress up over her head and removed it, to reveal that she was completely naked but for pink stockings. Her titties were a fine sight — plump and full, each one more than a man's handful. Randolph stared at them in fascination, and she took his hands and laid them on her fleshy bounties, for him to feel.

Her hand moved over his trousers outside, to gauge the length and girth of his shaft as it rose upright in salutation to her naked beauty. He told her he was dying to have her, and with a laugh of pleasure she lay on the bed for him. His heart pounded like a drum at the sight of her parted legs, whilst he hastily took off his clothes.

What a sight for a man with an iron stand is a lovely young girl wearing no drawers! Miss Jane's soft, lovely, bare thighs were spread for Randolph, to display in full view the choicest flower of female beauty, the delightful plaything that nestled between her creamy white thighs! He could scarce restrain the murmur of approval that rose to his lips when he saw her thick bush of dark brown silky curls, and the soft lips of her pussy.

'I see now why Mrs Mary lets you out by the night,' said he, 'for you are so desirable, my dear, that no man would quit your side after only one poke!'

Miss Jane's jet-black eyes opened widely to gaze at him, and a fond smile spread over her lovely face. Her hand crept down her belly, until her slender fingers lingered at her pussy.

'Is it this what so attracts you?' she asked him, her words sending thrills of delight up his spine.

At the instant Randolph threw himself naked beside her on the bed, his mouth pressed to her bare belly in a kiss, she drew open her pussy a little way to display the delicate pink inner lips and the button standing proud at the soft threshold of her depths.

'I must have a feel of it!' Randolph exclaimed.

He could hardly speak for the intensity of the emotions this delicious girl had aroused in him, but he succeeded somehow to tell her how beautiful and tender a morsel was her pussy, and his intention to fill it brimful with his creamy spending. Then words failed as he set eager fingers to her youthful blossom in a long caress that seemed to draw the soul out of his body and send it adventuring in glory into her warm split ahead of his questing hand.

He heard the softest of sighs then, and happily he flicked between her parted pink pussy lips in their soft and dark brown nest, teasing at her little button until she made sweet sounds and moans of delight.

'You'll bring me off,' sighed she, her looks languid and her thighs ashiver.

'Very like,' he commented, with a wolfish grin. 'Do you know the lines by Mr Walter Savage Landor, the poet? They might have been written with foreknowledge of this very moment:

> *There on a downy bed they fondly lay*
> *Teasing each other's parts in amorous play,*
> *Till Nature seizing on their luscious game,*
> *To fiery lust did both of them inflame.*

He lay upon her in love's hot embrace,
And pressed his shaft deep in her yielding place,
They pant, they throb, their fierce convulsions start,
As through their limbs sensations quickly dart.

They thrust, they push, they tremble to their letch,
Then taste the truest joy, and gasping fetch,
Her wanton belly heaving up to his,
And as his juices spurt, she swoons in bliss.

Miss Jane had by now Randolph's stiff shaft in her hand and stroked it whilst she was pleasured. She sighed tiny breathless words of bliss whilst his fingers ravaged her with the divinest sensations. She rolled her bottom on the green counterpane, and her ample titties rose and fell vigorously to her heavy gasps.

There could be but one way of it now. Her loins twitched in a rapid motion and her whole body shook convulsively, from crown to heel. A shriek of joy escaped her and she came off, rubbing her wet pussy against Randolph's fingers. At that he could bear no more — with an exclamation of urgent need he hurled himself on Miss Jane. A single hard push took him deep into her pussy, his shaft buried in her up to the hilt.

Miss Jane cried out again to feel herself so deeply plumbed, for she was still fetching off from the ministrations of his fingers. Whilst he rogered her hard and fast, she continued to come off, crying out in her bliss without stop, her mouth hard on his and her tongue thrust in deep in the enthusiasm of her lust to be done.

Her wet pussy seemed to suck at Randolph's throbbing shaft in its avid thirst for his essence, and incoherent exclamations of delight too deep for words escaped from him. No man, be he ever so strong, no human organism, male or female, could long bear a blissfulness so devastating, and sensations so immense! A moan fled from Randolph's mouth into the girl's clinging mouth as he felt his sap surging in great spasms into her pulsating pussy.

There ensued a period of languorous contentment, the two of them lying side by side, her hand lightly holding his dwindling shaft and his hand between her warm thighs. Soon his interest returned, and in pursuit of his everlasting curiosity about the sensual nature of females, he asked Miss Jane to confide in him the circumstance of her first coming-off, if she recalled that event clearly enough.

'Remember – how can I ever forget it!' cried she. 'For I was a young girl, orphaned by the sad death of my doting parents in a railway train collision near Stoke Poges. In this sad plight I was taken into the service of Lord and Lady Grantonby, as an undermaid. I was, without wishing to sound in the least vain, a pretty child, and soon noticed in the household. There seemed never a day to pass but a footman or a groom did not try to get me into a corner alone and slide his hand up my clothes to feel my pussy.'

'Servants' morals are a disgrace,' said Randolph. 'It ought to be clearly understood that maids are to remain virgins till the master of the house, or the sons, avail themselves of it. I find it damnable that so many young maidenheads are thrown away and wasted on low-class scullions and boot-boys!'

'Then you will be pleased to hear that I eluded all attempts on my virtue by the male servants,' said Miss Jane, tugging his shaft to see if it was ready to stand hard-on again, 'but only to find myself pursued by Lord Grantonby himself. He is a short gentleman, of thirty-five or forty years of age, and almost bald before his time. He caught me one evening at bedtime, busy with my duties upstairs, and had his hand on my pussy before I could say him nay.'

'It was your clear duty to say yes to him,' Randolph told her with a slight frown. 'Young female servants are supposed to be used by gentlemen. Your person was his to do as he chose with.'

'Whether it was or not,' said Miss Jane, 'I had no intention of letting him poke me. I slipped out of his grasp and escaped along the passage, His Lordship in pursuit. At the bend of the stairs I concealed myself behind a half-open door to the sewing room. At once an arm encircled my waist from behind and I near screamed out.'

'Did he throw you down across a bed to have his will of you, or was he too hot to wait, and had you on the stair?' Randolph asked, his curiosity greatly aroused.

'Neither, for it was not His Lordship,' she replied. 'A soft female voice whispered close to my ear, *There is no need to be afraid, Jane. It is I, Lady Grantonby, and I shall save you from being ravished by my husband*.

As you may imagine, I was greatly relieved at that, and stood silent, waiting for instructions. *We must not try to move from here yet*, said Her Ladyship, *for I can hear him grumbling up and down the passage as he searches for you. We must wait a little until he gives up and retires to his room*.'

'This is very strange,' said Randolph, turning to face Jane, so that he could play with her ample titties, 'why should Lady Grantonby care whether His Lordship poked his servants or not? Is she a jealous woman by nature?'

'The same question was in my own mind then,' said Miss Jane, 'and it was soon answered, though in a way I did not expect. We stood silent together, Her Ladyship and me, she pressing close to my back, and her arm tight round my waist.

109

Then of a sudden she was handling my titties through my dress, and sighing loud. I was near to crying out in my astonishment, but to be heard by His Lordship and dragged off to his bedroom was not to be borne at any price, and so I smothered my cry and controlled myself.'

'By George!' said Randolph, 'Her Ladyship's appetite is for young girls, is it?'

'So I found,' Miss Jane confirmed, 'for her other hand slid under my dress and explored between my thighs. I squirmed about a little at the unusual touch, and felt my bottom rub against Her Ladyship's thighs. *Little minx*, she whispered, *do that again*. An instant later her fingers were at my pussy and it was as if a bolt of lightning flashed through my body to feel her dainty hand open my soft split. She laid her middle finger along the slit between the lips and pressed gently inside to tickle my little button.'

The effect of Jane's story was to bring Randolph's shaft up hard-on in her clasping hand, whilst he to emulate her former employer, laid a finger between her parted cunny lips.

'What happened then you may well guess,' said Jane, 'for Her Ladyship's delicate touch on my button undid me almost at once, and a dozen tiny caresses sufficed to bring me off with ease.'

With a long moan, Randolph rolled Jane over face down on the bed, raised her hips and pushed his hard shaft into her pussy from behind, lying over her back, his hands clasping her plump titties. As when Jane had stood leaning back against the Lady Grantonby, so now he came off in less than a dozen strokes, and gushed his hot elixir into her.

'My word, that was quick!' said she, when he released her to turn over and face him again. 'It appears that the adventures of my girlhood have a strong attraction for you.

Though nothing much out of the way took place, merely the rub of fingers in a pussy to the point of coming off. Would you have been so hot to roger me if it had been the footman handling me?'

'Why no — that would have been shameful,' Randolph told her firmly. 'But what of Her Ladyship after? Was her kindness to you repeated?'

'Hardly ten minutes passed before she wished to make me the recipient of another charitable act,' said Jane with a smile, 'for as soon as we were sure His Lordship had gone to his room to sulk, she made me go with her to her own bedchamber. It was winter and there was a comfortable blaze in the fireplace, and a brocaded armchair pulled close to it. Her Ladyship sat at her ease and pulled me on to her lap. *You're a fine well-grown girl*, said she, her hand undoing my clothes to make bare my titties and play with them.

'I stared down at what she was doing to me, half coming off in the bliss of being caressed by this aristocratic lady. She bent her long slender neck to worry at my titties with her lips and tongue, and I could feel her hand under my clothes probing ever deeper into my hot little slit. Her face was flushed red with emotion and I knew I could, with impunity, touch her body then. I slipped a hand down the front of her low-cut evening gown and devoted myself to playing with her titties and the little hard teats that crowned them. I wondered if I could bring her off by stimulating her titties only, perhaps at the same moment that she fetched me off.'

Randolph's shaft was at the stand again, and twitching within Jane's loose grasp.

'And were you successful?' he gasped.

'Almost — for soon Her Ladyship began to wriggle her

bottom on the chair and heave her belly up and down in nervous rhythm. *You saucy little baggage!* she sighed. *I gave you no permission to touch me — and I'm half coming off already. You must pay for your impertinence!* With that she rubbed my secret button fast until my body shuddered and my pussy wept tears of sheer joy — in short, she caused me to dissolve in the spasms of coming-off yet again. I pinched her teats hard in my fingers and she too called out, *Ah, yes!* in the sweetness of the paroxysm.'

It was perhaps the simple and sincere way in which Jane told her story of girlish lust, or perhaps the cool and gentle touch of her hand on Randolph's swollen shaft, or perhaps it was some combination of the intellectual and the physical stimulation — for as she described the event of Lady Grantonby's coming off, he gave a long sigh, his body shook, and spurts of his creamy liquor flew from his leaping shaft into her palm.

'Good Lord!' said Jane in amused surprise. 'How easily you come off! Will you rest a little now?'

'Needs must,' Randolph answered her, surprised himself by his fast and full response. 'Turn over with your back to me, Jane.'

She obliged him by putting her ivory-skinned back to him and drawing up her knees, so that he could lie against her like two spoons, her bottom against his belly and loins, his arms about her and his hands cupping her titties.

'I think I may take forty winks to restore my strength before I roger you again,' he murmured. 'Lull me to sleep, my dear, with a continuation of your truly charming tale of Lady Grantonby's seduction of her little undermaid.'

'If it will please you,' said Jane, wriggling about the soft cheeks of her bottom in Randolph's lap to settle herself. 'When Her Ladyship had somewhat recovered from the sweet fatigue of coming off she asked me to help her to undress, not wanting to send for her personal maid and interrupt our games. I was glad of the chance to see what fine garments a great lady wore, and assisted her to remove her stylish evening gown, to marvel then at the delicacy of her underskirts and petticoat, and at the wealth of fine lace on her chemise.'

'I know what underclothes ladies wear,' said Randolph, 'for I have undressed more of them than you. Get to the point.'

'As you wish,' Jane agreed in perfect good humour. 'Suffice it to say that before long Her Ladyship was seated on the side of her bed in her fine batiste nightgown, and I knelt at her feet to roll down her stockings for her. The skin of her legs was so very smooth and fine that I was unable to refrain from running my fingers up and down, from ankle to knee, until seeing that she was flattered rather than annoyed by this piece of presumption, I became greatly daring and caressed lightly above the knees also.'

'And higher still, I hope,' Randolph said with a yawn, 'when did you get to her cunny?'

'As soon as Her Ladyship encouraged my boldness by opening up her thighs,' Jane replied. 'My searching hand found her pussy — and her face began to blush a pretty pink at the touch of my fingers on the moist lips. Soon after that, before I could bring her off, she lay on the bed and asked me to pull her nightgown up to her neck.'

'Ah, she showed herself to you naked,' said Randolph with a sigh of pleasure, 'and you were still fully clothed, I take it. Is she a pretty woman, Lady Grantonby? For I cannot recall ever meeting her in society.'

'A well-made lady,' Jane replied, 'with an excellent pair of titties for her age, which is approaching thirty years, I think. She is flat-bellied and somewhat broad across the hips, which may sound a trifle ungainly, but I can assure you that when she lies on her back she is as arousing as any woman on earth, for she seems to be made especially for the sensual act.'

'But does Lord Grantonby think so?' Randolph enquired.

'Why no, His Lordship is averse to sinking his aristocratic shaft in any female over twenty, being so inclined by Nature.'

'Continue,' Randolph urged.

'Her Ladyship had me kneel on her bed, my head down between her parted thighs, to lick her curly haired cunny. I ministered to her button with my tongue, till soon enough it throbbed most voluptuously and became slippery wet with the honey dew of high excitement of love. *Ah, Jane*, she gasped faintly, *I've never been tongued so delicately before – how delicious are the sensations you offer me! I'm sure you will fetch me off in a minute . . .*'

Randolph's ever-eager shaft had grown hard again, and to keep it still while he heard the remainder of Jane's account of her night of seduction, he slipped it between her closed thighs. He was tempted to insert it into her wet pussy, offered temptingly to him by her position, but refrained. He was well aware that he would come off in seconds if once he broached her, and for a while he wished to retain the flow of his sap to hear her out.

'The very idea of bringing off Her Ladyship aroused me to the peak of frenzy,' said Jane, squeezing Randolph's shaft between her soft thighs. 'I had done it once by stimulating her teats, but that was almost by chance. Now she had given herself to me completely, and lay on her back fully exposed to me. She moaned and sighed to the flick of my tongue on her button, and bounded upward to push her open pussy at me. I had wrought her up to a state of lustful impatience, and I delighted in the sound of her gasping at the tremors that darted through her beneath my urgent caress. And then! Ah, never shall I forget that moment – Her Ladyship's smooth bare legs kicked upwards on either side of me, advising the supreme moment was at hand.'

Randolph's sleepiness had vanished, as morning mist before a rising sun, and he was again ablaze with passion. His shaft was of itself jerking in the gentle clasp of Jane's thighs, and he knew he would not long hold out.

'Yes, yes!' he gasped. 'She came off – tell me of it!'

'She came off hard,' Jane agreed with a little laugh at his impatience. 'She uttered a loud shriek and heaved up her belly, gripped my head between her thighs and shook to the convulsions of her climactic pleasure.'

'And so must I!' Randolph exclaimed. 'On your back, quick!'

'What an impetuous gentleman you are, to be sure!' said Jane in a tone of understanding and acceptance. 'I know some lines that Lady Grantonby taught me before I left her service to make my fortune. She said they were written by the celebrated poetess Mrs Felicia Hemans:

Oh come, beloved, lay your body down
Upon your darling's naked belly white,
And rapture shall our dear embraces crown,
As stroking pussy brings us true delight!

Such spasms of desire I have for you,
Who lead me down the blissful ways of love,
I welcome everything you mean to do,
When I am underneath, and you above!

Smiling lustfully, Jane moved swiftly to place herself on her back for him, and even as he got his belly on hers, she used her dainty white fingers to open the pouting lips of her love-split. With a shaking hand he guided the head of his throbbing shaft to the entrance to Paradise and lodged it within.

He took a deep breath and pushed straight — and in the same instant Jane pushed up to meet him. In a long and delicious slide his shaft was embedded as deep in her wet cunny as a man could ever desire. He rogered in and out, enjoying to the full the sensual pressure of her tightly clasping pussy.

'Great Heaven, the sensation!' cried Jane, her ardour as his own in intensity.

Randolph rammed hard and furious until he felt the floodgates yield within his belly. He uttered a triumphant cry to the feel of a torrent of hot sap racing from his tight pompoms up his jerking shaft.

He was thinking to himself, in as much as any man is capable of rational thought at the moment of fetching off, that what it was that most delighted him and raised his pleasure to unknown summits, was to roger a pliant young female like Miss Jane, not a demanding virago like Alice Hamilton. His pleasure was to use and ravish a female, not to be used by one. From this it was a small step to renew his resolve to be the master always.

'Ah, ah!' he cried, and spent his lust in Jane's pussy.

CHAPTER 8
The Keeping of
a Resolution

The resolution Randolph had renewed when he was ensconced in Miss Jane's person was not put to the test during the next day, for after his night in her bed, he lacked his customary energy to pursue young females for the use of their pussies. In his mind was a warning passage he had read in Dr Acton's celebrated book, *The Functions and Disorders of the Reproductive Organs*. On a memorable occasion advice was sought of the learned doctor by a colleague suffering from a general debility, an inaptitude for work, disinclination for sexual intercourse, and a most ominous dimming of his eyesight.

In answer to Dr Acton's questioning, the sufferer admitted to connection with his wife *several* times a week, ever since their marriage seven years ago, and often *more than once a night*. The doctor at once informed him that this excess accounted for his troubles. Though he had been a hearty, healthy man at the time of his marriage, he had by over-indulgence in the conjugal act brought himself to this sorry pass!

Randolph bore it in mind that the sufferer was a middle-class sort of person, and therefore by Nature unable to sustain equal performance with a member of the titled classes, such as he was himself. Nevertheless, after poking Miss Jane six times during the course of a night, he felt it prudent to rest, till all his normal ebullience was restored. Therefore he passed much of the day quietly at his club in St James, where he dozed all morning in an armchair over the newspapers, and then after a sustaining luncheon, played a hand or two of cards.

On the following morning he awoke in his own bed in Cavendish Square, feeling much refreshed and ready for any friskiness, so long as it ended in rogering. When the under-maid brought in his morning tea, he was already up and out of bed, and standing at the window in his long dressing-gown, watching female servants at work washing the steps of houses all round the square.

'Put the tray down, Lizzie,' said he, turning from the sights that had held his interest. 'I have not seen you since I went to the poking-match, to tell you that it was a fine spectacle.'

The girl blushed faintly, her eyes looking down at the floor. Randolph smiled to see the effect he had on her, and determined to pursue it further, to assert himself as master of the girl's cunny, if he chose to make use of it. He undid the front of his frogged dressing-gown and let it fall open.

'See here, Lizzie,' said he, drawing up his nightshirt front to bare his shaft to her.

It was in a condition of readiness, standing hard-on, as the result of his contemplation through the window of a wench down on hands and knees scrubbing the steps of Number 14 next door. Young though she was, she had a good fat behind, the cheeks presented roundly through her dress because of her position on the steps. He had amused himself by imagining how it might be to come up behind the skivvy and poke her from the rear.

Fair-haired Lizzie gasped and put a hand to her mouth to see his shaft so boldly displayed. He was, whether or no the wench appreciated the fact, well endowed in the matter of his sexual part. He had not given the nickname of Mr Percival Proud to it without good reason.

This thick and long shaft pointed strongly upward toward her face, attracted her glance, whatever her confusion and dismay.

'If you were a pretty little trollop, such as hawks her wares in the West End,' said Randolph, smiling to see the scarlet of Lizzie's cheeks, 'and for a sovereign or two you had conducted me to a convenient room, then at the sight of my shaft standing forth uncovered like this, you would by now have knelt and put your arms about my loins . . .'

He paused momentarily to savour Lizzie's loud gasp of dread, then continued:

'Your tongue would flick out to tease the head of my hard-on shaft, till it oozed tiny droplets of love juice. Whereupon I would take your head between my hands and pull your face toward me, and you would draw a good half of my shaft into your mouth.

'Sir, sir — stop it!' Lizzie gasped, seemingly rooted to the spot in her agony of mind.

'No little trull who stops when she has a man's shaft in her mouth, before she brings him off, is worth a light!' said he. 'Nor would I allow you to pull way from me. I would hold your head firmly whilst you sucked at my throbbing muscle. And then what bliss — my elixir would start to gush forth, bringing on those ecstatic sensations which melt the soul in bliss.'

'Can I go now, sir?' Lizzie asked in desperation.

'Go? What the devil do you mean?'

She gulped and turned to leave the room without permission, at which Randolph strode smartly across the carpet, to reach out and seize hold of her by the nape of her neck. He whirled her about and pushed her towards the bed, until her legs were against the side of it. She squirmed in his grasp and begged to be released, but Randolph was enjoying the scene greatly.

'Don't be a ninny, girl,' said he, 'I've had you before, and mean to have you again. Why this show of resistance, when there is no cause for alarm? You were no virgin the first time I poked you, and who shall miss another slice off a cut loaf?'

'Don't, sir,' Lizzie pleaded.

Randolph was overjoyed at her reluctance and the opportunity it provided him to deploy his strength and mastery to poke her. He told her to climb up on the side of the bed on her hands and knees, with her bottom towards him. The tone of dominance that she detected in his voice evidently carried some weight, for no further protest escaped her lips as she did what he required of her. She placed herself on her knees, her face crimson with the shame of it, and he turned her dress and petticoats up over her back, to reveal her drawers.

It was the work of a moment to pry open with avid fingers the rearward slit of her undergarment. He stood in contemplation of the pale cheeks of Lizzie's backside sticking out towards him, and her brown-curled split. She stared over her shoulder, her expression troubled and yet also puzzled, that he merely looked at her secret parts, and made no move to touch them.

He for his part was rapt in thought, standing naked, for he had by then removed his dressing-gown and nightshirt. His hand slid along his stiff shaft, teasing Mr Percival to his maximum dimension, as a prelude to sinking him in the wench's slit. The moment was delightful to him — he had a female at the mercy of his hard-on shaft, and she was his to poke or not to poke, in whichever hole he pleased.

Lizzie summoned up the courage to enquire if he meant to do her like that, on her knees, or whether she should lie on her back for him. She asked without interest, and in resignation, to get it over with as soon as could be.

Randolph ignored her question, and stared at her bottom and parts to his full content. By then Mr Percival was leaping hard in his manipulating hand, and he bounded faster when Randolph put his other hand to Lizzie's hairy slit, to spread apart the lips and finger the button till he had made it slippy.

Lizzie was by then shivering and sighing, and Randolph came to understand that he had aroused her so that she wanted to be done. He found her attitude impudent in the extreme, and became annoyed with the girl for her presumption.

'Damme!' he exclaimed. 'I'm not here for your benefit! If I choose to finger your slit, it is for my pleasure, not yours! How dare you allow yourself to get into this condition!'

'I'm sorry, sir,' Lizzie gasped, 'I never meant to, but there was no way I can stop myself when you touch me.'

'You are a little trollop, and you let your cunny be felt by every manservant in the house!' Randolph accused her. 'A dozen times a day you're fingered and poked, I'm sure of it!'

'No, sir, I really don't,' she stammered, not knowing what he wanted of her, whether to scold her or have her.

'Lying will not serve you,' said he, his fingers probing into her wet pussy to add to her confusion. 'Tell me the truth now — when was the last time this common slit of yours was poked and spent in? Last night, I'll be bound.'

'Oh no, sir! The last time was when you did me, I swear.'

'Then who last fingered you?' Randolph demanded. 'Out with it, my girl — which of the servants was it?'

'If you please, sir,' said she haltingly, 'it was James, the second footman, who tried to interfere with me yesterday in the afternoon, when all the family were out of the house and most of the servants too. He caught me in the still-room, and had me seated on the table and his hand up my clothes so suddenly that I had no time to complain.'

'The filthy beast!' Randolph exclaimed. 'What did he do?'

'He wanted to do *me*,' Lizzie confessed, 'for he had my skirts up to my waist and his hand in my drawers to feel my parts. Two fingers together he pressed into my slit, groping for the most sensitive spot of all which, when he found, he rubbed, for all my protestations and struggling.'

'How dare the fellow make free of what belongs by right to his betters!' said Randolph. 'Did he have the effrontery to bring you off?'

'No, sir, I swear he didn't, for he was too eager to get into my pussy. Out came his shaft, as stiff as a poker, and he held it in his hand and stroked it while he boasted that he would have it up me to the limit. Now I, to put him down, said that I had never before seen so miserably small a shaft on a grown man — and he was mortified and jerked at it to bring it up longer and harder before pushing it in me.'

'Was it more than usually small?'

Lizzie blushed furiously and declared that she had seen very few male parts and had not the experience to judge.

'Well, was it smaller than mine?' Randolph demanded.

'Oh yes, a good deal shorter! I've never seen another as big as yours,' said the girl, though whether she spoke the truth or whether she spoke to please the young master, there was no way to be certain.

'It felt small inside you?' asked Randolph.

'He never got it inside me − I've told you that already, sir. What with rubbing at it to make it swell up bigger, James went further than he intended, and with a sudden cry, he spent and his sap flew out over my thigh, and wet my drawers through.'

'Where?' Randolph gasped, his arms about the girl to fumble at the fronts of her thighs, 'show me where he wet you. Was it here, close up to your pussy, or lower on your thigh, nearer to your knee?'

'It was about where your fingers are now,' said Lizzie.

'So near!' said Randolph, whose fingers were in her groin, 'An inch higher and the foul beast would have fetched off right over your pussy! Did he leave you then?'

'He swore at me, saying I had made him spill his tallow on my leg instead of in my cunny, but he let me go, for his bolt was shot and he could do no more.'

'Common people are not endowed with the natural strength and virility of the upper classes,' Randolph informed her loftily. 'I can come off twice in a row, as you have experienced, but an ordinary person is limited to once by a beneficent Deity.'

His fingers were toying with Lizzie's rearward-facing cunny the whole time he spoke, and she was squirming to sensations of pleasure that he had forbidden to her, and which she attempted to conceal.

'Why is there this difference between master and man, sir?' she asked, a trifle breathlessly. 'What is the reason?'

'Poking is the supreme pleasure in life,' Randolph told her, 'and Nature encourages persons of title and quality to indulge freely. This abundance of pleasure is denied to the labouring classes, who would neglect their work otherwise, to the great detriment of the Nation and the production of its wealth. Among the lower classes, the sole purpose of poking is reproduction of the species, to perpetuate the supply of labour required by titled families as servants, and by the business classes for their manufactories, and by landed gentry for agricultural work and as beaters for shooting parties. Now do you understand?'

'Yes, you have made it plain for me. Thank you, sir.'

'For the reasons I have adduced,' Randolph continued, 'it is given to males of the lower classes to come off but once within a period of several hours. This curtails the duration of their poking, so that their time is available for more useful tasks.'

Even as he spoke, the unanswered question entered Randolph's head — what was the period of hours required for a labourer to recover the power to roger? There was no doubt in his mind as to the truth of his statement, for commonsense required that no common persons should enjoy poking in the same way the upper classes did. Sexual intercourse was, to put it simply, far too damned good for servants and labourers!

The sense of self-satisfaction that pervaded his being at the conclusion of this train of thought so elated Randolph that, at a stroke, he put Sir Percival Proud's velvet-purple head to the female slit confronting him, and pushed him strongly in. Lizzie uttered a slight moan, to feel herself thus invaded, and then braced herself on hands and knees to receive the assault.

Randolph gripped her tight at the hips, to steady her for his thrusting.

'Lizzie — I hope that you appreciate the considerable honour bestowed upon you by having a gentleman's shaft up your pussy — and the even greater honour of his essence deposited in it!'

He waited on no reply while he slid Sir Percival in fast and rhythmic shoves into her. Her head turned, and she stared over her shoulder at him, her eyes pleading with him not to come off in her, lest he put her in the family way, to lose her position and be turned out into the streets, big-bellied and penniless. Her very helplessness added to Randolph's enjoyment, adding to his awareness of being the master, to use females as he willed.

'By God — I'm fetching off!' he cried, his sensations beyond compare delicious.

In another instant his belly heaved and he squirted his juice into her slit, and slumped over her back in trembling bliss, a condition which extended itself to several minutes. All through his spasms of delight Lizzie bore his weight on her back, and his belly against her bottom. She never moved, nor complained, but remained still and solid on her hands and knees, careful to do nothing to detract in any way from Randolph's pleasure, lest he become angry with her.

After luncheon, Randolph strolled forth to take the air, well contented with himself for the way he had asserted his mastery that morning. It was a pleasant day, the sun warm but not hot, and the rain clouds of the previous day passed over and gone, and in black frock coat and shiny top hat, he was elegant and perfectly comfortable. From Cavendish Square he walked south by Regent Street, pausing to purchase a small white flower for his buttonhole from a fat woman in a shawl on the corner. At Beak Street he turned into that district known as Soho, and before he had gone above a hundred steps along the narrow street, there were whores plucking at his sleeve and offering him the freedom of their persons for a guinea.

It was not in search of cunny that he had come to Soho, and he declined all that was offered, and sauntered on. He went by the church, where he caught a glimpse of a gentleman, to judge by his clothes, and a street woman, pressed hard against each other in the church porch. A religious poke, thought he with a smile, with the benefit of the Church, if not of the clergy.

In the next street, through a ground floor window of a house, he sighted a pair of bare titties, and a thick-bodied woman who wore nothing but her blue drawers, beckoning to him to come to the door. He halted for a moment, tempted in spite of himself, but the titties, although large and round, looked well-handled, and the woman was above thirty and had a foreign appearance. After a moment or two, he shook his head and walked on.

He was making for Greek Street, and the premises of Mr Avery, a bookseller of note. The volumes displayed in his dusty window and on the shelves inside the shop were unexceptional − sermons by celebrated preachers, bound up together, books of verse by esteemed poets such as Lord Tennyson and Mrs Elizabeth Barrett Browning, three volume novels by Mr Thackeray and other damned long-winded writers.

No doubt Mr Avery sold a book or two to innocent passers-by now and then, but to rely on lawful sales of wholesome and uplifting publications would have driven him into bankruptcy in double-quick time. The truth of it was that, for gentlemen he knew and in whom he could place his trust, Avery brought out from his back room books of particular interest. In the strict definition of law, these special books were reckoned lewd and obscene, dealing as they did frankly with sexual matters likely to catch the interest of gentlemen.

Nor was Randolph disappointed on this visit. After assuring himself that there was no constable to be seen outside in the street, Avery handed him a handsomely bound volume, which had on the title page an engraving of a naked man and woman in the act of coition together, standing under a palm tree. This, the bookseller told Randolph, was a learned and yet amusing work, a tome that dealt with unusual aspects of the act of generation. The author was a well-travelled gentleman, it appeared, who had an eye for oddity.

Randolph studied the engraving, noting that the man's organ must be at least a foot long, for the top part was thrust into his female partner's cunny, and he was shown in the very throes of fetching off, an expression of foolish delight on his face, yet he stood far enough away from the woman for their bellies not to touch. Such anomalies were known in the East, Randolph knew from previous reading, and a male organ of twelve and a half inches from root to head, in full erection, was thought to be the world's largest. He turned to the Table of Contents, which testified to many strange and little-known facts the author had noticed:

- *Colloquial names given to the male organ (various)*
- *Emergence of the sexual impulse in English females*
- *Earliest growth of hair on the female parts*
- *Copulation with Bombay women rendered difficult by an excessive development of the clitoris*
- *Heaviest female breasts by weight and race*
- *Signs of virginity from Antiquity to the present day*
- *Luxuriance of hair on the private parts of women*
- *Sodomy committed in three ways in Portugal*
- *Erections at the age of three in Bulgarian infants*

Without reading further down the Table, Randolph determined to make an assessment of the thoroughness or otherwise of the author's researches, and took at random a subject, turning to the page indicated. There with much quickening of his interest he read:

Madame Regnier was tall and thin, with expressive eyes and a sensuous appearance. She was a brunette, hairy as to her parts, had a long clitoris, a vigorous anus, slight bosom, passionate temperament, and cruel desires. She gave herself to every vice, offering her body to women as well as to men, whom she preferred to make use of her rear orifice. From which it may be seen as a characteristic of extremely erotic women that they have an abundance of hair on their sexual parts. It has been noted also they have a brilliant gleam of the eyes, and thick red lips.

It was the custom of Madame Regnier to lead her lovers to an alcove whose walls she had ordered to be covered with mirrors. There she repeated a thousand times all the different positions of love, so that the other party could see any part of her body and the most appealing postures for sexual congress . . .

There was much more, and the interesting statement that the volume was embellished with seventeen engravings, executed under the direction of the author, from his own sketches. Randolph told the bookseller that he would take it, and enquired whether he had in stock any new novel, romance or treatise dealing with a long-standing concern of his – namely, the strict and proper education of young ladies at boarding schools?

Avery smiled and put into his hand a book entitled *Selina Simcott, or The Tribulations of Virtue*, saying it had come in a day or two day before, being printed in Antwerp, and excellent value at three pounds.

Randolph opened the book at random and read:

Selina jumped in bed with her, and Susy nestled up close to her bosom, as if to keep warm, but in truth to feel the size of her titties. She passed her hand over these delicious globes a score of times, then asked Selina to open her nightdress, that she might lay her face against them. Thinking only to please, and without taint of sensuality in her motives, Selina let her bedfellow do as she wished, and soon Susy's inquisitive hands were wandering in a searching manner about her person, handling her soft plump titties, her round belly and bottom, her touches seeming to set her blood on fire and rouse every voluptuous emotion . . .

'Damme, Avery,' said Randolph, with a smirk, 'you've hit just the thing for my taste. How does it continue – let me read down to the end of the page.'

Judge of Selina's indescribable horror when the door was flung open and there stood Miss Rodwell with a candle in her hand to light the scene, and a swishy cane in the other. With a fierce jerk she pulled away the bedclothes, revealing Selina on her back, with her nightdress about her waist, and Susy's hand between her rosy thighs, her finger at the very slit of Venus.

'Upon my word,' exclaimed Miss Rodwell, 'I find you debauching a maidservant, Selina! Have you no shame, miss?'

Randolph's eye fell to the bottom of the page, to know what was the outcome of the schoolmistress's discovery. Nor

was he disappointed, for he saw that Miss Rodwell, forcing
a reluctant Susy to assist her, tied Selina's hands to the
bedpost, and her ankles to a heavy chest which stood handy
at the end of the bed so that she was well stretched-out.

*'Your bare posterior shall pay for your lubricity,' said Miss
Rodwell, nor would she listen to Selina's plea for forgiveness
or in any way abate her wrath. She cut her bare bottom five
or six times, each blow leaving a long thin red line and
bringing to the soft cheeks a peach-like bloom and glow.*

*Tears of shame and mortification welled from Selina's
eyes, but her loudest outcry was wrung from her when Miss
Rodwell put aside her cane and thrust her hand between her
victim's legs.*

*'How far had matters progressed between you and this
wretched maidservant?' she demanded. 'Had you
succumbed to the sensual paroxysm? Ah, there is a moisture
here between the lips that ought not to be present. It betrays
your condition of arousal before I so fortunately interrupted
your antics!'*

*'Ah no, no, Miss Rodwell − do not handle me in so
indecent a way, I implore you,' cried Selina, her plump
bottom wriggling about as she sought to escape the fingers
that probed into her virgin pussy.*

*'It is my duty to find out if you have been brought off,
as it is commonly called. Lie still, girl!' said her tormentor,
stimulating her secret button with a busy fingertip, with
more zeal than her avowed investigation warranted. The
outcome could not be long in doubt − the sensual spasm
seized on the pinioned girl, and with a long moan she came
off.*

*'What!' Miss Rodwell exclaimed. 'You dare allow
yourself to do that in my presence? Hand me my cane, Susy,*

I must thrash her behind until she repents and promises to reform her ways!'

'No, Miss!' cried Susy, 'for you will only arouse her again, and make her fetch off a second time!'

'Keep your insolent remarks to yourself,' Miss Rodwell said, 'her bottom shall suffer the cane until she has learned in pain and humiliation her lesson, and can come off no more when I put my hand between her thighs.'

Avery wrapped the two books carefully, to conceal from prying eyes their titles, and Randolph paid him and left the shop. He had gone only a short distance, his thoughts engrossed in what he had read, before he was accosted by a young girl. She said nothing, but stared knowingly at the long bulge in his clothing where Percival Proud stood hard and stiff from the misfortunes of Miss Selina Simcott.

'I wish I could spare the time,' said Randolph, 'but I am in somewhat of a hurry.'

'Won't take but a minute, the state you're in,' she answered pertly. 'In here.'

As if in a dream, he followed her into a narrow entry between two houses. The street was but a few steps away, where draymen passed with their loads, and pedestrians were walking by. That notwithstanding, the girl put her hand under Randolph's elegant frock coat and opened his trouser buttons all the way down. She pulled his shirt up out of the way, to take his hot and hard shaft in her hand.

'Two shillings, and I'll put him to rest for you,' said she.

'Done,' Randolph accepted.

'Not yet, but you will be in a minute,' she said with a grin. He leaned his back against the wall behind him and spread his feet apart a little. The girl jerked Percival Proud briskly up and down, making Randolph sigh at the pleasant feelings the simple action provided.

'Stand close,' he said, 'let me feel your cunny.'

She hitched up her threadbare brown skirt to let him slide a hand into her drawers and finger her between the legs. By the use of imagination he summoned up the memory of how he had that morning imposed his will on the undermaid Lizzie's pussy, shown to him as she knelt on his bed, quavering in her fright.

'What's your name, girl?' he asked the wielder of his shaft.

'Peg,' said she. 'You've a good-sized thing on you, sir. It's been up plenty of girls' cunnies, I'll be bound.'

Mr Percival was twitching in delight at the way he was being handled, and also from the lewd pleasure Randolph gained from feeling the girl's sparsely fledged pussy. He pressed a finger into it and rubbed her tiny button.

'Do you poke, Peg?' he asked.

'How much would you give me?' she said.

'Another day,' he sighed, 'I'm almost coming off already.'

'That you are,' Peg agreed, 'your hairy monster's jumping in my hand like a chicken with its neck wrung!'

Her hand rubbed at his straining shaft strongly, and Randolph felt his heart beating faster as the moment came closer for his passions to be relieved in wet spasms of delight. A fine frenzy of sensation seized upon him then, and his knees turned shaky under him, as his essence gushed in long jets up his belly, and soaked his shirt.

'Now I've done you!' the girl exclaimed.

CHAPTER 9
A Young Lady
Is Shamelessly Abused

After the young trollop in Greek Street had completed, wholly to Randolph's satisfaction, the process of inducing Mr Percival Proud to throb and spurt, she released her sticky hold to grin and ask for her money. Randolph put his clothes to rights, then paid her the two shillings he had agreed, bestowing a word or two of commendation for her skill in handling a gentleman's part so agreeably, after which he strolled on into Shaftesbury Avenue, thinking to find a cab.

To his surprise he was hailed by a dulcet female voice as he crossed the pavement and, turning, he saw leaving a milliner's shop none other than pretty Miss Dorothy Harker, accompanied by her brother Devlin. Randolph raised his top hat and returned the greeting. She looked deuced pretty, he thought, in a short jacket that buttoned tightly over her bosom, making her titties prominent. Her hat had small flowers sewn on it, and under her arm she carried a rolled umbrella with a round ebony knob for a handle. After the usual exchange of trivial remarks required on social occasions, Miss Harker declared that she veritably believed that Randolph had neglected her brother and herself.

'We have been in London for two weeks or more,' said

she, 'in which time you have never once visited to pay your respects. Do you find our company tedious, Mr Joynes?'

'Lord no,' he replied, 'but my time has been so taken up with family matters that I have neglected all my friends. I shall do my best to make amends by calling on you tomorrow, before noon, if you will be so good as to inform me where you are staying.'

'There is no need to wait until tomorrow,' said the sprightly Miss Harker, 'for you can accompany us to our lodgings now and take tea with us, mayn't he, Devlin?'

'Of course he may, but I've just remembered that I am to meet Lorimer at his club at four. Do you mind seeing my sister safe home, Mr Joynes, while I dash off?'

'With the greatest of pleasure,' said Randolph, offering his arm politely to Miss Harker.

It seemed to him that Devlin Harker had the look of a man who is intent on searching out a pussy to make use of, and not one going to meet another man in a boring club.

'Walk down Haymarket,' he advised, 'and through Jermyn Street towards Lorimer's club. There are fine wares displayed for sale along there, and you may well see something you like. I shall enjoy a cup of tea meanwhile with Miss Harker.'

In the hansom cab that bore them towards Paddington Green, where the Harkers had taken an apartment for their stay, she prattled happily of the many things she and her brother had seen in London, and of the excellent shops and the clothes she had bought. Randolph smiled encouragingly the whole time, even though his thoughts were on quite another topic.

He was pondering, in deep amusement, what this pretty nineteen-year-old virgin from Warwickshire might say if he were suddenly to inform her that, not ten minutes ago, he had been fetched off by the hand of a little trull in a Soho alley? Or what if he seized Dorothy Harker's hand now and thrust it down the front of his trousers, to make her feel the wetness of his spasm on his shirt, and his shaft lying limp between his thighs?

This sweet-smelling, smooth-skinned, soft-spoken young lady had never seen a male sexual organ in her life, of that he was certain. No thought ever entered her head that men she spoke to were eager to put their hard-on shafts up into the secret slit between her legs, and shoot their sap into it. Surely she would die of shame outright, if that were suggested to her face!

By dint of stretching his faculty of imagination, Randolph envisaged, under Miss Harker's snuff-coloured satin dress, legs encased in thin white drawers, ivory-skinned thighs and a dark-haired plump pussy nestling between. Mr Percival Proud approved wholeheartedly of the fantastical vision, and rose in readiness to his full height, inside Randolph's trousers.

Whatever strictures Dr William Acton might place on the over-frequent repetition of the sensual paroxysm and its harmful effect on the human organism, Randolph had formed a great letch to finger the maiden pussy of this untouched young gentlewoman, and gush his elixir into it. He knew perfectly well that there was not the least chance she would let him do so, or even speak of it, and that knowledge brought his emotions to the boil. His whole being yearned to roger Miss Dorothy Harker.

The pleasure would reside wholly in the physical conquest and the knowledge of being the first to spend in her, he knew, for often there was precious little more than the bare satisfaction of fetching off to be had with English gentlewomen, married or single. This Randolph had learned from his own experience, and it accounted for his predilection for whores. Quite the most beautiful woman he had ever rogered, disgraceful though it may be thought to admit it, was his sister-in-law, Lady Turringby, the wife of his eldest brother, who would inherit the earldom.

Randolph stayed often enough at his brother's country home in Surrey, and on one occasion had paid an unexpected visit during the hour when the household was dressing for dinner on lovely Gertrude in her room. She turned pale to see him there, though he had flirted with her for two days before this, and she had accepted his suit, though discreetly. Now the moment for action was at hand, she seemed to draw back, looking timid, and would have wished him to leave her.

This was not to be — as soon as the door was shut behind him, Randolph caught her in his arms and gave her a lengthy kiss of the most passionate nature. At this her reserve melted, and she clung to him, one arm clasped about his waist, the other around his neck, her dainty fingers playing in his curly hair. There was little time to spare on the delicacies of courtship with a married woman, and Randolph squeezed her titties through the lace-edged *robe-de-chambre* she wore.

'You do not love me,' she said, gazing deep into his eyes, 'I fear all you want of me is to make use of my person for you coarse pleasure. How banal that seems to me, how unworthy!'

She spoke the truth, of course, but that had little enough to with the matter. Without troubling to answer her, Randolph drew her tongue into his mouth, hugging her close in his arms, until she was breathless and ready for anything.

'I was hasty,' she murmured, her eyes searching his face, 'I see now that perhaps you do love me a little . . .'

Before she could go further into foolishness, Randolph slid a hand into her robe below the sash and felt quickly upwards between her thighs, to find the opening of her drawers and slip inside, to touch her soft skin.

'Ah now!' said she. 'Is that love, Randolph?'

'The fiercest, most passionate kind!' he declared.

His fingers were twining in the fine curly locks that covered her pussy. She continued to hold her legs together, especially when his fingertips stroked her moist lips. Eventually there came a relaxation of her muscles, as pleasant sensations manifested themselves within her, and he was able to press his finger into her pussy and tease her secret bud.

After some moments of this pleasant manipulation, he took her to the bedside and laid her on it. He got between her legs, fully dressed as he was, ripped open his trousers and brought Mr Percival Proud up to the mark. With one thrust he introduced that twitching gentleman into Gertrude's cunny, and rogered her with short hard strokes. Beneath him, her eyes were wide open to stare into his face, and she was so beautiful to look at that Randolph almost forgot what he was about. She did nothing to stir his blood, but lay passive on her back, her legs apart, allowing him to do what he wanted to her, almost as if her soul was elsewhere and only her body at his disposal.

'Do you like to be rogered, Gertrude?' he asked, panting.

She made no reply, but blushed fearfully at the suggestion, for all the world as if she were a young virgin with a shaft in her for the first time, and not the twenty-nine-year-old mother of three small children.

'Randolph – do not despise me!' she sighed.

Her words meant nothing to him. He rogered her strongly, and soon his creamy fluid came rushing out in thick jets, gushing up her pussy, and he squirmed in the bliss of fetching-off. But Gertrude, thus flooded, lay still, breathing perhaps a little more quickly but otherwise unaffected.

Since that time Randolph had made use of her commodity often but never once had he had the success of bringing her off, not by the use of his shaft, of his fingers, or of his tongue. It was because Gertrude was such a stunner in looks and figure that he was drawn to her and wanted to poke her each and every time he could, but her beauty was as nothing, he learned, for by Nature she was unreceptive, and he could as easily have been poking a dressmaker's dummy.

Nor was Gertrude the only woman of his acquaintance who was disappointing when her drawers were down. He had made trial of enough married gentlewomen to find that out. For some reason he could not understand, it was as Dr William Acton claimed – that as a general rule, a well-born, gently nurtured, virtuous woman desired little or no sexual gratification. She submitted to her husband or her lover only to please him and, except for the fear of losing him, she would far rather be relieved from his attentions.

Ladies like Alice Hamilton, who delighted in being poked by night and day, were all too few and far between, Randolph knew. It was in his thoughts that he had been hasty in breaking off with her, for she had given him some damned fine poking. Yet it had irked him that she wished to play the man's part and take the lead; it offended his manhood to be used for her pleasure, and he set his face against a return to her bed.

In the meantime, there was Dorothy Harker to think about, and if there was any chance of getting his hard-on shaft into her. If he did, it was extremely unlikely that he would be ever able to make her come off, English gentlewomen being too ashamed of their bodily functions, it appeared, to permit themselves to be gratified by poking. Yet it would be amusing to try.

The apartment Harker and his sister had taken for their stay in London had a large drawing room that overlooked the Green. Dorothy took off her bonnet and rang for tea, which was brought in by a maid with a bosom so well-developed that Randolph could scarce take his eye off her whilst she remained in the room.

Miss Harker poured him a cup and offered him a slice of fruit cake, and they chatted through the institution of afternoon tea until the social conventions had been sufficiently respected, in Randolph's opinion. A delicate and soft glow on Dorothy's face suggested to him that she was at her ease and well-disposed to him. Not that she would be receptive to his sexual advances, of that he was pretty sure, but at least he might make some little progress before she cried a halt.

They were seated side by side on a sofa, and he reached out boldly to take her hand in his own. At once her pretty face was suffused with the pink blush of modesty.

'Fie, Mr Joynes!' she exclaimed, trying to free herself from his grasp. 'What on earth can you be thinking of, to take this liberty!'

'Calm your distress, my dear Miss Harker,' said he, 'there is something of vast importance that I must ask you — and I hope you trust me sufficiently to take my question in good faith and answer it truthfully.'

'You must leave at once,' she told him firmly, 'release my hand that I may ring for the maid to show you out.'

'Do not be so hasty,' he said, 'the matter holds the greatest importance for you, and for me also.'

So saying, he slid a hand lightly over the full bodice of her dress, feeling the swell of her bosom. Had she been

139

dressed for the evening, with gown cut low, he would have slipped his hand down the front to clasp a titty and press it warmly. But in her high-necked walking-out dress, he could do no more than handle her titties through the satin.

'Dearest Dorothy,' said he, 'are you familiar with the lines written by Mr Leigh Hunt, the celebrated poet?'

> *Stolen sweets are always sweeter,*
> *Stolen kisses much completer,*
> *Sly feels of titties never pall,*
> *But stolen pokes the best of all.*

He saw Dorothy's mouth open to reprove him severely, and to prevent her outcry, he moved closer to her along the sofa and pressed a kiss to her lips.

'Unhand me!' she cried in alarm, jerking her head back from his to deny the touch of his mouth. 'This is a monstrous abuse of hospitality! Know, sir, that your friend Mr Lorimer Mawby has made me a proposal of marriage. I am to give him his answer at the weekend.'

'Dorothy — you must listen to me for one moment, and then I will release you,' said Randolph, smiling at her protest. 'Tell me truthfully now — have you allowed Lorimer, under the guise of a promise of marriage, to roger you? I have every faith in your maidenly virtue, and do not believe you have let him, even if he begged on his knees for it.'

She stared at him speechless, and he was very pleased by the strong effect his words had on her.

'Put aside this futile coyness,' said he, 'speak out freely — has Lorimer not put his hand under your clothes, and up between your legs, to feel your pussy, at least?'

'Oh!' she gasped, almost swooning from the excess of her

140

emotions, her eyes half-closed, while Randolph treated himself to a good feel of her big soft bubbies.

She would had risen to her feet, to escape from his insults, but Randolph threw himself to his knees before her and thrust both hands up her skirts. She cried out in horror, to feel his hands on her thighs, and attempted to press her clothes down on her knees, to prevent him from turning her hem up to her lap to uncover her knees and her stockinged legs.

'Stop this at once!' she cried, her face flushed scarlet as she stared down at him.

Randolph had not the least concern for decency or modesty just at that moment for, as the proverb informs us, *A standing shaft knows no pang of conscience*. His eyes glowed and his mouth was open in delight to observe how provocatively the fine material of Dorothy's drawers clung to her well-rounded thighs. Mr Proud bounded iron-hard inside his trousers, and without a moment of hesitation, Randolph tried to force his hand between her thighs to get at the opening of her drawers.

She pressed her legs tightly together to thwart him, and it was with the liveliest gratification that he heard her gasp of disbelief and dismay.

'For shame, sir!' she cried out. 'You must desist from this unspeakable indecency!'

Alas for outraged modesty, Randolph was by far the stronger, and his hand forced its way between her thighs, until he could slide forward on his knees and wedge her legs apart by placing his body between them. She struggled all the more then, to halt the vile advantage he was taking of her person, but in the grip of lust he was remorseless.

'You seem not to be a lover of poetry,' said he, panting with lust, 'but there are a few descriptive lines by the celebrated Mr Thomas Moore which bear exactly on our situation:

There is not in this wide world a valley more sweet
Than the vale where the thighs of a naked girl meet,
Oh, the last ray of feeling and life must depart,
Ere the love for that valley shall fade from my heart.

Miss Harker was in no mood for poetry at that time, not even if it were from the pen of the Poet Laureate himself.

'I shall scream to summon the servants unless you cease this infamous conduct!' she warned him. 'A constable shall be sent for and you given in charge!'

'I shall say that you spread your legs and asked me to feel you, but drew back when I begged to roger you,' he replied, to counter her threat.

It was in any case too late for warnings and consequences. His fleshy shaft was leaping so wildly in trousers that without a second thought he ripped open his buttons and let it stick out nakedly. He gripped it laxly between thumb and forefinger, stroking it suggestively to attract Dorothy's attention to its condition of readiness to devirginise her. At the sight of his thick and strenuously jerking implement, she uttered a long cry of dismay and collapsed against the sofa-back in a deep swoon.

Randolph stared at her with fierce delight, thinking how very fresh and pretty she was. Her eyes were closed and her cheeks pale, and she looked calm and pure. Her mouth was a little open to show her small white teeth, her breathing so light as to be almost imperceptible, hardly stirring her bosom. He panted in lewd desire, whilst he parted the slit of her drawers to bare her plump pussy, with its profusion of silky brown curls.

He did not hesitate, but pressed the tip of his middle finger to the soft lips and opened them, to gaze at the delicate pink of the interior, and her unbroken little maidenhead. His blood raced in his veins and he felt for a moment that he too might swoon, though in sheer bliss, at the sight of Dorothy's girlish pussy, so utterly at his mercy.

He slid forward on his knees, forcing her legs ever wider, to where he was close enough to present the swollen purple head of Mr Percival Proud to the lips of her cunny. One long straight push would take him into her, and his would be the first shaft ever to penetrate that beauteous pussy! One bold shove was all it would take to give him possession of her innermost charms! A dozen or twenty short stabs and his essence would gush up her deflowered slit, and the deed would be done!

Even on the very brink of his victory, something caused him to pause, though he could scarce breathe for the raging sensual emotions that had him in an inescapable grip. If Dorothy were of no more account than a common girl picked up and paid for along the streets of the East End, or out in the suburbs of Hampstead or Balham, he would have no qualm. More than once he had bought the use of a young virgin from her family and rogered her with merciless thrusts, her cries and sobs adding to his delight. It was beyond question that the daughters of the labouring classes had no higher destiny than to be poked by the gentry.

That notwithstanding, the uncomfortable fact was that Dorothy Harker was not a daughter of common people, but of a well-to-do land-owning family in Warwickshire. If she were deprived of her maidenhood outside marriage, there would be a devil of a fuss. In agony of mind, unable to go forward or back, Randolph stared at the sweet young pussy before him, while his trembling hand slid up and down the length of his throbbing shaft.

The sexual impulse was overpowering and would not be denied. With a moan of mingled joy and sorrow, Randolph fetched off to the wild jerking of his hand, and spurted his creamy sap on the soft white belly that lay bare above Dorothy's virgin cunny.

'Oh, oh!' he moaned, 'how blissful the sensations — but how mortifying that my essence is *on* her, and not *in* her!'

He sank back to sit on his folded legs, Mr Proud still in his hand, and stared in deep fascination at the white trickle down Dorothy's belly, into the silky curls that adorned her *motte*. A dissatisfaction possessed him, for there came into his mind the disgraceful story Lizzie had told him, of the attempt by James, the second footman, to interfere with her.

The damned fellow had pulled out his shaft, as bold as brass, and shown it to the under-maid bragging that she would shortly have it up her. He had stroked it to make it bigger, whilst at the same time he fingered the girl's slit — which was not his to use for his pleasure, he being only a servant in the house. Some such consideration must have entered his head, for he had brought himself off by hand and squirted his sap on to Lizzie's thigh. She believed it was by accident, but Randolph guessed at another reason — James had done it deliberately, to relieve his emotions without trespassing further on what was reserved to his betters.

Where now was the difference? For Randolph too had allowed his will to action to become *sicklied over with the pale cast of thought* as the Bard of Stratford put it, so that *enterprises of great pith and moment, with this regard their current turn awry, and lose the name of action*. He had behaved like a lackey in diverting his divine lust from its

144

natural receptacle and letting it dissipate itself in a cowardly gesture. Meanwhile, the swooning girl lay pale and still, mercifully unaware of the great danger that threatened her.

'Damned if I'll be fobbed off like a flunkey!' cried Randolph in his anger and mortification.

Reckless of what might befall, he jumped to his feet, seized Dorothy by the hips, and turned her over to lie face down, her bosom supported on the sofa and her knees on the floor. Only an instant was required to turn up her skirt and petticoats to her waist and reveal her round bottom, clad only in thin drawers of fine white linen. Randolph flung himself down on his knees near this provocative vista of young female charm, and in a trice he had her drawers wide open behind, and was running his fingers up and down the charming cleft between the soft cheeks he had so brutally uncovered.

Although he had spent less than five minutes before, Percival Proud was standing to attention once more, eager to assert his mastery over the senseless girl who lay before him. Nor was he to be denied his raging desire – Randolph took him in hand and steered him bare-headed into the rearward slit of Dorothy's drawers. He bounded like a stag when he touched the smooth skin of her bare bottom. Then he was at the mark, and after taking a deep breath, Randolph pushed slowly forward into the puckered little pink knot-hole between his victim's nether cheeks.

He sighed to feel felt the tight sheath of forbidden flesh on his shaft, for it contracted in nervous spasms that imparted a succession of delicious sensations to the male organ it held so fast. He passed his hands under Dorothy's thighs, to finger her sweet little pussy while he poked her backside with short sharp digs. Delightful sensations flooded through him, emanating not only from the sliding pressure on Mr Percival's embedded head, but equally from the savage pleasure Randolph took from his act of perverse domination of the girl.

'Here's a new conundrum to ask the chaps at the club,' said he in panting glee as he worked at his shameful task, '*How can a girl be rogered and spent in, yet remain a virgin?* That will baffle a noddle or two!'

The rapid thrusts of his shaft and the feel of Dorothy's warm pussy under his fingers combined to rouse him to the very peak of pleasure in double time. He began to gasp in time with his strokes, and rub his belly against her backside as his emotions became intensified to near-delirium.

'Oh, Dorothy – I'm spending in your knot-hole!' he cried.

She heard him not at all, lying as if lifeless all the time he wreaked his will on her defenceless person. But he spoke the simple truth – his body was racked with ecstatic feeling, sighs were torn from his lips, and then he shuddered mightily whilst he discharged his sap into her ravished bottom.

He lay trembling on her back, his limbs relaxed in the sweet lethargy of satisfied lust. He was satisfied that he could not be accused now of acting like a timorous lackey, fearful of the consequences of his own desire. He was a gentleman who insisted on taking whatever he wanted, from young lady or slut alike. A faint groan beneath him brought him to his senses. At once he leaped to his feet, thrusting Mr Percival into his trousers, to fasten up his buttons, before lifting Dorothy in his arms, and placing her fully on the sofa, her head propped up on a cushion and her clothes decently arranged.

Her eyelids were fluttering, and he noted a slight

movement of her fingers. She was regaining her senses, and he did not wish to be there when she became aware of the ravaged condition of her knot-hole. He rang the bell urgently for the maid.

Bella of the big bosom came into the room and gasped with her hand to her mouth to see Dorothy stretched out on the sofa at full length, with her feet a little apart still.

'Oh sir, what has happened?' she asked, her eyes darting in curiosity from Miss Harker to Randolph and back again.

'Your mistress has fainted away,' he told her, 'I have placed her on the sofa, so that she may recover.'

'So I see, sir,' said Bella, her tone implying more than her words, whilst her gaze rested in turn on every smallest detail of the young lady's clothing, looking for signs of disturbance.

'Bring the *sal volatile* and assist her,' said Randolph. 'She must be kept quiet and rest for an hour or two – it is better if I leave, not to be in the way.'

'I'm sure you're right, sir,' said Bella.

She looked as if she might, excepting for the gravity of the circumstances, have smiled a little at the unusual scene that lay before her – the young lady flat on her back and bereft of her senses, the young gentleman flushed of face and with his frock coat only half-buttoned. It needed no very extraordinary powers of intellect to make out what had happened here on the drawing-room sofa.

She stared at Randolph with such knowing eyes that he dipped into his waistcoat pocket and found a gold sovereign.

'That's for your trouble,' said he, and he pressed it into her hand and folded her fingers over it, smiling at her.

'Leave everything to me, sir,' she said. 'I'll take good care of Miss Harker. Look – her eyes are starting to open.'

147

Randolph reached out to give Bella's enormous titties a quick squeeze through her clothes, then skipped out of the room. He collected his topper in the hall, and left in prudent haste.

CHAPTER 10
A Gentleman Goes Shopping for Ladies' Apparel

When Randolph walked out at midday, he proposed to take lunch at his cub and enjoy a day amongst men friends, away from all female influences and interests. The train of his thought while he strolled down the length of Regent Street was complex — for him, at least, for he preferred a simple approach to life and to rogering. His adventure with Dorothy Harker had been, it ought to be said, outside his past range of sensual experience, and puzzling, even to himself.

He was strolling past the Cafe Royal, looking the devil of a swell in his nipped-in frock coat, his top hat and shiny patent leather boots, when he became aware that his thinking had taken him on further — in his imagination he had reached Shaftesbury Avenue, and the shop where he had by chance met Dorothy and her brother Devlin, on the fateful day when he violated her bottom.

As he remembered, it was a milliner's shop Dorothy had been leaving when he passed, looking for a cab to take him home with his newly-purchased books, after he had been brought-off by a young trollop in an alley. The reason he recalled the shop was because he had dreamed of having

Dorothy against the window of it, leaning forward with her hands on the glass, her clothes up over her bottom, and he standing close to roger her.

Randolph was not a man much given to philosophising, or even to an examination of his motives, particularly not those having to do with poking girls. To his way of thinking, the pleasure of the poke was reason enough to do it, and no further debate was necessary, nor even desirable. That said, there were times when his curiosity was aroused beyond the ordinary — and this was just such a time.

He had dreamed of poking Dorothy Harker — all well and good. But why outside that particular shop? Why had he not dreamed of poking her in a hansom cab on the way to Paddington Green? Or in the privacy of her own lodgings? Randolph did not much believe in random events — there had of necessity, he argued to himself, to be a sufficient reason for his sleeping choice of location. In brief, there was something about the shop itself which had caused him to select it for his dream-poke.

Needless to say, the matter could not be left unresolved like that. Lunch could wait, while he walked round to Shaftesbury Avenue to look at the shop and see if anything occurred to him. Surely more must be involved than merely the name of the street — a thoroughfare for shafting in!

On the occasion of meeting Dorothy coming out of the shop, he had given it scant attention. The first discovery of interest he made now that he regarded it closely was that it was not, as he had assumed, a milliner's shop at all, selling only hats and gloves and ribbons, but an establishment that provided ladies with those items of underwear in general described as *lingerie*.

That was enough to set lewd speculations stirring in his mind for the most interesting item of lingerie was female drawers — a garment on which Randolph could never think without going yet further and summoning up visions of those choice parts of young ladies which were contained in drawers, and the uses to which these delightful parts could be put. Evidently he had noted the shop's true character when first he saw Dorothy Harker emerging it, and in his dream mind had spun a fantasy of rogering.

When he pushed the door open to enter, a little bell set on a spring tinkled merrily, bringing a smile of welcome to the lips of a young lady standing behind the long counter. She wore a white blouse with a high neck, and a dark skirt, the business-like severity of the ensemble mitigated by the merest touch of lace beneath her chin and at her thin wrists.

'Good day to you, miss,' said Randolph politely, tipping his hat to her, for though she was only an employee, and therefore rated not much higher than a servant, she was well-turned out, pretty, and eminently pokable, given the right circumstances.

She returned his greeting pleasantly and asked how she could be of assistance.

'I am the Hon Randolph Joynes,' said he grandly, 'and my pater is the Earl of Broadwater. A female friend of mine was in your premises a couple of days ago, in the afternoon. The young lady's name is Miss Dorothy Harker, and she was wearing a short blue jacket and a hat with small pink flowers around the brim. Under the jacket she had a high-necked walking-out dress in a lighter shade of blue. And I think she may have been carrying a rolled umbrella, though I cannot swear to it. Do you perchance remember the lady?'

Why he was asking this question, Randolph was not sure, but he wished to engage the pretty shop assistant in conversation and to make enquiries of a customer seemed as good a way as any he could invent. Nor was his sudden interest to be wondered at, the shop girl was a ravishing brunette, twenty-two or twenty-three years of age, erect of carriage, gracefully shaped, with a full bosom and a wasp waist, an engagingly pert smile on her pretty face. There was neither engagement ring nor wedding band on her finger, but she was a girl who knew herself to be attractive to men, and who treated every man as a possible admirer.

'So many young ladies come into the shop to buy,' she said, 'that it is hard to recall one in particular. Of course, if we delivered her purchases, her address will be recorded. What was her name, did you say?'

'Harker,' he answered, 'with an address in Paddington Green. If I may enquire, what is *your* name, my dear? I have told you mine, and it seems awkward not to complete the introduction.'

'My name is Maria Peabody,' said the shop girl, with a smile that struck Randolph as pleasingly coquettish. 'If you will wait for one moment, sir, I will consult the sales ledger.'

She departed through a door behind the counter into a room at the back of the shop, leaving Randolph to look about him. Very little of what the shop sold could be put on display, owing to the intimate nature of the garments, but he looked at morning wraps and neck scarves and imagined the rest.

Miss Peabody returned quite soon, to confirm that Miss Harker had made a purchase, and it had been delivered to her the same day at an address in Paddington. Finding the transaction in her ledger had jogged Miss Peabody's memory, and she said she could recall Miss Harker clearly.

'What did she buy?' Randolph asked idly.

'I am sorry, Mr Joynes, but I am not at liberty to discuss a customer's purchases,' said Maria.

'Not even to a very close and trusted friend of hers?'

Maria's dark eyebrows rose slightly up her smooth-skinned and ivory forehead in amusement, and she said:

'If you are as close a friend of the young lady's as you say, then you may already have seen her purchases for yourself — or if not, then that pleasure may be yours shortly.'

Randolph grinned at her across the counter.

'Drawers, was it?' he asked, with his accustomed boldness to females. 'Your finest drawers for her soft thighs and delicious belly. With a hand-stitched slit for a hand to enter and have a feel of her pussy?'

'Oh sir!' Maria exclaimed, suppressing her laughter. 'What a thing to say! I ought to ask you to leave at once, but I hate prudery, so I shall let you remain, if you will give your word not to make any more immodest remarks.'

'You have my word,' he agreed at once. 'Now, Maria, my dear, I wish to see a pair of drawers similar to those bought by Miss Harker for herself.'

'Is it your intention to buy them?' she enquired. 'Or is it only a gentleman's interest that prompts this request? Mr Wyck would not wish me to pass time showing goods unless you mean to purchase something.'

'This Mr Wyck — is he the owner of the shop? Where is he?'

'He is the proprietor,' she confirmed, 'and he is today about his regular weekly visit to Spitalfields in East London, where many of the garments we stock are sewn.'

'Really?' said Randolph. 'I rather thought these charming little garments to clothe young ladies' delicious naughtiness were brought from Paris. Nevertheless, show me a pair of these drawers made by London seamstresses.'

'How can I do that?' Maria protested. 'Suppose that garments of so confidential a nature were to be spread out here on the counter for your examination, and in walked another customer, most probably a lady — how would that look? You must see that it is out of the question, though I would oblige if I could.'

'But of course you can, my dear,' said Randolph, 'turn the key in the door and the shop is closed for the lunch hour. Then we can go into the stock room at the back and you can show me in complete privacy what I wish to see.'

His choice of words made Maria look at him closely. When she still hesitated, he plunged on boldly, having nothing to lose.

'Look here, Maria, you can trust me. Are you Wyck's mistress? For I have been told that employers normally take advantage of the girls who work for them. Does he treat you well? Does he provide for your welfare? Does he pay you a proper wage?'

'What a cheek!' Maria exclaimed. 'You walk in here from the street and ask questions like that! How do I know you're what you say you are? For all I know you could be a coal-heaver in stolen clothes!'

Randolph drew out his card case and pressed into her hand his handsomely engraved calling card, showing his name and status. He removed his black silk top hat and honoured the girl with a little bow, smiling at her the while, letting his good looks and easy manner impress her.

'Well,' said she at last, 'it is highly irregular, but seeing that you are a gentleman of standing, and have the intention of making a purchase, I shall depart from my strict instructions and let you into the back room to inspect our merchandise.'

She was perfectly correct to call him a gentleman of standing — Mr Percival Proud was standing hard-on in his grey trousers and had been for some time. Furthermore, the prospect of being alone with the pretty young shop assistant in the back room was cheering enough to make him twitch mightily, as if it were then a foregone conclusion that he would soon be into her pussy. As the common saying has it, but with more truth than elegance, a standing shaft is ever an optimist.

Unaware of these considerations, or as unaware as a charming young girl who is no maiden can ever be when a gentleman shows his partiality towards her person, Maria gestured with a graceful hand that Randolph should walk round the open end of the counter, but before he did so, she went to the street door and locked it and bolted it top and bottom.

Randolph followed her into the back room, which was larger than he had supposed. It was fitted with shelves stacked with cardboard boxes along two sides, but under a window there stood an oblong writing desk littered with bills and lists and other commercial papers. The view from the window was into a small paved yard, where empty boxes lay higgledy-piggledy.

Randolph turned the straight-backed chair out from the desk and sat himself on it, crossing his legs and settling himself comfortably, while he was waited on. Maria took down a long box from a shelf, removed the top and held out for his inspection a pair of female drawers of finest white cambric, with pink rose bud ribbons threaded through the ends of the legs.

'Very pretty,' said Randolph, nodding in approval, 'are these what Miss Harker bought when she was here?'

'Three pairs,' said Maria, with approval in her tone.

'Are they the style you wear yourself?' he asked.

'At four shillings and sixpence a pair!' she cried, a tinge

of blush pink on her pretty cheeks, 'you must think my wages of Mr Wyck exceptional!'

'What!' said Randolph in pretended outrage. 'Do you mean to say the damned skinflint doesn't furnish a charming and sweet-natured young person like you with the best his shop has to offer? The man must be wholly deficient in decency and common goodwill! How can his pride as a shopkeeper, if such a thing can be in so low a calling as commerce, allow him, with a clear conscience, to slip his hand into your drawers for a feel of your pussy in the knowledge that your darling bum is encased in an inferior garment?'

'You go too far, Mr Joynes!' she reproved him.

'No, damn it all, let us speak frankly to each other. To me it is very apparent that this Wyck indulges himself in fullest use of your pussy, but hasn't the decency to dress you or pay you as you deserve. If I owned a shop — which I never would, it being beneath my station in life to engage myself in trade — I would say to you: *Maria — you are to pick whatever you choose from the stock, for the pleasure I have in rogering you is made all the keener by first undressing you and releasing your soft and delightful body from the prettiest undergarments that we stock!*'

'Heavens above! I think you must be a poet!' said Maria.

'Alas, not myself, though I have a great liking for poetry and number a poet or two amongst my acquaintance,' he replied. 'I have more than once got drunk with Mr Rossetti, who is also a painter of pictures, besides being a poet. Shall I recite a line or two of his for you?

Fain would I feel my darling's dainty leg.
Which is as white and hairless as an egg,
Fain would I kiss her titties' rose-red tips,
And feel the curls upon her pussy lips.

156

It continues for several verses in this vein, but I shall stop there until we know each other better, Maria, for the poet then becomes exceedingly personal in his address to his beloved, and what he wishes to do to her.'

'Lord!' said she. 'I am surprised there is much more for him to say. Now, sir, I have shown you what gentlemen are not shown ordinarily of our stock — do you mean to buy this pair?'

'I mean to buy half-a-dozen pairs,' he replied, in a briskly cheerful tone.

'Your intentions towards the young lady are not hard to guess at,' Maria commented with a half-smile. 'Six pairs of finest cambric drawers comes to . . . let me see . . . one pound and seven shillings. Do you wish them to be delivered to the same address as before in Paddington, or will you take them with you?'

'Neither, my dear,' said Randolph, 'for I mean them as a gift for *you*. But there is a small condition attached.'

The shopgirl's pretty face blushed a delicate pink at that.

'I am not entirely an innocent, Mr Joynes,' said she, 'and I am perfectly well aware of what you would be at. I must decline your gift, for I have an arrangement with my employer, Mr Wyck, and I cannot contemplate an act of disloyalty towards him.'

'What tomfoolery!' cried Randolph. 'What loyalty can there be to a tradesman who deals with you meanly? I have formed a high opinion of you, Maria, and it irks me to see you ill-used by your employer. How many times in a week does he roger you?'

'You have no right to ask such a question!' she retorted.

'My concern for your welfare gives me every right,' he said 'Wyck is a man in his middle years, I dare say, like almost all shopkeepers I have ever seen, and is from a pretty common sort of family. He is surely married and has six or seven children. I put his capacity for poking, even with a girl as delicious as you, at not above twice a week. Is my supposition correct?'

'I cannot divulge information about my employer,' said Maria, now blushing furiously.

'No need, for it has not the least importance. Your agitation confirms all that I said. But to revert to more interesting and immediate matters — you have refused my gift before hearing the condition attached to it. Are you not curious, Maria?'

'I am quite sure I can guess what condition an upper-class gentlemen like you would attach to a gift of undergarments.'

'You have a nicely lascivious fancy,' Randolph told her, with warm approval in his voice, 'but you run ahead too fast. I only want to see you wearing a pair of these very superior drawers, no more than that, and the half-dozen become yours.'

Maria found it difficult to believe that he would settle for that, and make her a gift costing as much as she earned a week from her employment with the absent Mr Wyck. Randolph took care to give her assurances — that she should stand out of his reach to display herself to him, and that he would remain seated on the chair the whole time. In return, she would allow him to see her with her skirt raised for as long as he wished.

That settled, she removed herself to the far end of the room and turned her back to him while she bent over to raise up her long black skirt, drop the drawers she was wearing and replace them with the expensive new pair. When all was to her liking, she turned herself to face Randolph, who sat at ease to enjoy the spectacle.

'Now, Miss Maria, if you are quite ready,' said he,

gesturing with a hand to indicate she should lift her skirt.

With only the faintest hint of a blush, she stooped to grasp the hem of her skirt and raise it slowly. Randolph stared with eager eyes, as if watching the curtain going up at the theatre. Maria wore plain black stockings, and the slow lifting of her skirt revealed that, above well-polished but not new footwear she had trim ankles and well-rounded calves. A little below the knee, her stockings disappeared up inside the fine white cambric drawers, where the rosebud pink ribbons were threaded through the legs.

'How utterly delightful,' said Randolph to encourage her, 'a pair of legs that would grace the greatest ballerina!'

Maria seemed to preen herself a little at the compliment, and slowly she raised her skirt higher yet. Now came into view her thighs, and concealed inside the thin white drawers though they were, their round fullness could not be hid. She stood so that they were pressed close together, and Randolph sighed happily to imagine himself slipping a hand between them and feeling her warm flesh through the linen.

'Oh Maria,' said he, 'you are even lovelier than I could guess — how very tragic that so much youthful female charm should be thrown away on a miserable shopkeeper! Why do you let him, my dear, when you could advance yourself so much higher?'

'Could I?' she asked coolly. 'How would I set about that?'

'Why, I am certain there must be scores of gentlemen about London — perhaps even hundreds — who would take you out of this dreary shop and keep you in style, if you consented to it.'

'The gentlemen I have met so far have been interested only in giving me a couple of guineas if I will let them have me for a short time,' she answered. 'I find such offers insulting to my good name, for I am not a street girl of the sort who stand on the corner by Piccadilly and sell themselves to any who ask.'

'Certainly not!' Randolph exclaimed, feeling the throb of Mr Percival Proud in his trousers. 'But continue, if you please, for I have not yet seen all of my gift to you.'

Maria poked out her pink tongue at him, and lifted her skirt up to her wasp waist, revealing the drawers fully. He stared in open admiration at the provocative curve of her belly under the fine material, and at the place where her thighs met.

'There — that's what you want to see, isn't it?' she cried.

Randolph could not speak for the intensity of his emotions. His gaze was fixed on the closed slit in the drawers, the long opening into paradise, the place of concealment of the tender morsel that could give such rapture to a man. Maria saw that he was strongly affected, and perhaps in a condition of mind that could be prevailed on to her own advantage, always bearing in mind that she would do nothing against Mr Wyck's interests.

'Of what does a gentleman think when he sees a female in her drawers, posing for him in secret?' she asked with a smile.

'He thinks of this, and its satisfaction,' Randolph answered, bold as brass now that his power of speech had returned to him.

So saying, with nimble fingers he undid his coat and then his waistcoat, leaned back in the chair, stretched out his legs to their full length, opened his trousers wide and pulled up his shirt. Maria stared astonished to see him extricate from out of his gaping trousers his shaft, and finger it without the least sign of embarrassment.

While she stared at it, and he at her face, he took firm

hold of his shaft and stroked it up to its full height, so that it stood stiffly.

'See how very hard-on he has grown,' Randolph exhorted her, speaking in all seriousness, but smiling, 'not a minute's rest will he allow me now until he has discharged his desire.'

'A trouble-maker, is he?' Maria asked softly, mesmerised by the frank display of a hard male organ.

'No, he's a pleasure-maker!' said Randolph, and staring hard at where Maria's white drawers covered her pussy, he began to rub up and down his cockstand firmly.

'Stop,' Maria cried out, 'this won't do at all. Stop, please, Mr Joynes, or I shall lower my skirt.'

'We made a bargain,' he replied, 'you are to stand there for as long as I require, with your clothes up.'

His fingers moved faster on his straining shaft, the movement sending such thrills through him that he sighed aloud, whilst his legs twitched.

'This is not what I agreed to,' Maria complained, though not in earnest, seeing advantages to herself in Randolph's lack of self-control at the mere sight of her drawers. 'No gentleman exposes his person and abuses himself before a helpless female, only low drunks outside public houses on Saturday night.'

'Drunk or sober,' said Randolph, 'a cockstand brooks no delay or denial — it insists on spending.'

'Be careful, or you'll soil your shirt front,' Maria warned in a solicitous tone. 'Here, make use of these!'

With those words she let go of her raised skirt with one hand to pull from the box in which they rested another pair of the expensive drawers, and throw them fluttering across the space between herself and him, to land in Randolph's lap.

'Maria — you are a perfect angel!' he exclaimed, seizing on the intimate garment and draping it over his jerking shaft.

A frenzy seized on him at once, his hand slid up and down rapidly, then he cried out as the sexual spasm took him in its unbreakable grasp. His body was jerking to the spurting of his essence, which soaked at once through the fine cambric of the drawers, to make a dark wet stain that spread quickly.

'My word,' said Maria, when he had finished spending and sat tranquil again, 'I never thought to see a gentleman do that to himself! Mr Wyck would rather die than abuse himself in the presence of a female.'

'Wyck is a prudish clod,' said Randolph. 'All his class are. I doubt if he even knows how to poke properly. Does he bring you off when he rogers you?'

'I shall answer no questions about my employer,' she said at once. 'Are you on the slack now you have spent?'

'Almost,' he replied, removing the drawers to display his wet and softening shaft. 'How very pleasurable it was – I am much indebted to you for your help, Maria. Tell me something – if a rich gentleman came into the shop and asked your advice on what gift he should send to a female friend who had conducted him up to the very peak of bliss, what would you say to him?'

Maria let her clothes slide down her legs to conceal all but the toes of her shoes. Randolph made no complementary move – he lolled on his chair, trousers agape, his soft shaft lying limp in full view.

'What I would advise such a gentleman is this,' said Maria in a thoughtful tone of voice, but with a cheeky smile, 'he should send his female friend a complete set of undergarments. By that I mean several pairs of fine stockings, two or three chemises with lace edging, a petticoat or two with flounces on – and as many pairs of our best drawers as he thought suitable.'

'Capital advice,' Randolph returned.

'But only for a free-spending gentleman,' she added, 'for the cost of all that would run to ten pounds or even more, which few would want to expend on undergarments, however close the friendship.'

'I am a very free-spending gentleman,' Randolph informed her with a smile, 'for I spend in the pussy of any pretty girl who takes my fancy. But that apart, you must break out of this confined way of thinking. To a common person like your employer the thought of buying a girl ten pounds worth of underwear may bring on an apoplexy, but to a man about town it is hardly more than an amusing gesture. You, dear Maria, shall have all that you mentioned, and at my expense, in return for a small favour.'

'If you wish to spend freely here, then it must be in money,' she retorted, 'for nothing else will be accepted.'

'Gad, if you were my female friend I'd treat you with respect and affection and give you everything you desired,' he replied, pleased by her ready wit to turn his joke back on himself.

'You must not try to subvert my loyalty to Mr Wyck by bribery and seduction,' she said, her tone slightly rueful. 'He has my word that no other male shall be allowed to take advantage of me whilst I remain in his employ. Do not tempt me, Mr Joynes.'

'By Jove, you are a pearl amongst women!' Randolph exclaimed in delight. 'Never have I come across such loyalty in a female — would the object of it were more worthy of you! But have no fear, dear girl, for I will not insult your integrity by trying to roger you, much though I would enjoy it. The favour I ask in return for the vast deal of underwear you mentioned does not require you to let me poke you.'

'Then what is it?' she asked him, somewhat surprised.

'Only this — hold up your clothes again and let me kiss your darling pussy. There — that is no betrayal of your loyalty to Wyck, is it?'

'You wish to kiss me *between my legs*?' she asked, hardly able to believe what she heard.

This was something no man had ever yet done to her, and it seemed to her very strange, and almost unnatural. Neither Wyck nor the man before him who had her maidenhead ever tried more than a straight poke — a moment or two fingering her pussy till it was wet, then his hard-on shaft up her and a fast poke to a spend. Nevertheless, Maria Peabody was a young woman able to learn fast, and if a titled gentleman had an urge to kiss her pussy, then it must be perfectly all right.

'Just that?' she asked. 'A kiss? You give me your word you would not try to force me?'

'A warm kiss of affection and respect,' said he, 'no more.'

Privately, Maria thought it almost too good to be true, but she had seen Randolph come off, and basing her estimate of all men on Mr Wyck's limited capabilities, she thought it safe to accept Randolph's offer. She gave him permission and raised her skirt waist-high once more.

Randolph knelt at her feet, opened the hand-stitched slit of her drawers, and pressed his lips to the soft and yielding pink cunny that was the heart of her female nature. He heard above his head the softest of sounds then, a half-stifled sigh that was almost a gasp, and he guessed he was the first man to kiss her cunny. He guessed further, in view of her ready response to it, that she had a hot nature, which she concealed.

He clasped her bottom in both hands whilst his tongue flicked up and down between delicious parted pink lips in the nut-brown little nest of her curls. The sighs he elicited

164

were louder now and even more emotional, and after some hesitation she placed her hands on his shoulders to support herself.

'Surely you've kissed me enough now!' he heard her gasp out, but he ignored her words and continued to ravish her with his wet tongue, pervading her with sensations so divine that she swayed on legs that had become weak.

'Oh, this is so improper!' she sighed, 'and yet so nice . . .'

There could be only one way of it then — Maria's belly began to jib forward in rapid little thrusts to press her open pussy against his mouth, and she shook convulsively from head to toe. A shriek escaped her lips and she came off briskly and would have fallen helpless to the floor but for Randolph's arms about her, supporting her staunchly whilst he squeezed the cheeks of her plump bottom, and rubbed a fingertip over the puckered little knot between them.

'Oh my dear lord!' she exclaimed, when she was able to speak again. 'Now you've done it! You promised not to take advantage of me if I let you kiss me.'

'Nor have I,' he retorted pleasantly, 'for I have not rogered you, my dear, nor fingered your pussy — your bond of loyalty to your miserable employer is unbroken.'

'But you brought me off!' she protested.

'What of that?' he asked. 'I'm sure you come off on many an occasion without the benefit of Wyck's shaft up you. When you play with yourself in bed, for example, and when you wash your darling little pussy and dry it. That you fetched off because I kissed you is neither here nor there — it cannot be construed a breach of your trust.'

'I suppose you're right,' said she, relief in her voice, 'but all the same, if you were given half a chance, you would be up me like a shot — admit it now!'

'I freely admit it,' he said, 'but until you of your own

free will invite me to roger you, I shall restrain the force of my natural desire for your beautiful person.'

'Perhaps I am a fool,' she said, 'but I trust you.'

'Excellent!' he cried. 'Now we have agreed that I shall not attempt to get my shaft into your pussy, that delight being the sole prerogative of the undeserving Wyck, nothing stops us from giving each other pleasure in other possible ways. The logic of that must surely be acceptable to you, my dear. I am aware that the eminent Dr Acton disagrees with me on this point, but it is my considered opinion that two pokes a week from a decrepit and decaying shopkeeper cannot be enough to satisfy a warm-natured young female like you. Does he poke you here behind the shop, after hours?'

'I have said I will not answer questions about Mr Wyck,' said Maria firmly.

'Then I'm right, and he must do it to you on this desk, there being no other convenient place here in your stockroom. But as the desk is not large enough for you to lie on, he must sit you on the edge and stand between your legs to poke you.'

There was a trace of pink on Maria's cheeks that informed him he had arrived at the truth of the matter. He took her hand and led her to the desk, sat her on the edge and raised her skirt to her lap.

'A sad waste,' said he with a sigh, 'poking in a back room! A pretty girl should be delicately and lovingly and frequently rogered in a four-poster bed, on a swansdown-stuffed mattress, between sheets of purest linen, wearing a nightgown of silk, pulled up above her titties for her lover to lie on her belly.'

'What are you doing!' she exclaimed. 'Remember your promise not to touch my pussy!'

'Nor shall I,' he said reassuringly, his hands busy with the buttons of her blouse, 'I gave my word not to put either shaft or fingers into your pussy, but there is no reason in the world not to have a feel of your bare titties.'

In a trice he had her blouse open, her chemise pulled down, and her warm and plump titties bare for his hands to fondle. In this she gave him no argument, for she enjoyed having them felt and Mr Wyck rarely obliged her in this, being in too much of a hurry to get his shaft up her. She put her hands on Randolph's hips whilst he stroked and squeezed and touched her. Soon her teats were standing stiff, and she was sighing a little. As if by chance, her hands moved from their resting place and found the gaping entrance of Randolph's trousers.

'Oh, you are stiff again!' she exclaimed, staring curiously into his handsome face.

'How could I not be,' he said, 'with so delectable a pair of titties in my hands?'

In a little while Maria's slender body was trembling from the force of the sensations he roused by his skilled handling of her, and he too began to shake gently — for she held in a warm palm his hairy pompoms, and her other hand was clasped about his cockstand and slid up and down it with affection and lust.

'As long as you make no attempt to get this furious thing up my pussy, Mr Wyck is not being deprived of his rights,' gasped she, making a pious attempt to salvage her sense of duty as she was fast approaching the culmination of her pleasure.

Randolph made no reply, for he was past rational expression. Mr Percival Proud had swelled himself up to his thickest girth and his maximum length, and was hard as a broom handle. Maria's pussy was wet and open, and her hips were making little thrusts as she sat on the edge of the desk, as if inviting a shaft to plunge into it.

It amused Randolph to keep his word, and instead of sliding his hard-on shaft straight into her and coming off before she could push him off, which would have been the most sensible and natural course of action for a gentleman to take, he kept his hands away from her cunny and continued his stimulation of her titties. It took him some time to bring her off thus, but eventually the pleasurable sensations became more than her frame could withstand.

She cried out and came off furiously, and the sliding of her hand on Randolph's jerking shaft carried him up to the peak of bliss. He moaned joyfully to feel the fast surge of his sap up the length of his pulsating shaft, and in nervous and urgent spasms he gushed his creamy essence over her bared pussy.

CHAPTER 11
A Messenger is Given an Unexpected Answer

At half past ten o'clock in the morning Randolph left Cavendish Square with the intention of calling on his tailor to place an order for a *suit of clothes*, as the new style for gentlemen had been named. This consisted of a short jacket and trousers made of the same material, instead of a black frock coat and sombre grey trousers. It seemed dashing, even audacious, to depart so far from tradition, but Randolph liked to think of himself as a bold spirit, eager for novelty.

On the corner of the Square, where Wigmore Street ran, he saw standing on the pavement in an attitude of watchfulness a woman he recognised from a distance and approaching more nearly he saw that he had been correct, for it was none other than Miss Dorothy Harker's maid — Bella of the huge titties.

When he drew level with her, he naturally did not raise his hat to a mere servant, but stared at her. Her eyes dropped to a suitable abased position, and she addressed him humbly:

'Mr Joynes — excuse me, sir, for the liberty of speaking to you in the street, but I have been entrusted with an important message by a young lady whose name I need not mention.'

169

'The devil you have!' Randolph exclaimed, astonished by this act of insolence on the part, not only of the maid, but also of her mistress in sending her to accost him in a public place.

'The young lady is in the gravest of conditions, sir — I beg you to listen to what she has sent me to say. It will take but a few minutes.'

Randolph paid no attention to what Bella said. It was only to be expected, though devilish irksome, that Miss Harker desired to have some words of reproach delivered to him. He had, truth to tell, been daily expecting to receive a tearful letter of remonstrance from her. That would have been irksome enough, but to send a maidservant was past the limits of all decent behaviour!

Nevertheless, it had to be admitted that Bella sported as big a pair of titties as Randolph had ever seen on a young woman in his life. Concealed though they were under the cloak of greenish-grey wool she wore, they looked devilish inviting to the hands.

'I cannot be seen talking to you in the street,' said he, cutting off her words. 'What on earth would people think! But I am a reasonable man, and I will give you five minutes of my time to deliver your mistress's message. Do you know where Holywell Street lies?'

'No, sir, for I am a stranger to London, being here with Miss Harker for the first time in my life.'

'It runs off the Strand,' Randolph informed her. 'I have most important business to conduct at this moment, but afterwards I will go there, at great inconvenience, I may say, to hear you in private. In Holywell Street you will find Black's Temperance Coffee House. Ask for me there at twelve noon.'

Without waiting for a response, he walked on, swinging

his silver-knobbed stick in jaunty fashion, sure that Bella would be there to meet him, when he had completed his business with his tailor. In this his assumption was correct – he found her standing outside the coffee house when he got there. Hardly pausing, he instructed her to wait for ten minutes and then to go inside and ask for him of the waiter.

Rooms to accommodate couples desiring an hour or two's privacy were to be found in every part of London. Some were in lodging-houses, where half a dozen lettings a day produced a superior profit to the owner than to have a regular tenant. The easiest to find, and the least costly, were the many coffee houses that showed a sign in the window saying *Beds*. The respectable world at large took this to mean that bona-fide travellers unable to afford the price of a hotel room could be accommodated cheaply for the night, but the true significance of the sign was that a room might be had for rogering at any time of day.

The waiter's name was Will, an elderly man with a fringe of white hair. A few words sufficed, five shillings changed hands for the room, and another shilling for Will himself, then Randolph was directed upstairs. A glance about showed him that the room was adequate to his requirements, being clean furnished with a large bed. Randolph seated himself on a cane-bottomed chair, his top hat pushed to the back of his head, his hands resting one above the other on the silver knob of his stick.

Soon there came a tap at the door, and Bella entered. Black had only two rooms to rent out, and the other was unoccupied so early on in the day, so she had needed little guidance to find Randolph. She closed the door, and at his order bolted it, then stood in before him in a respectful posture, hands folded, eyes downcast.

'Well?' he demanded, eyeing her natural abundance greedily.

'First, sir, I am to return this to you,' said she, fetching out from under her loose cloak a wrapped parcel Randolph knew — it was the books he had bought from Avery and, in his hurry to quit the Harker apartment, he quite forgot them and left them behind in the drawing room. He had missed the parcel before he reached home, but could think of no easy way of retrieving his precious bundle.

'I'm obliged to Miss Harker for the return of my property. Is there more, or was that your whole errand?' he said, hoping to embarrass Bella further.

'No, sir, there is more.'

'I trust that your mistress has made a full recovery from her fainting spell.'

The tone of his enquiry was casual in the extreme, though his eyes never once left the impressive rotundities beneath Bella's clothing. He had determined that she would not leave the room before he had viewed them bare and felt them very thoroughly.

'She keeps her bed, sir, feeling weak and unsettled, and out of sorts. Mr Devlin wanted to send for a doctor to attend her, but she refuses that. What ails her is distress of mind, sir, and uncertainty.'

'I'm sorry to hear it,' said Randolph off-handedly, 'but what has it to do with me?'

'I think you know that, sir,' Bella answered, her voice firm.

'Do I? What do you mean?'

'After you left the house, I assisted Miss Dorothy up to her room, and put her to bed, to rest. There was a wetness about her undergarments that betrayed what had been done to the poor young lady, while she lay helpless in a swoon.'

'Damme! Do you accuse me of taking advantage of her?' cried Randolph, in a fine show of virtuous outrage.

Secretly he was wondering if, when Bella's dress was taken off, her massive titties would hang down low and slack to her belly-button, or were they still young and firm enough to stay in place, with only a provocative dangle.

'It's not my place to make accusations, sir,' Bella replied, unabashed, 'but the signs were clear that a gentleman had spent on her belly, for her drawers were soaked through.'

'Oho!' said Randolph with a grin. 'It appears to me that you know more than you ought about these matters, for an unmarried woman. How old are you, Bella?'

'Twenty-six years of age,' said she.

'And you have experience of men coming off in your drawers?'

'That's as may be, sir,' she replied impertinently, 'but what is troubling Miss Harker is that she thinks she was ravished by you while she lay fainting. She fears she is a maiden no longer and in her ruined condition may not wed Mr Mawby, who has asked her to become his wife.'

'And do you believe that I ravished her, Bella?'

'No, sir,' said she, looking him in the eye, 'that is, not in the usual way of ravishing, so to say. I bathed Miss Dorothy's parts in warm water before I put her to bed, and examined them closely. Her curls were wet with a man's spending, and stuck to her skin, so at first I thought the ravisher had pulled out in time to avoid putting her in the family way. I feared the worst but a closer inspection showed me that she is a maiden still, as the world reckons these things.'

'Then there is no more to say,' cried Randolph.

'Ah, but there is, sir, for virgin she may be, but untouched she is not. To be frank and open with you at the risk of

173

giving offence, Miss Dorothy has been unnaturally used in her rearward passage. She, poor innocent, has yet formed no suspicion of her plight, being concerned entirely with the honour of her other opening remaining intact. She knows that something unlawful was done to her, for a gentleman's amusement, but not what.'

'Then there is no reason to tell her,' Randolph suggested. 'A disclosure of something unfamiliar to her way of thought might only distress her to the point of upsetting the balance of her mind and casting her into a fit of the vapours. My advice is to leave well alone — what harm can there be to her from a bung-holing, if what you suspect is true.'

'If only it were that simple!' said Bella. 'But Miss Dorothy is certain in her mind that you interfered with her in some way and that she is, as a result, unworthy to marry Mr Mawby. She will answer him no when he comes on Saturday for her response to his proposal of marriage, as she will answer no in future to any other gentleman who seeks her hand. She feels that she is consigned to lifelong spinsterhood by what you have done to her, and is greatly agitated.'

'This is ridiculous!' Randolph exclaimed. 'Her pussy is pure as the driven snow, for aught I did to it! A feel, perhaps, no more than that. Neither finger nor shaft did I put into it.'

'Yes, sir, I truly believe that,' said Bella, 'but it is not the point. The trouble lies in Miss Dorothy's mind, not between her legs. What can be done about it, sir?'

'Damned if I know!' he replied. 'Will she tell anyone of her misgivings, do you suppose?'

'Not at first, sir, for she is too ashamed to confide in any but me. But with the passing of time, and her continuing misery of mind, her family will take note, and she will be pressed by her mother or her father to speak out. When she does, I greatly fear that you will be called to reckoning, Mr Joynes. It is no light matter to ravage a young lady's backside while she lies swooning on her own sofa. In fact, sir, should it be brought to the notice of a magistrate, then I have been told that to have unnatural connection with either woman or man is held a fearful crime, and punished by long years in prison, with hard labour.'

'But why should there be any question of magistrates, Bella? The dishonour of being named in open court as victim would be too great for Miss Harker to bear, I am convinced.'

'I hope that you're right, sir,' said Bella, pursing her lips tightly and shaking her head, 'but it must be remembered that the young lady's own father is a Justice of the Peace out where we live in Warwickshire.'

'Damnation take it!' Randolph cried. 'Here's a fine kettle of fish! What's best to do, I wonder, bearing in mind that the well-being and good name of Miss Harker are the main concern in this. Sit down, Bella, and give me the benefit of your advice.'

There being only one chair in the room, and he sitting on it, Bella seated herself on the edge of the bed, removing her cloak at last, as he had hoped. She wore the usual maid's plain black dress, without the usual white apron, since she was out of the house. Her great bosom swelled out the bodice of the dress and set Mr Percival Proud to twitching lightly.

'Whilst we discuss how to promote Miss Harker's happiness, it is in your hands to do me a considerable favour,' said Randolph with an encouraging smile.

In truth, he was not overly concerned at the hidden threat of Mr Harker Senior, Justice of the Peace, learning that his dear daughter had been briskly bung-holed. At any threat from that quarter, Randolph was ready to skip across the

Channel to Paris and enjoy himself there for a year or two. Indignation cannot last forever, and his madcap escapade with Miss Harker would be forgotten in an eighteen-month at most. On the other hand, he wished to keep Bella beside him for a while yet, to implement his lewd designs on her, and so he pretended to take seriously Miss Dorothy's predicament.

When Bella asked him what the favour might be that he wanted of her, he told her that he had an unquenchable desire to view her titties. If she would bare herself to the waist to give him sight of them, she would find him particularly grateful. Bella blushed a little at his words, but only for form's sake, before she unbuttoned her bodice all the way down from neck to waist, and slipped her arms out of the sleeves.

'Ah!' he sighed in blissful anticipation, his shaft swaying under his shirt like a metronome beating time.

Bella smiled at him, a meaningless smile, though that he did not notice in his eagerness to see her bubbies. His eyes shone lustfully to see her slide the ribbons of her chemise off her shoulders and pull it down, exposing her bare titties to him.

'By Jove!' Randolph said emotionally. 'What whoppers!'

Bella was thin of form, her arms and shoulders very slender and fragile of appearance. This emphasised the contrast with the fullness of her titties, which were the size of fully grown pumpkins, vast globes of soft white flesh, looking for all the world like over-ripe fruit depending from a bough.

Seen thus in all their fleshy glory, Randolph confessed that never had he laid eyes on a more letch-provoking pair. This he told to her, and she smiled at him with her knowing eyes, and asked if looking was enough for him.

It was obvious to Randolph that she recalled his generosity of the preceding day, when he had put a golden sovereign in her hand — and she undoubtedly expected more where that came from. *Why not*? thought he to himself, for he had never in his life grudged full payment to any girl or woman who made him an offer of her bodily charms. Smiling, he asked Bella to come and kneel between his legs — *and to bring her titties with her*!

She knew what he was after, for he was by no means the first gentleman who had sought the same thing from her. She left the bed to come forward and kneel on the floor, as he had asked. His legs were spread wide apart, his trouser buttons undone, his hard-on shaft sticking out and up for Bella to clasp in her hand.

'Good Heavens — then this is the monstrous thing that forced an entry into poor Miss Dorothy's bottom!' she exclaimed. 'How long and thick it is! How pitiful she must have seemed, while you were at your wicked task!'

Her skilful hand sliding firmly up and down Mr Percival was like to have brought that quivering gentleman off, but she refrained from inducing the sensual spasm too soon.

'There is something I do not understand,' said she, gazing up into Randolph's face. 'You spent on Miss Dorothy's belly, for her drawers and chemise were wet through. Yet you also spent in her bottom, for when I washed it, your sap came trickling out. You were alone with her for only twenty minutes or so — how can it be possible that you fetched off twice in so short a time?'

'Why, when my rogering mood takes me and I have a pretty girl at the end of my shaft, I can come off in her cunny, or on her belly, or any other part of her, five or six times in a row,' said he boastfully. 'Your mistress was not the only female to be the recipient of my cream yesterday — there were two more.'

He did not tell her that one was a servant like herself, and the other a young trollop in Soho, but left her to assume that he had rogered three gentlewomen.

'My word! To spend so often, and still have a shaft standing up stiff again the next day!' Bella sighed.

She pressed herself close in between his open legs, and laid his leaping shaft between her massive soft titties, stroking it with her hand and making her globes close upon it, until he was able to slide it between them. That, she knew well, was what he wanted for that was what every gentleman who had laid bare her bubbies had wanted — to roger them.

'There now, he's in a warm and cosy place,' she said, 'is it to his liking, or would he rather be in me elsewhere?'

'For now he's happy with his billet,' Randolph sighed, as he tupped up and down against her smooth skin, 'later on he will try out other parts of you, my dear, to see which he prefers.'

The sight and feel in his hands, and about his shaft, of her huge titties made him as eager as if he had not had a poke for a week or more. To see Mr Percival rubbing himself in between those cushions of soft flesh brought on blissful sensations and soon overcame him. He cried out in rapture to the spasms that shook his body so furiously that his topper fell from his head and rolled on the floor behind him. *Ah! Ah!* he went, emitting a profuse flow into the warm hiding-place between her titties.

'Well!' Bella commented brightly. 'What a lot he has given, after spending with three ladies yesterday — and twice with at least one of them! If the truth has been told, that is.'

Her words instigated in Randolph a determination to show this sceptical maidservant that she was in the presence of

178

a virility she had never encountered among men of her own class. The last drop was scarcely out of his twitching shaft than he rose from the chair, dragged Bella upright and took her quickly across to the bed.

'Lie down,' he commanded, 'on your back.'

'Oh, sir, surely you must rest for a while,' said she pertly, 'for your shaft will be soft and useless in a minute, and needs time to regain its stiffness before you can think of repeating your spending.'

'Nonsense,' said Randolph with a sneer, 'I need no rest.'

He gave her no opportunity to delay or disobey him, being resolved to demonstrate his male superiority. With a hand that shook a little from his recent exertion, he pushed her down to sit on the bedside, and then to lie on her back with her legs hanging over the edge. Her vast titties rolled slackly towards her armpits, spreading themselves widely apart, as if forming a mattress on which his weight should rest while he did her.

He raised her skirt in front until he had a full view of her legs, encased in cheap black stockings, and her slender thighs in her white drawers. Through the forward slit he touched her sparse dark bush, then pushed her knees wide apart. In mounting desire, he untied the string of her drawers and laid bare her white-skinned belly, and pressed his mouth to it in hot kisses. He gazed in fascination at her bare pussy, fingering the warm fleshy lips with one hand, whilst with the other he massaged Mr Percival strongly, to restore his hardness.

'Oh, sir!' Bella murmured. 'You're standing hard again!'

'Did you dare doubt my word?' he cried.

He brought the hard-on shaft jutting from his trousers close to the moist lips of her slit. With a sharp jerk of his loins he pushed Mr Percival Proud's shiny unhooded head inside, and then with determined thrusts, slid into her right to the limit. As his curls lay tight to hers, he threw himself forward on to her belly and seized her bare breasts where they hung slackly on her chest, whilst he rogered her furiously. After three or four strokes, she returned push for push, to urge him on.

'Oh what bliss!' she sighed. 'It's as stiff as a cast-iron poker in me — you're a marvel, sir!'

Her thin-cheeked bottom heaved and squirmed on the bed, the while she uttered exclamations of pleasure. At another time, he would have taken deep offence at a servant expressing enjoyment in so open and disrespectful a way, but his present intention was to impress on Bella his utter mastery, and her cries were tributes to his achievement in that respect.

Her cries grew shriller as he reached the short strokes, then turned to open-mouthed gasping when she received the hot gush of his lust. She made no effort to hide it, but came off loudly and with gusto, then lay trembling and spent beneath him.

She thought he was finished with her then, having fetched off twice, but he had other plans, and refused to let her depart. To her protestation that Miss Dorothy was awaiting, in agony of mind, her return with news, he said brutally that she must wait longer, and that another hour or two wouldn't hurt her. He made Bella strip naked and sit up on the bed for him to look at, for he was greatly taken by the piquancy of her monumentally large titties on her thin frame, and wished to study her further.

To render himself more comfortable, he removed his clothing and sat beside her in only his shirt, whilst he handled her big bubbies, lifting them on his palms and rolling them, fascinated by their fleshiness. Bella let him do as he pleased, for in her mind she was sure that she had caught him with her titties, and stood to profit considerably.

'Do you know what is in the parcel you returned to me?' he asked her, his shaft beginning to stir again between his legs.

'No, sir, but from the weight of it, books, I would say.'

'Your inference is correct,' said he, reaching for the parcel which lay close to hand on the bed, where he had cast it aside earlier.

'Have you been taught to read?' he enquired.

'Why yes, sir,' Bella answered, 'for although my father could not afford the twopence a day to send me with my brother to the village school, they taught me free at Sunday School, so that I can read the Scriptures.'

Randolph opened the parcel, and selected the volume entitled *Selina Simcott, or The Tribulations of Virtue* and handed it to Bella.

'This is a tale of girls at school,' he explained, 'though it is not a Sunday school but a boarding-school, where games are played with pussies. Open the book at random and read aloud to me, while I stroke your titties.'

'I've heard about books like this,' said she, grinning, 'but I never expected to see one.'

She let the book fall open where it would, smoothed down the page and began to read, somewhat hesitatingly, but with a note of interest in her voice that more than compensated for a lack of fluency:

'Come closer, girl,' said Miss Rodwell.
Selina moved toward the high-backed chair on which the schoolmistress was seated. At once Miss Rodwell reached out to pass an arm about Selina's waist and hold her fast, whilst with her other hand she opened the startled girl's long

181

dressing-gown and raised her nightdress up to her waist, laying bar the expanse of her thighs and belly. Before Selina could collect herself to utter a respectful protest, Miss Rodwell's hand was playing freely between her thighs and over her sweet and soft-haired pussy.

'Without the word of a lie,' Miss Rodwell declared, 'you have the prettiest cunny in the school, and the smoothest, whitest pair of thighs. You may believe my words — there is not a girl in the school, from Juniors to Sixth Form and Prefects, that I haven't inspected in person, and handled thoroughly.'

All the while she was running her hand across Selina's naked flesh, in the most shameless manner, causing the mortified girl to blush scarlet.

'Oh!' she cried out then, to feel Miss Rodwell pressing with a gentle middle finger on the junction of her thighs.

'Good gracious!' exclaimed Bella, looking up from the book at Randolph, her face a fiery red, 'This schoolmarm is a beast who handles the girls for her own pleasure, under pretence of correcting them!'

'Indeed she does,' Randolph agreed, his tongue flickering over his lips to wet them, 'read on, my dear, for there can be little doubt now that Selina will be made to undergo the final ordeal of being brought off in Miss Rodwell's hand.'

Miss Rodwell's finger fluttered and lingered, seeking out the maiden slit within the mossy bower of Selina's silky curls. It found what it sought so insistently, and began caressing and teasing.

'Oh, Miss Rodwell,' murmured Selina, 'I beg you, for the love of all that is wholesome and precious, do not make me undergo this shameful ordeal!'

She spoke in vain, for the older woman's fingertip slid up to that sensitive spot at the top of her slit, where sensation is the greatest. Selina twitched and squealed, but Miss Rodwell held her firm while she spurred her agitation to fever pitch.

'Shameful ordeal, do you say?' she exclaimed. 'You did not think it shameful to get into the maidservant's bed the other night and allow her to feel you! Why is it shameful now — am I less worthy than a servant to play with your pussy?'

'No, Miss Rodwell, that is not what I meant!' gasped Selina in her confusion. 'I did not know what Susy was doing, when she put her hand between my thighs, I swear it!'

'But you knew soon enough when you came off at her touch, you wicked girl! Do you think I'm a fool, to believe that you were innocent of why pussies are felt?'

'Oh, sir,' Bella gasped, 'do you believe that she really let the maid bring her off — or is this another contrivance of the teacher's to finger her?'

'A contrivance, of course,' Randolph replied at once. 'Selina will be brought off shortly, as also will you!'

Whilst Miss Rodwell spoke thus unfeelingly, she rubbed with her immodest finger at Selina's button and the lewd movement grew ever faster and faster. The victim's breath came in short gasps, interspersed with incoherent words that she had little or no knowledge of uttering:

'Oh no, Miss Rodwell . . . oh Heavens . . . I am near to coming off . . . stop . . . do not make me do that . . . too late, too late!'

Her hips jerked and her uncovered thighs quivered. For some seconds she seemed quite to lose control of her limbs, and but for Miss Rodwell's supporting arm about her waist it is certain she would have collapsed in a heap on the floor.

To hear Bella reading affected Randolph greatly, His colour became heightened, as also did his fleshy shaft, which bounded hard-on between his thighs, uncovered by his shirt, which he had drawn up to his belly-button. His hand had crept down from Bella's enormous titties, over her smooth belly, and between her parted thighs. In the same way that the lascivious schoolmistress manipulated Selina's parts, so he addressed himself to Bella's, delighting to feel the slippery wetness he caused to descend over her secret button.

'Oh, what a wicked girl it is to fetch off so quickly,' Miss Rodwell exclaimed. 'The feel of your tender pussy has undone me and I must have you again, little Selina.' So saying, she pulled the half-fainting girl down on to her lap and thrust her tongue into her mouth. She opened the front of Selina's nightdress, to handle her smooth soft titties and tickle their rose-pink teats.

'Tonight you shall sleep in my bed, Selina,' said she, 'and by morning we shall have brought each other off a dozen or more times and sleep through tomorrow morning in the languor of love satisfied.'

Randolph's fingers had done their work well, and spasms of an ecstasy beyond the ordinary seized Bella, making her belly rise as she came off. Randolph gave her no opportunity to enjoy her paroxysm in peace — he was on her immediately, thrusting up his shaft into her twitching pussy, while her throes yet shook her. He was greatly aroused by the sight of her coming off, and he lunged in and out of her slippery cunny zestfully.

'You're killing me!' cried Bella, her belly writhing beneath him, yet sustaining his hard tupping with an enthusiasm that equalled to his own.

'Die then!' cried he. 'Yield up your life to the stabbing of my shaft in you!'

Needless to say, she did not die, but returned his thrusts in good measure, with upheavals of her belly and slidings of her wet pussy on his shaft, showing herself to be as lively as any gentleman could hope for. With a cry of bliss, Randolph gushed his ardent lust deep into her, and she too dissolved in joy to feel the sudden surge in her belly.

Bella Gurney, it must be said, for all her lasciviousness of spirit, was a well-trained servant who had her mistress's good at heart. She waited for Randolph to recover himself, lying at her side, his head cushioned on her bare titties, before coming back to the reason for her presence with him in Black's Coffee House.

'What am I to tell Miss Dorothy?' she enquired, her tone now respectful again since her sensual throes had faded. 'She is in a pitiable state of mind, sir, and unless she can be calmed by good news of some sort, I fear she may sink into a decline.'

'Tell her?' said Randolph lazily. 'You may tell her I am not unsympathetic to the inconvenience in which she finds herself. But you must add that I have no immediate solution to offer for the relief of her predicament, as she alone sees it, except to guarantee that, for aught I have done, she is a virgin intact. If she feels herself unable to rely on the word of a gentleman, then she may consult her medical adviser, who will inspect her parts and confirm what I have said.'

'Then you do not offer to make amends, sir?'

'What the devil do you mean, *amends*? Does Miss Harker

think I have some sort of duty towards her to offer her marriage − is that what she hints at?'

'I won't go so far as to say an offer of marriage on your part would make her happy, if you'll excuse the liberty,' said Bella, 'for happiness will remain a stranger to her for many a year to come, I believe. But a proposal from you would set her mind wonderfully at rest, when she declines Mr Mawby.'

'Marry a chit of a girl on account of a quick bung-holing?' Randolph expostulated. 'I've never heard such confounded nonsense in my life! Let her marry Mawby and be done with it. He's not a hot-blooded man − the use of her cunny twice a week will content him, and he'll have no interest in other orifices, even if she becomes inquisitive as to their use.'

'That she can no longer in good conscience do, sir. She holds Mr Mawby too honourable a gentleman to deceive by fobbing him off with part-worn goods. She looks to you to help her out of her difficulty.'

'Damnation take it all!' Randolph exclaimed. 'If any more is needful, then you may tell Miss Harker that I will think about the matter further, when opportunity serves, and may reach some useful resolution in a few days. If so, then I shall send word for you to meet me here and hear the outcome.'

'Very good, sir,' said Bella, 'on behalf of Miss Dorothy, may I say that's very kind-hearted of you. If you've finished with me for now, sir, I will dress myself and return in haste to Paddington Green, to convey your message to my mistress.'

'Not so fast,' said he, catching her between the legs with a clasping hand to keep her on the bed with him, 'you have other warm openings I have not yet made use of, Bella, and it would be a pity to let them go to waste. A guinea a hole — that's the price I'm giving today. You've earned two guineas and you've two more orifices yet untouched. What do you say?'

'At that rate of pay you can use me as you like,' said she.

'Capital! Roll over, girl, and brace yourself!'

CHAPTER 12
Some Slight Feelings of Guilt are Purged

After Randolph had his full four guineas worth of Bella's orifices it might be thought that he would sleep like a top that night, and wake up next day with a zest for life and a hearty appetite for breakfast. On the other hand, the followers of Dr William Acton would no doubt insist that he fell into a comatose state of senselessness, brought on by reckless over-indulgence in the sexual spasm, and lay twitching and moaning all night long in a clammy sweat, tormented by incoherent dreams of dark despair.

In the event, neither opinion held any truth. When Randolph retired to his bed that night, he fell asleep at once, as well might be expected after his lustful exertions, but he was made restless by dreams throughout the night, and woke several times in dismay.

Nevertheless, though he dreamed, he was not troubled by the nightmares that Dr Acton believes to be the lot of a gentleman who has rogered four times in the course of a single day, whose nervous system is thereby exhausted and like to collapse into invalidism. Randolph's dreams were odd and puzzling visions, but not frightening, and Miss Dorothy Harker played a leading, if ill-defined, part in them.

At one moment he thought he stood at the foot of a staircase, down which she came towards him, a candlestick in her hand to light the way. He hoped she meant to lead him upstairs to her bed, for he had a letch to poke her, but she halted when she reached the lowest stair. She stared at him mournfully, asking why he had ravished her bottom, for no decent person would have her to wife now that her person had been defiled.

Later in the night, when Randolph's dreaming returned, he and Dorothy were looking into the window of the milliner's shop in Shaftesbury Avenue where he had met her. For no reason he knew, she undid the tight buttons of her short jacket and opened it wide, to show him she wore no blouse underneath, and above the waistband of her skirt, she was stark naked.

Randolph stared at her titties, and though she would not let him feel them, she turned to place her hands flat on the glass and lean forward a little. He tipped his hat in salute, before raising her clothes behind to her waist and parting the rear slit of her drawers. He slipped his hard-on shaft into her, but whether he rogered her pussy or her knot-hole, he could not say in his dreaming state, nor did it matter.

Towards dawn he woke again, gripped by a vision of Dorothy down on her knees before Lorimer Mawby. She was fully dressed, but he had removed his trousers and she held his stiff shaft in her hand and toyed with it. Randolph wished to call out to her, to advise her not to continue, but he was unable to speak, and in another moment she had taken Lorimer's shaft into her mouth.

When he finally awoke, roused by Lizzie with his morning tea, his mood was unsettled and uneasy. His powers of concentration were in abeyance, for he could not turn his thoughts away from Dorothy. He had himself accused her of allowing Lorimer to put his hand up her clothes and feel her pussy, but it was only to put her out of countenance, and he had not believed it for even an instant. Yet in his dream she was sucking Lorimer's shaft to bring him off!

It was damnably confusing and made him irritable and lacking in his normal confidence. Lizzie handed him his cup of tea and stood at the bedside while he drank it, humbly waiting for him to pull her down on the bed and roger her. Yet with so much on his mind, Randolph had no heart to fumble with a servant girl, and he sent her packing.

He passed the morning in solitude at his club, over brandies and soda and the newspapers, having no desire to converse with anyone. After a frugal lunch, his mind was made up — he needed to seek advice over his confusion of mind. Naturally, it would have been the act of a complete cad to risk exposing the good name of a lady by consulting any of his old chums at the club. After much agitated thought, he made up his mind to seek advice of a person whose knowledge of sexual matters was unrivalled — namely, Mrs Mary Jeffries.

Soon after two o'clock in the afternoon he took a cab to her house in Chelsea. She thought at first he'd come to further his acquaintance with Miss Jane, who had slept through the morning and was well-rested and available to receive visitors. Randolph explained that it was advice he sought, which made Mrs Jeffries frown, until he made it clear he was prepared to pay cash for the benefit of her counsel. That being understood, she took him to her private parlour, sent for a bottle of brandy and asked how she could be of service.

Randolph stared at her in thought for a moment, uncertain how much he might prudently reveal to her. She had a respectable look about her, seated opposite him in her genteel black satin, almost like a kindly aunt, but her knowledge of fornication and its attendant problems must surely be without equal, she being the kept woman of an eccentric peer of the realm for ten or more years, and procuress to the gentry for another ten after that.

'Dear kind Mrs Jeffries – I am sure that you will understand my predicament very well,' said Randolph, settling himself into an armchair. 'Any consolation you are able to give me at a most difficult time will be very gratefully received by me.'

He went on to relate to her, mentioning no names, something of his unusual interlude with a certain young lady of quality, after she had swooned on her sofa. He did not tell all – some vestige of an unfamiliar sense of embarrassment acted on him to curb his tongue. Mrs Jeffries listened with a look of interest on her face. When he fell silent, she offered some comfort:

'I can't say I'm surprised that a hot-blooded gentleman like yourself found it hard to resist the temptation of exploring a little, when you were alone with a beautiful girl and she quite senseless on her back,' said Mrs Jeffries, her voice warm and sympathetic. 'How far did you go with her – did you have a feel of her titties?'

'I did,' he answered, 'but only through her clothes. They were divinely full and firm, satiny globes that my soul yearned to lay bare and kiss.'

'Hmm! No harm done so far!' said Mrs Jeffries. 'Did you put your hand up the young lady's clothes?'

'Yes,' said he, a little more able to discuss the matter now that he had made a start on his confession. 'And more – I felt her thighs, so smooth and firm to the touch!'

'Ah, I understand now,' exclaimed Mrs Jeffries. 'You had

her clothes up round her waist and your hand in her drawers.'

'My hand lay between her thighs and I fingered her warm and silky-tufted mound,' he answered proudly.

'Silky-tufted, eh? You've a dash of the poet about you, Mr Joynes,' said she. 'That's an excellent thing in a gentleman of your years. Older gentlemen lose all fine power of discernment and see a cunny as no more than a handy place to shove into and unburden their carnal lust, not caring whether it has hair like silk over it or coarse carroty bristles, or is as bare as the palm of your hand.'

'Can you keep a confidence, Mrs Jeffries?' he asked. 'When I parted the slit of the lady's drawers and looked at her pussy, gracefully adorned with a profusion of silky brown curls, the delicate pink lips and the virginal bloom that lay over all, it seemed to me then that never in my life had I seen so lovely a female organ. I have seen hundreds, large and small, dark, fair and ginger, and poked them! Yet this dear lady's pretty little toy caused me to experience an exceptional intensity of emotion – indeed, my blood raced in my veins and I was dizzy from sheer lustful joy.'

'Well!' said Mrs Jeffries softly, beginning to understand a little of what ailed Randolph. 'You had a good feel between the young lady's legs. And why not? Did she go wet and slippy when you interfered with her?'

'A little,' he replied. 'I played with her delicious cunny – oh, if only I had words to describe how perfectly formed are the lips, how delightful to touch! I thought I was about to come off in my trousers.'

'You have a very warm nature,' Mrs Jeffries said, 'and that is a source of much enjoyment to any gentleman. So she became a little wet, you say, from your handling?'

'Her heavenly little pussy became slippery with a sweet dew of love, and I was desperate to thrust my shaft up it.'

'You poked her? Is that what troubles you?'

'No, I refrained,' said he, 'though Heaven alone knows where I found the strength to contain myself at that moment.'

He made no mention of the fact that he'd rubbed at his shaft until he fetched off on Dorothy's belly, for that was the act of a timorous underling, not of a gentleman.

'Then if you did no such thing,' said Mrs Jeffries, sounding puzzled, 'why are you now concerned? I'm sure a little gentle tampering with a swooning young lady's privates is nothing to be troubled about. You held back and behaved very properly, far more so than many another would have in your position, in that you respected the young lady's virginity.'

'I did something I have not yet told you,' Randolph admitted with a touch of reluctance now he had reached the crucial point of his confession.

'Whatever can that be?' she cried. 'Are you telling me that you took advantage of her after all – that you did *not* refrain from plucking her bloom? Are you saying that you poked her?'

'Mrs Jeffries, please try to understand,' he said, hardly able to get the words out, 'the beauty of her face and form so aroused my passions that I had no choice at all but to do as I did. When I felt her sweet moisture on my fingers, it was quite impossible to hold back – I had to make her mine! I turned her over on the sofa, bared the cheeks of her darling bottom, and did the forbidden deed.'

'What? You back-buttoned her?' exclaimed Mrs Jeffries.

'Yes,' he said simply, 'I ravished her bum, since which time I have been uneasy. What shall I do?'

'Does she know what was done? When she recovered from her swoon, did she feel the effect of your ravishment?'

'She is aware that something was done to her lower parts, but not what,' he said, 'for she is wholly innocent and without any thought that a bung-hole may be used for copulation.'

'Then you must leave her in fortunate ignorance. The memory will fade and she will resume her life as if nothing happened, mark my words. But as for you — the difficulty sticks in your mind and must be dislodged. An hour or two's rogering upstairs with Miss Jane will bring you back to your normal self.'

'I think not,' said Randolph morosely, 'for yesterday I poked a girl four times, and even that was not sufficient to drive away the sombre thoughts that disturb me. In fact, it served only to make them stronger and more abiding, so that they intruded into my sleep in curious dreams.'

'What I can discern here is a feeling of guilt,' Mrs Jeffries pronounced. 'You wish now you hadn't bung-holed the lady, nice as it was at the time. Am I right?'

'Guilt?' he exclaimed. 'Damn it all, guilt is for the lower classes, not for persons like myself! I've never felt any sort of guilt in my life, and certainly not over poking women, not even when a near relation was involved. You are incorrect.'

'Pardon my error, Mr Joynes,' said she hastily. 'Guilt is not for the ruling classes — who should understand that better than I, who for many a year was the close companion of a noble lord, now sadly deceased. His Lordship with complete equanimity did such things as would cause a common person to sob with remorse and pray for forgiveness. You are of the same aristocratic turn of mind as he, and could roger a virgin in a church without the least pang of moral discomfort. This is a valuable and useful quality to have and makes for a contented life.'

'Thank you,' said Randolph, mollified by what she had said, 'guilt is a cheap emotion which plays no part in my being. Yet for some reason I fail to understand, I am troubled with qualms of some sort and cannot rid myself of them.'

'As you say, they are mere qualms, of no importance at all to you,' said Mrs Jeffries, sounding most understanding. 'It is my opinion that they can be quickly made to vanish, with the right treatment applied.'

'Then what do you suggest?' he enquired.

'You've come to the right place for advice,' said the smiling bawd. 'In your mind you half believe that there is something to set right, though not the trivial matter of button-holing your female acquaintance. The best and quickest way to put at peace these odd emotions is to have your backside properly tanned. If you laugh at my suggestion, I shall not be offended at all, but you may believe me, Mr Joynes, when I say I've seen it dozens of times – gentlemen like yourself arriving here burdened with heavy and oppressive feelings and after a sound thrashing, off they go relieved and contented.'

'Damme, but I think you may be right!' he exclaimed. 'A good whipping, such as I've not had since leaving school! Capital – the very thing to ease my mind! Can you arrange it at once?'

In Mrs Jeffries's house anything could be provided at shortest notice to visitors with enough gold sovereigns in their pocket. The housemaid was sent for – a sturdy young woman named Martha – and orders given to prepare the whipping room at once and ask Miss Emily to present herself there, ready to employ her skill with the instruments of punishment.

'Emily?' Randolph asked. 'I do not remember her. Is she new to the house, Mrs Jeffries?'

'Why no, sir, she has been in my service these three years or more. You have not met her yet during your visits here, for the reason that you have not required to be chastised, that being Emily's especial talent to satisfy gentlemen by.'

'Is she young?'

'You'll take to her,' Mrs Jeffries assured him. 'She is a fine example of female flesh, not yet thirty years of age, strong as she needs must be for her particular work. You will see her shortly for yourself, but until then, I can tell you that she has a pair of titties on her big enough to put your face between — if she would let you. As to her cunny, I shall say nothing, for if she likes the look of you, she may just give you a glimpse when she toils at punishing you.'

'Does she not poke, then?' Randolph asked, surprised.

'Not often. I see you are astonished at that, to find one in my house who does not lie all day on her back. Yet Emily earns her keep by the use of her strong right arm, and for the rest I let her do as she pleases. A few gentlemen make request for her services outside the whipping-room, and are content to pay very highly for the pleasure.'

'What sort of gentlemen are they?' Randolph asked curiously.

'Why, the sort who like to be roughly treated for pleasure by a female, who enjoy being abused and mistreated. The sort who like to lie underneath in rogering, and have Emily's weight lie above them to thump them into the mattress with her belly and thighs till they fetch off and are satisfied.'

On another occasion Randolph would have been so taken by what Mrs Jeffries told him that he would have asked questions about this strange-sounding form of poking, so very far removed from his own pleasure in domineering and browbeating a helpless girl and vanquishing her with his manly shaft. But his spirits were low and he said nothing, but waited for the whipping room to be made ready to receive him.

In less than ten minutes Martha returned to tell Mrs Jeffries that all was prepared, and that Miss Emily was in there and at the gentleman's disposal. On hearing this, Randolph glanced at the mistress of the house in a condition of mind akin to sudden panic, though he would never admit such a thing, not even to himself. Fortunately, Mrs Jeffries was too wise in the ways of men not to interpret his look correctly and immediately she spoke to reassure him:

'Come with me now, Mr Joynes, and we will put all to rights for you. I shall remain with you, to supervise the proceedings, so that you do not feel yourself put into strange hands for the treatment. Trust me now – all shall be done properly and wholly to your satisfaction.'

Randolph thanked her and followed her from her parlour into a room on the top floor of the house, at the back. Though large, it was sparsely furnished, containing no more than a couple of straight-backed wooden chairs and – there near one end, upright and fixed firmly to the bees-waxed wooden floor, the *whipping frame*! Randolph stared at it as if fascinated, having not seen such a piece of equipment before. It was a frame of heavy wood, the posts joined across at top and bottom, so that no amount of heaving or writhing would shake it, and the four corners were provided with black leather straps to pinion wrists and ankles. Close by this fearful apparatus stood a raven-haired woman, dark-eyed and strongly built. Mrs Jeffries presented her to Randolph as Miss Emily, and as he acknowledged her with a slight nod, she smiled cruelly at him. As to her attire, she was clad in only a short chemise ending halfway down to her knees and she wore neither stockings nor drawers, a particular which went some way to reconcile Randolph to the ordeal which faced him.

The plain linen chemise was thin enough for him to note that Emily had good-sized titties inside it, and a fat round belly. Even while he was observing her, and she standing still to let him, the maid performed a valet's part in assisting him out of his frock coat and his waistcoat, his silk cravat and his tall stiff collar. Mrs Jeffries meanwhile took a seat on one of the chairs, set back some little way from the whipping frame, yet close enough for all that went on to be seen and directed.

The maid was down on her knees now in front of Randolph, to take off his elastic-sided boots and his black silk socks. She was a heavily made woman of about the same age as Miss Emily, he observed, with the trace of an impertinent grin permanently about her broad face. Had she been his servant, he would have disciplined her severely to bring her to a proper appreciation of her place in life. At that moment, she undid his braces and buttons and pulled his trousers down his legs — her incipient grin blossoming forth into a hearty smile.

Randolph scowled down at her, thinking it insolent beyond any acceptable bounds for a lowly female servant to wear any facial expression at all when waiting on a gentleman, even if she was staring at close quarters at his dangling shaft. The moment his feet were clear of his trousers, he stepped away from the woman and turned to face Mrs Jeffries and saw that Emily was at her side, bending down to bring her ear close to her employer and catch her whisper.

The leaning posture drew up Emily's short chemise at the rear and afforded Randolph a good view of much of her sturdy thighs. He pondered a moment on the bountiful curve of her bottom, and wondered what it would be like to be rolled on and brutalised by her. The memory came into his mind of the poking bouts that he had seen at The Ratcatcher's Arms in Marylebone, and it occurred to him Emily would make an amusing contestant — and one who was hard to beat and poke by the look of her!

Mrs Jeffries stared at him and told him that his shirt must be removed before he was strapped into the whipping frame, so that he was naked for the kiss of the lash.

'Damned if I like the look of the thing,' said he. 'It's more like a flogging post for criminals in prison than anything else — and that does not please me.'

'There is something in what you say,' Mrs Jeffries agreed, at once, for to her way of thinking, gentlemen with cash to spend were invariably correct, however improbable their opinions.

'It is a pity we no longer have the secret of the celebrated Mrs Berkley's chastisement frame,' she continued. 'It was her own invention, fifty years ago, and in great demand by gentlemen who visited her house in Charlotte Street.'

'Who was she?' Randolph enquired.

'Why, sir, Theresa Berkley was the queen of the profession in her day,' cried Mrs Jeffries. 'Noblemen and the gentry were her patrons and, it is reported, royalty also, for King George IV when he was yet Prince of Wales went to her house, besides the Duke of Queensberry, and many another.'

'She procured by Royal appointment, eh?' said he. 'Did she put the Royal coat of arms on the wall outside her door too?'

'She was a very discreet woman,' said Mrs Jeffries, 'and

she could hold her tongue about her visitors, including bishops and even a great lady or two whose taste ran that way. This I know from the lord in whose service I was, he being a client of hers at one period in his life.'

'This invention of hers, what was it like?' Randolph asked.

'It was reported to be in shape not unlike the human form, to accommodate the victim in comfort. But alas, when Mrs Berkley died, the frame was lost and never seen again. Her property and her fortune, which was considerable, passed to her only brother — a religious person who had been a missionary among the black savages of Australia. But he was too ashamed of his celebrated sister to accept, and in default everything went to her medical adviser. He took the cash and sold off the property, and it is believed that the frame was bought for a large sum of money by the keeper of a Paris brothel.'

'Confound all Frogs!' said Randolph, patriotically.

'They make good whores,' said Mrs Jeffries, 'hardworking and ingenious in poking. I employ them gladly when they apply here. But to conclude my story, my dear kind lord once told me that at Theresa Berkley's a gentleman could have himself whipped or birched, scourged, fustigated, caned, thrashed with stinging nettles, or whatever took his fancy, till he was fully spent and wrung out.'

'It sounds devilish painful to me,' said Randolph doubtfully.

'Lord love you, sir, each to his taste, and I see that yours is not that of gentlemen who find bliss only through agony. You are in a different way of things, as we have agreed, for you do not seek pleasure here today, but the removal of certain qualms that stick in your mind. That being so, it is my proposal that you be chastised on your bottom with

201

a cane, as when you were a schoolboy. Does that meet with your approval?'

'Excellent,' Randolph agreed, 'so long as I need not be hung in that evil-looking frame of yours.'

'No, sir, you shall be horsed on Martha's back, while you are chastised. Prepare yourself, Martha.'

'Yes, madam,' said the sturdy maid at once.

She bestowed on Randolph the benefit of her impertinent smile and said she was sure he would have no objection if she removed her dress, in case of accident. He did not take her meaning, and before he had time to ask what the Devil she meant, she had unbuttoned and unhooked herself and had her plain black servant garb off and across a chair with his own clothes. She stood in only chemise and drawers, her fat titties dangling inside and a wisp of brown hair visible through the slit of her drawers.

'Now, Mr Joynes, if you are quite ready,' said Mrs Jeffries.

Martha placed herself in front of him, her broad back turned towards him, her plump backside within an inch of his person.

'Put your hands on my shoulders, if you please, sir,' said she, glancing backwards at him.

Speechless now that the moment was at hand, Randolph obeyed, resting his hands on her shoulders. At once she reached up and back to take hold of his wrists and pull his arms over her, and down, her back now pressed hard against him. She bent forward sharply, lifting him right off his feet, and he hung helplessly on her back in the traditional posture of being horsed.

She was strong of grip, and her hold on his wrists was not to be broken. She had thrust his hands down the loose front of her chemise, to take hold of her plump titties, but he was prey to such emotions of fearful apprehension that the feel of her warm flesh went unnoticed in his clasping hands. He gasped to feel Emily's hands on him, tucking up his shirt tail to uncover his bottom and make it ready for the caning to come.

This touch of her hands on his rearward cheeks, to which she gave some moments of manual attention, smoothing her palms over them, pinching the flesh between forefinger and thumb, parting the cheeks to press her fingers into the crease between, had an effect on Mr Percival Proud, that forlorn and forgotten friend hanging down between Randolph's legs. He woke up from his long sleep, shook himself, and raised his head.

'Is the gentleman ready yet?' Mrs Jeffries enquired.

'Almost,' said Emily, her fingers busy between the cheeks of Randolph's bottom in a way that made him squirm against Martha.

Then Emily pressed her belly against his bottom, both arms round his waist, so that he was squeezed between two big female bodies as if in a human sandwich, they the bread slices and he the meat in the middle. It was a peculiar feeling, and one that he found very agreeable. Emily slid her hands between him and Martha, and took hold of stiff and twitching Mr Percival. She held his pompoms in one cupped palm, and ran her fingers up and down the hard-on shaft, handling it with contempt — and yet the touch excited Randolph beyond words.

Finally, she arranged his cockstand neatly against Martha's well-filled chemise, where it was trapped and held firm. Then at last she stood back and picked up the long cane that leaned upright against a chair. Randolph turned his head to stare hard at her, and his heart leaped to see her stern face and sombre dark eyes regarding him with an

203

expression of disdain. Her full titties and belly filled out her thin chemise in a provocative manner that caused Mr Percival to jerk furiously.

'I hope all is to your liking, now you find yourself prepared for your punishment,' said Mrs Jeffries from where she sat down the room. 'Miss Emily will wield the cane very briskly, you may take my word for it.'

'I hardly know what to think,' replied Randolph, his voice shaking to the intensity of his emotions, his hands squeezing Martha's big bare titties and rolling them about in her chemise so that she grinned and grunted.

'You are about to find out, not by any words of mine, but by virtue of suffering pain, that some things ought not to be done — and if they are, then they are to be forgotten quickly. Have you understood me?'

'I take your meaning,' he answered, 'and it is to be hoped an outcome as satisfactory as you promise will result — though by keeping me waiting you add to my suspense.'

Truth to tell, now that Mr Percival was at hard-on stand once more, Randolph was no longer certain that he wished to proceed with being caned. A good poke or two with Miss Jane was surely a better remedy for his low spirits. He considered asking to be released, but decided that was the act of a coward, and set his face against it.

'Begin, Emily!' said Mrs Jeffries.

Randolph, his head turned to the side, watched Emily raise her arm high above her head, so that her heavy breasts rolled and slid under her chemise, and a tuft of jet-black hair showed in her armpit. A moment later she brought the cane down across his behind, making him jerk to the cut, whilst the fierce pain made him cry out, *Oh no, no*! Again she caned him, the rod whistling through the air as it descended, to end in a loud crack across his flesh. In desperation he tried to kick backwards and pull his wrists free, but Martha held him firmly. Miss Emily struck again, making his bottom feel as if it were wrapped in a sheet of fire. In his suffering he was unaware how his shaft was swollen to tremendous size and stiffness, for it was trapped tightly between him and Martha's back, squeezed between his belly and her chemise, on which it rubbed to the writhing of his body as once more the cane cut savagely through the air and cracked across his tormented backside.

Excruciating though the pain was, Randolph could not help but notice that Emily's short chemise was now hitched up around her waist, to permit her legs to move freely as she swung the cane. He saw her full round snow-white belly, inset with the tiniest of buttons, and below, her cunny, almost hairless and with lips no larger than those of a young girl not yet poked. Yet Emily could be no virgin, living in this house. Was her pleasure to come off with other women, Randolph wondered — with the lovely Miss Jane, perhaps?

'Oh!' he exclaimed. 'Your little pussy is adorable, Emily — I want to roger you!'

'Be silent, sir, and take your punishment like a gentleman,' Mrs Jeffries said. 'You will thank me for driving out of your mind the unwelcome memory of interfering with a young lady when she lay in a faint and at your mercy! Ah, how shameful — not a proper ravishing in her cunny, even, but a furtive approach by the back door! Lay on hard, Emily, turn his backside scarlet.'

'Yes, Mrs Jeffries,' Emily answered, 'and it is my intention after I've reddened his bottom to give his shaft a good beating to teach it to mend its ways.'

'Capital idea!' said Mrs Jeffries. 'How many's he had — six of the best? That will do his bum for the time being — punish his offending part!'

Emily ceased to cane him and, to Randolph's horror, she slid a hand between him and Martha to take hold of Mr Proud and tug hard at him, as if to stretch further his already impressive length.

'Yes, half a dozen cuts across this will reduce his conceit,' Emily agreed. 'The cheek of it — to say he wants to put this up me and fetch off! Am I to continue, Mrs Jeffries?'

'You cannot mean to beat me there,' Randolph cried. 'You may thrash my backside all you will, for it might perhaps be argued that I have deserved no better — but do not inflict pain upon me there! It could maim me for life! Spare me this agony, and you shall be well rewarded, I promise you!'

'Maim, is it?' cried she, still handling him roughly. 'Some gentlemen who come here to appreciate my services like nothing better than to be bound to the frame and whipped on their shaft until it turns blue and red, being bruised and battered until they faint clean away.'

'Ah no, no!' Randolph moaned.

He need not have feared, for he was in the hands of experts, the trio of females attending to him being highly experienced and skilled in ministering to the whims of gentlemen. Out from Randolph's caned bottom there had spread a hot glow to embrace his loins and raise Mr Percival to his extremity of erection.

Randolph's fingers were firmly clenched on the soft flesh of Martha's titties, and the rubbing of Emily's hand did the rest. A bolt of sensation passed through his body, as if he had been struck by a pistol shot and, with a shriek of unexpected bliss, he squibbed his hot sap on to the back of Martha's chemise so forcefully as to soak it almost up to her shoulder-blades.

When at last he lay calm, she stood upright and lowered

him to his feet, and Miss Emily passed a strong right arm about his waist to support him. He took advantage of the moment to reach under her chemise and have a feel of her maidenly looking cunny — and she did not prevent him, but stood with her feet apart to facilitate his groping.

Randolph, apart from the sting of his backside, was in high spirits. He sensed that whatever had ailed him had been set to right by the caning, that the slate was wiped clean, and there was nothing to trouble himself about further. In his elation he handed Mrs Jeffries a five pound Bank of England note, and announced an intention of poking the perspiring Miss Emily a time or two.

She at once delivered a smart smack of her hand on his bare backside and told him he was much mistaken, but that she would roger *him* to a standstill, if he so desired. Whereupon Randolph recalled the sporting match he had attended in Marylebone and offered to wrestle her the best of three pokes, and to that she agreed.

CHAPTER 13
A Most
Disconcerting Discovery

Randolph allowed the weekend to pass before getting word to the maid Bella that she was to meet him again at Black's Temperance Coffee House, there being a matter of some importance he wished to acquaint her with. She arrived promptly at half past two of the afternoon, eager for any least shred of comfort she could convey back to Miss Harker.

It is unnecessary to say that, having some experience now of the Hon Randolph Joynes' way with females, Bella came to the meeting in the expectation that she would be rogered. In this assumption she was correct — she had been in the upstairs room with him not even five minutes before he had her dress and drawers off, and she flat on her back on the bed, thighs apart and chemise up above her titties.

To demonstrate his authority over her, and to experience that high feeling of total domination he so much enjoyed, Randolph divested himself of none of his garments — not even his black silk topper, which remained clamped on his head during the entire operation! His frock coat stayed buttoned, only the flaps parted in front, and if he could have devised a way to do her without opening his trousers, he would, but that was beyond the wit of any man, and gaping wide they were to allow out his stiff shaft and plunge it into her pussy.

Once installed in her, he rogered her long and artfully, slow in thrusting yet deep and piercing, for he had a mind to poke her to the point of hysteria and prolong the duration of his pleasures that day. In this manner, Bella was driven almost out of her senses by the luxurious feelings that emanated from her well-filled cunny and spread throughout her body. She became lost in transports of ecstasy long before Randolph was ready to spend, and when at last his essence gushed into her, she gasped very loud and fell into paroxysms of bliss that almost caused her to lose consciousness.

After he had dismounted he sat upright on the side of the bed and gazed down at her thoughtfully, his sticky shaft back in his trousers and his topper a trifle askew on his head. Bella lay motionless, her legs spread wide and her heart filled with contentment. He smiled to see how her frame was shaken by an occasional tremor from the still-trembling strings of joy that had been plucked to sound out the melody that had enraptured her senses.

He was well pleased with what he had done to her, knowing she would be more amenable to his suggestions now that he had by means of his manly shaft carried her up to the very heights.

His conclusion proved true, for when Bella regained the power of speech, she turned on her side to stare at him in wonder and speak most flatteringly:

'Lord above, sir, I've never been done like that before,' she said. 'It's a pity you can't do it to Miss Dorothy, for I swear she would forget her troubles in an instant, if you brought her off as you have me.'

'There is much in what you say,' Randolph agreed, 'for in my own experience a good poke cures most of the concerns that ail humankind, and we aristocrats are very expert at it, as you may suppose. Is Miss Harker still dejected, then?'

'She is, for on Saturday Mr Mawby arrived by appointment for an answer to his proposal of marriage. She refused him, as she told me she would, and as I informed you when we met before.'

'How refused him? Briskly? Sadly? Indifferently?'

'Not without tears and sighs, sir, for she has an affection for Mr Mawby that is a neighbour to Love itself. He was first distressed, and sought to know why he was refused, enquiring if she thought him not good enough for her. But there was little enough Miss Dorothy could tell him of the reason why she felt herself unworthy of him, and he became angry and demanded to be told if there was someone else. I heard voices raised in the drawing room and was in fear for my poor mistress, but then Mr Mawby left in a huff, banging the door behind him.'

'Were you able to bring any comfort to her mind?' Randolph asked. 'Did you offer solace?'

'Comfort? What comfort could there be for one in her piteous condition? I do not understand what you mean, sir.'

'Then I shall explain myself, Bella,' said he, his hand lying on her uncovered titties, to feel them and toy with them whilst he spoke.

'When you came here before,' he continued, 'to acquaint me of the details of Miss Harkers misgivings, something you said lodged in my mind. I pondered for the next day or two what it might signify and finally, I reached a conclusion of interest.'

'What do you mean, sir?' Bella asked.

'In telling me of your actions when Miss Harker recovered at last from her swoon, you said that you conducted her into her bedroom and there bathed her parts in warm water. Is that so?'

'What of it? She was still half-swooning and unable to do anything for herself, and you had spent freely on her. I feared that if even a drop of the prolific juice trickled inside her, a calamitous result might make itself apparent in nine months time. Some gratitude must be due for saving you from paternity, sir. Or is that an impudent suggestion?'

'Not in the least,' he said cheerfully, 'and I shall remember your solicitude. But − be frank now, Bella − is it not an act of extraordinary intimacy for a servant to bathe her mistress's private parts, even in an urgent situation?'

The maid made no answer, and he squeezed her nearside titty whilst he spun the thread of his argument.

'To perform so intimate a function without hesitation, or any afterthought of embarrassment, implies to me that it was not at all the first time you had done it, Bella. I strongly suspect that you bathe Miss Dorothy's pussy for her regularly as part of your duties − am I not right?'

'What of it?' said Bella, giving away nothing.

'Well, my dear, I have seen Miss Dorothy's pussy, as you well know, and it is quite the prettiest little thing I have seen in many a year. In my opinion, Bella, in bathing it, you would not be able to resist touching it, and stroking it, and tickling it to make it pout. Do you deny taking these pleasures?'

'My word!' she exclaimed. 'However did you guess?'

'You gave yourself away, for when you read aloud to me of the tribulations of Selina at the hands of Miss Rodwell, there was a bright blush on your cheeks that showed the pleasure you took in hearing of a young girl's cunny being played with by another female intent on fetching her off.'

Bella smiled up at him and laid her hand flat over her own exposed cunny, and teased the wet lips a little with her middle finger as if in fond reminiscence of former bliss.

'Seeing the effect the book had on you, sir, when I read from it, I suppose you are curious to know more about Miss Dorothy's bedtime preparations.'

Randolph signified his enthusiasm to be better informed, and Bella launched into the story of her duties to Miss Harker.

'As you are aware, sir, I am no housemaid, but lady's maid to Miss Dorothy, and have been for three years now, since she passed sixteen and was thought old enough to have her own maid. At night it is my duty to undress her for bed, to help her out of dress and underskirts and drawers, until I have stripped her to chemise and stockings. To enable me to remove her stockings, she seats herself on the side of her bed, whilst I kneel down and reach under her chemise to roll down her stockings.'

'Ah, what a jolly scene!' Randolph sighed, aware of Percival stretching himself inside his closed trousers, and growing hard and thick. 'You feel her pussy – am I right?'

'She loves me to do so, sir, and has since she was a girl. My hands are out of sight up under her chemise, her legs are apart to let my hand between, and I treat her to a good feel, outside and in, and then with a fingertip on her secret button until her beautiful face begins to flush.'

'Do you bring her off fully?' Randolph asked.

'Oh yes, sir, I tickle her button until her back arches and she emits a long sigh and comes off. I let her recover while I remove her stockings, whereupon she stands up for her chemise to be taken off – and for a moment or two I see her lovely body as naked as day! Then I slip her nightgown over her head and she gets into bed, a contented smile on her face, and is asleep before I have cleared away her clothes and left the room.'

'And how often do you do this, Bella?'

'Every night.'

'Well, well,' said he, 'it seems that the innocent young Miss Dorothy Harker knows more about the joys of coming off than any unmarried gentlewoman of her age ought! Why then should she be upset to the extent you claim she is at being interfered with a little by me? There is something here out of place.'

Bella had two fingers within the soft lips of her pussy and was stroking slowly and with evident enjoyment.

'Miss Dorothy knows nothing at all about poking,' she said, a smile crossing her face at the thought. 'She believes that what I do to her — which she also does to herself most days, for I have observed her — is just something which ladies do to amuse themselves. She has not been instructed yet that her pussy is not only for playing with by hand, hers or mine, but is formed to be poked by a gentleman's hard-on shaft. Nor does her mama intend to tell her, until the evening before her wedding day. I fear that is put off, for she sent Mr Mawby away.'

'When do you bathe her cunny?' Randolph asked, being not at all interested in Lorimer Mawby and his disappointments. 'In the morning, I presume.'

'That's right, sir,' said Bella, a little breathless from the tremors of pleasure rippling through her uncovered belly from the movement of her finger in her open cunny.

'Tell me about it,' said Randolph, equally breathless, for Mr Percival was standing very firm and jumping about, so eager was he to get inside the wet split the maid was fingering.

'Miss Dorothy rises at nine o'clock,' said Bella, 'when the housemaid brings the hot water for her to wash in. I help her out of her nightgown and put down a towel on the rug in front of the washstand. She wakes in a sunny mood every day, and she smiles and chatters to me while she stands on the towel and I wash over her face and neck and under her arms with a soft facecloth.'

'Ah, I'd give a hundred pounds for one day of your duties,' said Randolph with a long sigh. 'Tell me you wash her lovely titties.'

'Of course I do — and a prettier pair you'll never lay eyes on — should you ever be so fortunate to see hers! I wash over them with my palm, very softly and gently, and her tiny pink teats stand proudly up beneath my touch.'

'By George!' he moaned 'I'll come off in another second if you continue like this! Tell me more, Bella, more!'

Mr Proud stood untouched by human hand inside Randolph's dark grey trousers, but bounding like a stag in full rut. The time was not far away when his hood would roll back to bare his head and he would discharge his creamy fluid in spurts of bliss.

'I bring a chair close to the washstand and on the seat put another towel,' said Bella, her words punctuated with sighs as she too approached the zenith of enjoyment. 'Miss Dorothy sits on this, her legs apart, and I place a bowl of clean warm water between her feet. Then I wash her pussy, using only my fingers, until it is perfectly sweet and pure, and she gasps and shakes and comes off.'

'Every morning?' Randolph asked hoarsely.

He was astonished that Bella without the least sign of shame was bringing herself off by hand in plain view. Paid-for doxies would do it on request, of course, but to see a maidservant do it to herself unasked was new to Randolph's experience. It was extremely arousing, and for that reason he enjoyed watching her — though in some part of his mind there was a nagging suspicion that Bella was stroking her pussy because she liked to be *seen* bringing herself off. And if she was merely using him for her own pleasure that would be unbelievably insolent and he would take punitive measures. He pushed the thought away, not wanting to spoil his own enjoyment.

'I give her a thrill every morning, and some mornings twice,' Bella whispered, her eyes closed and her hand moving fast on her own cunny. 'Often there are days when, after she is calm again, she insists that I have not done my duty diligently enough and orders me to wash her pussy better, and I bring her off a second time.'

With that, Bella moaned, her loins jerked hard upwards and she fetched off to her own fingers. Randolph watched her squirm and heave, enrapt by what he saw, feeling his own spasm about to overwhelm him. Was it possible that a man could come off and shoot his roe with no stimulation at all of his shaft, only the power of imagination at work in his mind? He had never heard of it happening, except of course in dreams, an involuntary joy severely condemned by Dr Acton.

Whether possible or not, he was not to discover that day, for no sooner had Bella's throes of passion faded, than she rolled over towards where he sat on the bedside, opened his frock coat with busy fingers and ripped apart his trouser buttons. His shirt was still bundled up round his belly, from when he had poked her before, and Mr Percival leaped out like a Jack-in-the-Box.

Without a pause, she brought her mouth to bear on the jerking shaft, drawing it in over her wet tongue and licking it fast. A sensation of extreme voluptuousness enveloped

Randolph — rarely had he been so aroused as now, to observe the maid's head down between his thighs and her tongue flickering at the head of his throbbing shaft. Almost at once he felt the supreme moment arriving — the most delicious spasms racked him, shaking him from head to foot like a sapling caught in a strong gale.

'I'm coming off, Bella!' he gasped, and his cream gushed out of his shaft and into her sucking mouth.

The afternoon passed very pleasantly, for he had her on her back and rogered her twice more before they parted. He told her how he wished her to prepare Miss Dorothy's mind for a meeting with him the next day, when he would endeavour to resolve her moral difficulties. Bella listened with care and attention, for she was wholly won over to him and entertained secret hopes he would marry Miss Dorothy, so that she and her mistress had the benefit of his poking on a daily basis.

Thus encouraged by what she saw as in her own interest, Bella did her work well. When Randolph presented himself at three the next afternoon at the Harkers' apartment in Paddington Green, he was shown up to the drawing room at once, where Miss Harker received him. Her face was pale of hue and her eyes downcast, her manner somewhat distant, but undoubtedly she wanted to hear whatever Randolph had to say to her. Tea was brought in and a cup poured for him, though he noted that she kept the tea table between her chair and his.

He spoke to her cheerfully and in a spirit of friendship and admiration for her many qualities, by degrees turning round the conversation to the particulars of her plight — or what it was she perceived as her plight. Knowing now that she was very well acquainted with the pleasures of the sexual spasm, even if only when induced by her maid's nimble fingers, he edged towards the topic never to be spoken of in polite society — the harmonious bodily relation between loving husbands and wives, and how this felicitous state of matrimony was accomplished.

'Of all that I am aware,' said Dorothy faintly, 'for in these past few days I have made it my business to find out what it is men want of women, and how they go about it.'

From this Randolph understood that Bella had obeyed him fully and had made some explanation to her innocent mistress of the mechanics of rogering, perhaps even making all clear by means of her finger playing, however inadequately, the penetrating role of the hard-on male shaft.

'Even now I know,' Dorothy continued, 'I confess to finding it next to impossible to believe a lady will allow a gentleman, even if he is her dearly beloved husband, to insert his fleshy organ of generation into any part of her person and discharge his vital fluid. Yet I needs must accept that this is what an All-Wise Deity has ordained, however distasteful it may seem, for the continuance of the human race.

'There's more to it than getting heirs,' said Randolph. 'That would require doing it no more than two or three times a year, to bring on pregnancy. You may not be aware, Miss Dorothy, that young married couples perform the marital act nightly, not just once but several times, and often by day also.'

'What you say is monstrous!' she cried out. 'It cannot be true. Why on earth should any modest wife permit her body to be abused so vilely, however much respect and love she may have?'

'Why, for the pleasure of it,' he replied. 'Perhaps you find it difficult to understand this, for you are a virtuous young lady who has never experienced the sensations of a hard-on male shaft inside her private parts.'

At that, Dorothy blushed crimson to the ears, and for a moment Randolph thought he had offended her past retrieval. Be that as it may, she did not rise and leave the room, but stayed to hear what he would say next.

'You have no experience,' said he, knowing that she had enjoyed years of it in Bella's hands, 'but you may believe me, the pleasure ladies find in coming off is intense and they wish to repeat it as often as their husbands can manage the affair.'

'Can this be true?' she asked thoughtfully, and he saw that he had scored a point.

'I give you my solemn assurance that it is,' said he. 'Surely it is obvious to all that the female body was formed to receive within itself the all-important male organ, not once or twice a year, but constantly. There are many medical cases on record of females being deprived of that bliss for which there is not in this world any substitute, and falling into melancholia.'

'I would rather have supposed the opposite,' Dorothy informed him. 'This so-called pleasure you talk of is surely reserved to gentlemen. It seems to me that ladies would be driven into deep and unbearable distress of mind by husbands enforcing marital rights on their hapless body with a frequency that destroys all dignity and trust.'

'Dear Miss Dorothy,' said Randolph, 'believe me, when you are a wife yourself, and lie abed at night by the side of a loving husband, you will come to an appreciation of the exact truth of my assertion. The sensations of the sexual spasm are common to men and women alike, as is the strong and wholesome desire for carnal pleasure. These divinely implanted instincts were never intended to be borne without relief — and the proper management of this relief lies within the union of the sexual parts. Has no hint, howsoever distant, ever imparted to you in sleep, when the mind ranges freely, the bliss to be found in intercourse?'

As he was well aware, Dorothy's custom was to experience the divine sensation night and morning, ministered to by her maid. Yet her face turned paler yet at his words, and she stammered:

'Shameful! What you suggest is shameful, Mr Joynes.'

Her agitation was great, and Randolph wondered whether she might be about to swoon. If she did, then he proposed to take full advantage of her, front and rear.

'Great Heavens!' he cried. 'That you should stigmatise the wondrous works of Nature as shameful! But you cannot be held responsible for this opinion, for it has been taught to you by others, who ought to know better. How infamous and hypocritical is the society in which we live, that allows the fresh beauty and youth of young ladies to be blasted by a withholding of the simple facts of Nature which would so much ease their minds!'

Common girls, he could have told her, suffered from no such ignorance, for by the time they were twelve years old they had been shown by their playmates in the alleys and courtyards the uses to which their hairless little cunnies could be put. Unhappily, they were soon in the family way thereby. Their problem lay in too much knowledge at too early an age, not in too little, as was the case with gentlewomen like Miss Dorothy Harker.

By the time the tea things were cleared away, Randolph felt that he was making great strides. Dorothy was listening avidly to his words, and she seemed to trust him — at least as far as not flinching when he crossed the room to seat himself at her side.

'Mr Joynes,' she said, somewhat timorously, 'will you tell me something truthfully? You speak with such easy familiarity of the union of the sexes that I cannot help but think that, even though you are a bachelor, you have tasted these pleasures. To be blunt, it seems to me that you must have experienced carnal connexion with at least one female. Is this so?'

Randolph acknowledged that it was, whereupon she pressed him with questions to know what females they were, and why they had allowed him ingress to their bodies.

'Dorothy, Dorothy,' he exclaimed, 'there is so much I could tell you, if I wished. But believe me, my dear, a single ounce of example is worth a half-ton of talk. Trust me, for I will do you no harm, I swear.'

With that he pressed her gently back on the sofa, and with a delicate hand, raised her clothes. Dorothy stared at him with eyes bulging with apprehension while he uncovered her drawers, and she kept her legs close together. He made no move towards the forward slit of her drawers and her hidden pussy, but tried to reassure her with soothing words.

'Do not be alarmed, dear Dorothy, I mean you no insult, only an explanation. Remain calm, while I reveal to you every secret that has been kept from you for so long.'

It was his intention to demonstrate to her what a gentleman's organ looked like, and say some words as to how it fitted into the female aperture. To this end, he pulled open the buttons of his trousers and brought out his fleshy shaft to show her. Then his face turned a fiery red with the humiliation of realising that he had no cockstand! Mr Percival Proud belied his name – for he was hanging his head in shame, without the least hint of stiffness in him, and he was shrunk to his smallest size.

Never in his life had Randolph found himself to be

unequal to sensual activity. He stared down in amazement at his limp part, wondering why this had come about. There was nothing he could think of to account for this feebleness. He had slept well, he had abstained from poking Lizzie when she woke him, he had made a hearty breakfast on porridge with cream, a brace of Scottish kippers and a pair of mutton chops.

He had no inconvenient feelings about having taken advantage of her when she lay in a swoon, for a sound caning had rid him of that nonsense. What the Devil could be amiss? Here at hand sat a young lady he found most provocative because of her youth and innocence, a choice example of female flesh! He had the strongest letch for her, to repeat in her cunny what he had done a few days before in her back door. That notwithstanding, his shaft lay meek and useless between his fingers.

'My God, what must you think of me!' he exclaimed in dread, hardly able to look Dorothy in the face, sure that she despised him for his unmanly weakness, 'I don't know what is the matter with me!'

Dorothy's words showed that she had not the least idea that anything was in the least wrong: 'Oh,' said she pleasantly, 'how small and tender is your . . . I hardly know what to call it . . . this part of your person. In my ignorance I imagined it to be enormously thick and hard, far too big to go into my modest opening, that being what I have been given to understand gentlemen do to females. I was afraid it would hurt me dreadfully, and perhaps even split my poor little thing wide open. Now I see it, there is nothing fearful about it at all. Rather the reverse, for I find it endearingly small and soft, and I would not be in the least afraid to hold it in my hand and dandle it.'

'Do so,' he begged her, hoping that the touch of her dainty

hand would stir Mr Percival into life and make him stand hard.

She stretched out her delicate white hand and took his shaft on her palm, raising it up to inspect in detail the first male organ she had ever been allowed to view. What she saw evidently pleased her, for very soon her other hand crept slowly forward until, with a fingertip, she could tickle Mr Percival Proud's head, for all the world as if he were a kitten to be petted and cuddled tenderly.

For reasons of her own, he understood, Dorothy had decided to entrust her honour to him, and allow him to roger her. Perhaps she thought that he then would feel obliged to ask her to marry him. Her reasoning was of no importance, only the physical fact of her surrender to him. In his mind he envisioned it complete − how his eager fingers would part the slit of her drawers and stroke her pretty pussy.

He longed to see that fleshy jewel of hers once more, to kiss the delicate pink lips of it, and press a gentle finger inside to seek out her tiny button, so sensitive to the manipulations of her maid, and tickle it until she near-fainted with excess of joy. Then he would lay her on her back, her firmly rounded thighs spread wide apart in a state of delightful anticipation, the globes of her titties heaving beneath her clothes.

He saw in his mind's eye how he would bring up his throbbing shaft to the charge and present the swollen head to the lips of her darling pussy. And then *Farewell* to her maidenhead, for with strong pushes he would force it into her, opening her out as he entered and penetrated her. She would tremble beneath him and stifle her little cries of pain, then with her tender cunny clasping Mr Percival like a velvet glove on a finger, he would roger her gently until he fetched off and flooded her with the warm balm of his spending.

The bliss of it would be ineffable! Moments like that came but rarely and were to be savoured. Randolph stared down into his lap, praying silently that Dorothy's soft touch and toying would infuse his shaft with vigour and cause it to grow strong and mighty. Nothing availed — it remained as lifeless as ever, a small limp stub of flesh that lay still on Dorothy's hand. He was utterly mortified and brought to an end the humiliating examination, tucking his childishly soft dangle swiftly into his trousers and taking his leave of Miss Dorothy.

Outside in the street he walked at random, not knowing where he was going, nor caring. The world had turned upside down and he had no thought but one — his dreadful incapacity! Nothing else held the least significance, compared to that. Into the travail of his mind came a recollection of the fearful ending a few years before of Captain Edward Sellon of the Indian Army who came home to write his memoirs.

To judge by what he wrote of his early life, Sellon went the pace with Indian women, finding that their smoothly bare-shaven cunnies aroused him to constant heights of lustfulness. Nor did he neglect the European ladies he met abroad, whose hairy slits were equally stimulating. On his return to England, he carried on in the course he had set himself — incessant poking by day and night, wife, servants, mistresses, whores.

So much so that, while still youngish in years, the gallant Captain found himself no longer capable to perform the sensual act, his shaft being too over-used and done to death to rise to any occasion again, as Randolph found himself now to be. The conclusion was fearful — Sellon despaired and shot himself to death in a hotel in Piccadilly.

'No!' Randolph exclaimed aloud to no one as he walked

along. 'Not that! There are doctors who specialise in the disorders of gentlemen. I shall consult the best of them, and I make no doubt that a course of treatment, rest and good food, will soon put me back in the way of rogering.'

Then he remembered what the most celebrated expert of all had said on this very subject, Dr William Acton:

'. . . *the morally purblind man indulges himself in the trivial pleasures of sexual indulgence, thinking nothing of the heavy penalties attached. He is unaware that, if the sexual desires are stimulated frequently, it will require a greater power of will to master them than falls to the lot of most men, and he will be a prisoner to the harmful habits of his own making. How foolish and short-sighted, to be insensible of the inescapable truth that an awful risk attends on frequent sexual intercourse − and not take heed that self-indulgence, long pursued, leads ultimately to insanity and self-destruction . . .'*

'I am lost,' Randolph groaned, 'consigned to perdition, cut off from the acme of all human felicity, never more to know the wondrous sensations of fetching off in a warm pussy!'

CHAPTER 14
An Opinion is Offered by a Titled Lady

In his sad confusion of mind, Randolph walked for a long time, following the pavement and making no deliberate choice of which way he turned but letting blind Chance direct his feet. It was only when he was called to by an angry voice that he came to an awareness of his whereabouts. He stood in New Bond Street and the voice that had called to him was that of Lorimer Mawby.

Randolph looked at his friend in some surprise, for the truth was that Lorimer's luxuriant mutton-chop whiskers bristled with rage and his eyes seemed to flash fire. He was accompanied by an elegant lady dressed all in bottle-green satin but he made no attempt to effect an introduction. Indeed, he took a step forward away from his charming companion, to confront Randolph.

'Lorimer, what the deuce is the matter?' Randolph asked, for he could think of no reason why the other should harbour hard feelings toward him.

'The matter? I'll tell you what the damn matter is!' cried Lorimer. 'The matter is that you are a low bounder, a scoundrel who deserves horse-whipping!'

'What on earth do you mean? What can I have possibly

227

done to offend you? I haven't laid eyes on you for ages.'

Lorimer seemed to swell up inside his smartly waisted frock coat, till Randolph thought the buttons would burst.

'You have tampered with the affections of a young lady whom I had reason to believe would accept my proposal of marriage! That's what you've done to offend me, you cur!'

'I have done nothing to interfere with your plan to marry Miss Harker,' Randolph insisted feebly, quite unwilling to accept the responsibility thrust upon him.

'You lie!' Lorimer bellowed, his face dark red with emotion. 'How you have achieved your evil end, and for what purpose you have ruined my prospects, I do not know! Nor do I care to, for it is certain that both means and motive are unspeakably vile. You are a cad and I shall have you blackballed at the Club and thrown out!'

'Now look here,' said Randolph, his dejection swept aside by this tirade of abuse, and his own temper rising fast, 'if Miss Harker doesn't want you, that's not my doing. I've seen her but twice since you introduced me, and that by chance. For what it may be worth, I have made no overtures of marriage to her, nor have I spoken slightingly to her of you. Are you sure it wasn't some action of your own that set her against you?'

'What the Devil do you mean, sir!' Lorimer said in a squawk. 'I have behaved with perfect propriety towards her!'

'So you say,' Randolph struck back verbally at his assailant, 'but why should I believe you, I who have seen you fumbling up skirts and squeezing female backsides? You are not entirely a paragon of purity and respectfulness, are you?'

'Damn you! That was with whores and well you know

it! With Miss Harker I have been the very model of etiquette!'

'What!' Randolph exclaimed, letting the grievance he had for his own incapacity deflect on to his friend. 'Did you believe you were with a whore when you rogered Mrs Hamilton on her own sofa? Or when you had Miss Violet Burkington-Hutchins in the conservatory at her coming-out ball?'

'You are no gentleman, sir, to mention the names of ladies in this offensive manner,' said Lorimer, his voice half-strangled with rage.

'You accuse me of God-knows-what in the street and then cry foul play when I remind you of your own misdeeds?' Randolph at once countered. 'I am sorry for your disappointed hopes, yet if they were dashed because you forgot yourself, there is none but yourself to blame.'

'Forget myself! Damn your eyes, Joynes, it is you who forget yourself. My manners have been exemplary towards Miss Harker.'

'Evidently not, if you have been turned way. Did you have a cockstand in your trousers while you wooed the lady, which gave her gentle nature cause for alarm? Or did you chance your luck and put a hand up her clothes for a feel of her pussy?'

At these outrageous suggestions, Lorimer became so incensed that he began to gobble like a Christmas turkey and shake his fist at Randolph.

'Ah, I see I have touched on the sensitive spot,' the latter crowed, enjoying the spectacle of his erstwhile friend reduced to fuming rage.

'You utter blackguard!' Lorimer screeched, scarce able to speak. 'I'll pay you out for that!'

Then, unable to contain himself longer and fearful he

would engage in fisticuffs there in the street like a common drayman, Lorimer turned on his heel and strode away across the road, and was almost run down by a four-wheeler passing by. Randolph eyed his retreating back with glee, and tipped his hat mockingly.

In the heat of his anger, Lorimer had stalked off without any thought for his fair companion, who stood pretending not to hear the altercation. Randolph looked at her properly at last and saw she was a lady of quality, dressed in the very height of fashion and *bon ton*, as the Froggies call style. She wore a thin summer coat of silk, with elegant leg-of-mutton sleeves, and a short train she held off the ground with one gloved and graceful hand. He put her age at between thirty and forty years, near to the latter rather than the former, although she was slender of form and face.

'Forgive me for addressing you without an introduction,' said Randolph, raising his topper, 'but Mawby went dashing off like a mad creature before doing the honours. May I present myself – I am the Hon Randolph Joynes. Please allow me to be of some assistance to you, for it would be unthinkable to leave a lady unescorted in a public place.'

'You are very kind, Mr Joynes,' said she, smiling politely at him. 'I am Lady Fotherington, and I am exceedingly vexed with Lorimer for abandoning me in the street. As to the uncommon way of our introducing ourselves without a third person present to conform to the niceties, perhaps it will help to know that you and I have friends in common, quite apart from Mr Mawby.'

'I am glad of it,' said he, wondering who these friends might be and what was the nature of her friendship with Lorimer.

'I cannot stand here in the street one moment longer,' said Lady Fotherington, 'for strangers are beginning to talk!

Pray be so good as to summon a hansom cab, Mr Joynes.'

That was soon done and when he handed her into it she requested him to escort her to her home, for she had hardly ever been out alone and needed a gentleman's superior knowledge to cope with the petty business of travel and shops. The unexpected row with Lorimer had bucked Randolph up a bit, and he sprang lightly into the hansom with the lady, who informed him that she lived in Belgrave Square.

He passed on the address to the cab driver up above, and the number. The cabbie cracked his whip, and the horse set out at a smart trot towards Piccadilly. Lady Fotherington then showed she had an ulterior motive in asking Randolph to accompany her, for she referred to his quarrel with Lorimer Mawby which polite manners required that she had not listened to – though it was very obvious she had.

'It is fearfully vulgar, I know,' she said, 'to overhear the conversation of others, but you and your friend were shouting so very loudly that I could not help but catch a word or two. I did not know that Mr Mawby had a sentimental interest in a lady and had proposed marriage to her.'

'Why yes, Miss Dorothy Harker, from Warwickshire,' Randolph confirmed.

'A young lady of fortune, do you know?'

'I believe I heard it said that she will have seven thousand pounds a year from her father when she marries,' said Randolph with complete disregard for the truth, but to land Lorimer deeper in trouble. The conclusion he had reached was that Lorimer was poking Lady Fotherington on the side while he courted Dorothy, and neither knew of the other's existence.

'He has not been open with me,' said Her Ladyship,

frowning, 'but no matter now, for I shall cut him dead in future.'

'After his extraordinary behaviour today, so shall I,' said Randolph. 'You cannot imagine my astonishment to be attacked by one I thought a good friend.'

'He holds you responsible for the collapse of his prospects with Miss Harker. Your denial was forthright, Mr Joynes, yet if I look at him and then look at you, I cannot help myself from wondering if there is not some grain of truth in the charge − or is that too fanciful?'

Randolph turned sideways on the cab seat they shared to look at her more closely. There was a smile on her long aristocratic face that betokened more than amusement.

'You accused him of having a *cockstand* in his trousers in the young lady's presence,' she continued, her smile broadening.

At her ready use of a word not thought to be known to ladies, he gasped, then recovered himself and gave as good as he got.

'You're very free of expression, for a lady of title,' said he, 'I also asked Lorimer if he'd put a hand up Miss Harker's clothes for a feel of her pussy, and he did not deny it.'

'Nor did he confirm it,' Lady Fotherington replied. 'And as for my openness of expression, why should I not have the same latitude as a gentleman? It requires two to poke, one to part her legs and one to push his shaft in. Then since both sexes do it, I see no reason why both cannot talk about it.'

'Damned if you'll not be wanting equal rights next!' said he with a hand on the lady's knee. 'What then − will you insist on lying on top every time, to prove you're as good as any man?'

'I shall do whatever gives me most pleasure,' she replied, 'I always have and I mean to go on in the same course. Now, this business of feeling Miss Harker — in my opinion it is much more likely to have been *your* hand on her pussy.'

'None but the lowest bounder would name a lady whose pussy he had felt,' Randolph cried. 'Tell me if you will, dear lady, who are the friends we have in common, for I am mighty curious.'

'As it happens, Miss Violet Burkington-Hutchins is a niece of mine and I was interested to hear you say that Mr Mawby poked her at her coming-out. I knew that you had, for she told me of a handsome young fellow named Randolph Joynes who rogered her when she was still in the schoolroom, before her debut into society. You had her virginity, I believe. She still speaks of you fondly, though she is married this twelve-month past to Lord Henry Chevening and six or seven months gone in the family way.'

'Damme! How a chap's sins do find him out!' Randolph said cheerfully, much taken by the lascivious way in which his new acquaintance spoke.

'More particularly, though,' she went on, 'Alice Hamilton is a dear friend of mine, and from her I have heard much about you — not all of it to your credit.'

'Surely she can have no complaint against me?' he said, 'for I rendered her sterling service in the days of our friendship.'

'Quite so,' Lady Fotherington agreed, 'she awards you high marks for rogering. Her grievance against you is that you left her after too short a time and did not return to continue your pleasant games together. But she is a woman of the world, not a stay-at-home, and she has replaced you with two or three Guards officers who rotate their attendance on her as if doing military duty.'

The hansom stopped outside her imposing town house and as he hoped, she invited Randolph to come inside to continue their conversation over a glass of champagne, the hour being past six o'clock. A footman in blue livery opened the door with a deep bow to Her Ladyship, and took Randolph's top hat and stick.

She led him up a curving marble staircase, two flights, into a cosy sitting room he took to be her private retreat. A lady's maid bustled in before he was even seated, and was sent away to instruct someone named Ronan to bring a bottle of Veuve Cliquot at once.

Divested of her summer coat, Lady Fotherington showed herself to be in the simplest of silk dresses, cut somewhat after the French Empire style close to her form, to display her shapely hips, and very high-waisted, to throw into prominence titties of only modest size. Thinking it best there should be no sudden and unwelcome surprises if their acquaintance were to develop into any loser acquaintance, he enquired as to the whereabouts of Lord Fotherington.

'Abroad,' she told him, 'in Baden-Baden, to take the waters for his liverishness. Or so he said when he left, though I rather suppose that he has gone to roger a German Baroness or two.'

Ronan proved to be another footman, who brought in a bottle of bubbly and glasses and poured it for them. When he was gone again Randolph raised his glass to the lady and drank to her. She suggested that he quit his chair and sit alongside her on the sofa, which he willingly did.

In the cab, he had put a hand on her knee, and she had let him do so without reproof. He did so again now, the instincts of his entire adult lifetime driving him on to make trial of the lady, even though he was wholly unsure whether he would be able to achieve anything. Mr Percival lay limp in his hiding-place, and appeared to be in deepest slumber, even when Randolph turned up Lady Fotherington's skirts over her knees.

His hands began to wander gently over the uncovered treasures and she moved her legs with artful thoughtlessness to provide a view of a charming portion of her person — two smooth bare thighs! The very thought that a lady of the upper classes went out into the streets of London wearing no drawers blazed like a fire in Randolph's mind. How deliciously audacious of her, how truly aristocratic, to hold in contempt the polite and petty conventions of lesser mortals!

If only he had known this of her when they rode together in the cab from Bond Street, he would have given her a feel on the journey!

At last his gliding fingers reached the join of her legs and touched the centre of delight, her warm hairy pussy. It seemed to throb and palpitate in his hand, like a living creature. At the touch of his fingers on her dearest part, she hitched high her skirts and opened wide her legs, until Randolph could see the entire length of her fine slender thighs and the fringe of dark-brown hair that covered her cunny.

'Dear Lady Fotherington — what can the world offer lovelier than a warm cunny waiting to be poked,' cried Randolph.

'To be poked? Fie, sir,' said she. 'Nothing has been said about poking — I have given you no permission to do so. But you may play with my cunny, and whilst you do so you may call me Henrietta.'

Truth to tell, Randolph was relieved to hear her words, there being as yet no flicker of life from his shaft. He tickled her cunny lips expertly, and pressed a finger between them to find her button and tease it.

'You do that with a noticeable loving care,' said Henrietta, 'I take it that you enjoy playing with cunnies as much as doing them — is that so?'

Before he could reply, she was up off her bottom and kneeling on the sofa, her legs astride his knees and her dress held round her hips. The furry join of her thighs was no more than a handbreadth from Randolph's face, and he stared in warm admiration at her bared belly and dark bush.

Ah, the bitter irony of that moment, the sad mockery of Fate, that Henrietta was revealing to him the lovely secret charms of her soft little belly in which the button was sunk deep and a long lipped cunny almost hid from sight in dark-brown curls. All this was wasted on Randolph, for his shaft made no response, not even a twitch. His mind was filled with lust, but his loins were feeble and neuter.

Almost driven to distraction by his plight, he leaned forward to open Henrietta's split with trembling fingers and plunge his tongue into her.

'Ah yes,' sighed she at once, 'Alice Hamilton told me you had a way with your tongue that threw her into a perfect delirium of sensation. Bring me off, Randolph.'

He clasped the bare cheeks of her bottom in his hands to hold her close while he licked her button speedily. Her loins jerked back and forth, and in moments she gasped that she was coming off. Randolph gripped her tightly, to support her throughout a long and voluptuous climax of bliss.

When she was calm once more, though her limbs still shook to tiny after-spasms, she sat herself across his lap and dragged open his trousers to take out Mr Percival — and found him limp and small in her hand.

'What!' she cried out. 'You dare to insult me? I permit you access to my person and you have no cockstand? What are you — a eunuch? Or are you a damned Molly, preferring boys' bottoms to a juicy cunny?'

'God damn it to black perdition!' Randolph groaned.

The caning of his bare backside had obviously not cured him of his lingering emotions of uneasiness about Dorothy's bottom and his unauthorised use of it. Shamefaced and stammering, he explained as best he knew how the dreadful misfortune that had befallen him only that day — after years of diligent poking. Lady Fotherington was not won round, for she was a lady who desired action and had no time for excuses.

'Confound you,' said she, annoyed by his condition, 'you've done me out of my pleasure! Lorimer would have managed one or two pokes, if you hadn't chased him away.'

'Believe me,' said Randolph miserably, 'you cannot be half as put out about my incapacity as I am. Yesterday afternoon I passed in rogering until my partner was half-dead with the exhaustion of coming off time after time — and today, yours is the second cunny I have felt and prepared for a poke, only to find myself in this wretched state.'

'Why?' Lady Fotherington demanded. 'Were you so wrung out yesterday that you have nothing left today — is that it?'

'No, it is more complex than that. Unless I mislead myself, I am paying in some way for taking advantage of Miss Harker when she lay in a swoon.'

'You claim that your conscience is preventing your shaft from doing its duty? Pish — what utter nonsense from a man of your reputation! Have you never before taken advantage of a young girl — what of Violet Burkington-

237

Hutchins? She was barely sixteen with not the least notion of what a male shaft could do to her, when you had her.'

'The truth is this, something held me back from taking young Miss Harker's maidenhead when she lay in my power and instead I ravished her bottom. Since then, it is as if a powerful spell has been laid on my mind, rendering me uneasy.'

'That be jiggered for a tale!' said Lady Fotherington, with more heat than propriety. 'I refuse to be cheated of my due without making my feelings known. Get down and kiss my ladylike backside, for that is all you are good for.'

So saying, she stood up and turned her back to him, raising her clothes to bare her small-cheeked aristocratic rump.

'At once!' she commanded briskly, as if he were a flunkey in her household, 'Do not keep me waiting in this, as well!'

His face scarlet with shame, Randolph slipped from the sofa to his knees behind her, grasped her thighs and kissed the twin cheeks of her bottom in submission.

'At least you know your place,' Lady Fotherington commented over her shoulder to him. 'Again, till I tell you to stop.'

He kissed her again, many times, then parted the cheeks and licked up the crease between them.

'I'll be damned, but you've got a letch for bung-holes!' Her Ladyship cried. 'You'll not roger mine, for I have no taste for backstairs poking. You shall pleasure me as before.'

She lowered herself gracefully on the sofa, sitting with her legs splayed wide and her summer dress up round her waist, the long lips of her pussy pulled slightly open by the posture to display the dewy moisture that gleamed inside. Randolph turned, still on his knees, and slid closer to stroke her bare belly.

'Still no cockstand?' she enquired, hoity-toity. 'How vexing for you. I can't be kept waiting, for I must come off again. If your shaft's no good, then use your tongue once more.'

Humiliated to be spoken to in this off-hand manner, Randolph slid his hands up her ivory-skinned thighs, which lay as fully open as a book to be read. He stared in disappointment at the soft pink lips that gleamed through her dark-haired thatch, and his fingers moved inexorably towards them to satisfy her and then leave, to hide his shame.

Henrietta Fotherington's pussy was neither tight virginal, nor yet loose and flabby, but somewhere nicely between – much used and ready, well adjusted to its purpose of engulfing stiff shafts and receiving the tribute of their gushing desire. Just the sort of pussy Randolph adored to poke if circumstances had been normal. Alas, they were not.

The tip of his middle finger titillated those enchanting lips to part them wider yet, and Henrietta awarded him a brief smile of encouragement. He bent forward, his face pressing between her naked thighs, and she spread her legs further to give him room in which to work. His mouth took possession of her pussy, causing a little cry of pleasure to spring from her as his tongue entered and rolled over her secret button.

For Lady Fotherington these were moments of bliss and triumph – she had a handsome young gentleman down on his knees before her, licking her cunny to bring her to the sexual spasm. After which she would rest for five minutes and then order him to do it again. Yet for Randolph these same moments were an ordeal – his once-proud shaft had betrayed him into an unmanly weakness, and in his debilitated condition he could do nothing more to this willing beauty than bring her off by use of his tongue!

Whether to hate her for using him as if he were a servant, or to admire her for allowing him to make such use of her person as he could, he was in doubt to decide. He wanted to vindicate his manhood by poking her, more than anything he ever wanted before in his life, yet Percival hung too soft and small even to thumb into a cunny.

Or did he? The stimulation of Henrietta's pussy seemed to be having some sort of mild effect — or was this the delusion of a mind tottering on the edge of complete breakdown? To settle the matter one way or the other, he put a hand down between his legs, opened his buttons and released his member. A tremor of hope passed through his mind, to find it somewhat engorged, though by no means stiff.

Her Ladyship lay back on the sofa, legs sprawling immodestly wide, her soul soaring up into the Celestial Sphere, lifted by the intensity of blissful emotion Randolph's tongue imparted. She neither knew nor cared what he did to himself, so long as he continued to tongue her towards the sensual paroxysm that she lived for.

Randolph's clasped hand slid up and down his part, to bring it to life, to make it go hard enough to plunge into the cunny he was licking. Perhaps because nothing else occupied his mind other than the process of bringing off Henrietta, his frantic efforts were rewarded with some measure of success. Mr Percival grew thicker and longer in his hand, and gratifyingly hard-on.

Henrietta was sobbing in joy as she fast approached the apex of felicity. For Randolph also, a crucial moment was close at hand. His tongue flicked furiously in the wet cunny before him and all his limbs shook from tremors that racked him from head to toe. His clasped hand gripped his shaft tightly, sliding up and down in quickstep rhythm.

At this moment there occurred the miracle he had prayed for. Mr Percival Proud leaped in his hand, whilst the pent-up desire in Randolph's belly swelled into an uncontrollable explosion. He thrust his tongue deep into Henrietta and heard her faint cry of bliss, at the instant that Mr Percival spurted the creamy fluid of virility in gushes, soaking the sofa cushion between Henrietta's parted thighs.

'Ah yes, yes, yes,' Randolph gasped into her hot palpitating pussy with each throb of his shaft, his soul relieved beyond measure that he had been able at last to come off and satisfy his tormented mind that his powers were undamaged.

When Henrietta became quiet, he pulled slowly away from her, to sit back on his heels. His sexual ejaculation had sprayed an inside thigh and she feeling the trickle on her flesh, reached down to rub her fingers in the warm slipperiness.

'Well!' she exclaimed. 'You did something after all!'

'Henrietta, you have put right whatever the Devil it was that ailed me,' Randolph said. 'I am more grateful than you can ever imagine — and if a good rogering is still to your liking, you shall have it.'

'Let me see this Lazarus raised from the tomb!' she cried.

She took him by the hand and drew him up to sit beside her on the sofa, then clasped Mr Percival in her soft hand and rolled him up and down.

'He isn't stiff enough yet,' said she, 'he's only half hard-on, after spending in the air. But if you are truly restored we shall not wait long for, according to Alice Hamilton, you've poked her four or five times in a row with scarce a pause for breath between. That's why I hoped for great things from you when I invited you here.'

'You shall not be disappointed, I swear it,' said Randolph, a degree of conviction he did not feel in his voice, being as yet uncertain as to his degree of manly strength.

'Properly spoken like a gallant gentleman!' said she. 'Lie on your back along the sofa, Randolph, so that I may render you every assistance in making a good recovery.'

Under her guidance, he stretched himself out on the sofa at full length, and Henrietta opened wide his waistcoat and tucked his shirt up to bare his belly and thighs — and his half-hard shaft, which she rubbed briskly. It was not long before she had induced that condition of useful stiffness she craved, and she requested Randolph to remain as he was, on his back, Percival straining upwards anxiously, whilst she sat over his hips, her knees either side of his waist, and spread her skirts over him.

Beneath the covering folds of her dress, her hand found his shaft and guided the head to her pussy, then impaled herself on it. Randolph heaved a long sigh of delight to feel the soft and velvet folds of her wet split enfolding him.

'Dear Lady Fotherington,' he said, 'my darling Henrietta, you are a saint direct from paradise to have brought on this happy transformation of my condition. When I entered this room with you, my shaft lay cold and lifeless and I veritably believed my joy in existence to be gone forever. Yet now the miracle has been worked and I feel the bodily spasm fast approaching, even though I have been lodged within your sweet cunny for so short a time! You have saved my sanity and I am in your debt.'

'Then you must pay your debt,' said she. 'Do not insult me by coming off the moment you are in me, as my husband used to in the days when I spread my legs for him. Instant discharge may satisfy a man, but it does nothing to gratify a woman's needs.'

'Have no fear!' he replied. 'Now I have regained control of myself, you shall have a full measure of sensation before the paroxysm overtakes you.'

He watched the smile of concentration on Henrietta's long and aristocratic face whilst she rode up and down on his embedded shaft, giving herself delicious tremors of bliss.

'How adorable you are!' he exclaimed. 'Mr Dobson's sublime lines express the situation admirably — you may know them:

> *Angelic creature, fashioned in such wise,*
> *With love-wan eyelids and love-wanton eyes,*
> *Unveil thy titties, show those wondrous toys,*
> *All naked to my hands, my lips. Our joys*
> *Shall endless be, I hear thy love-sick sighs*
> *And sink my shaft between thy rounded thighs,*
> *While on thy mouth I dote in loving kiss,*
> *And roger thee to soul-disturbing bliss!*

'Oh, how very romantic that is!' Henrietta cried. 'You shall put those lines on paper for me before you leave, so I may learn them by heart.'

Under the stimulation of her wet cunny sliding up and down on his shaft, it had grown thicker and longer, and throbbed in joy and gratitude for the pleasure it was receiving. Henrietta was staring down at his face, assessing the strength of his emotion and his nearness to the physical convulsion.

If at that moment a servant had entered the room, footman or maid, nothing of a sensual nature would have betrayed itself to inquisitive eyes, though Her Ladyship and her visitor were both only heartbeats away from the sexual spasm. True, his position lying on the sofa was very strange and hers, seated on his body, stranger still. But highly improper though their posture undoubtedly was, nothing of the truth was revealed, her skirts covering all — the intimate embrace of stiff shaft by wet cunny and the friction of wet flesh on wet flesh.

Lady Fotherington's face was flushed a bright pink and her breathing was rapid, for she like Randolph was at the brink of fetching off. She bounced on his shaft with frantic vigour, making the hard-used sofa creak beneath them, and Randolph felt the floodgates open in his belly and his essence surge free. The shudder through his body communicated itself to Henrietta, who at this supreme moment thrust her loins hard down on him to force his leaping shaft deep into her belly, and at the very instant his torrent of desire gushed out.

At the spurt of his hot elixir within her cunny, her eyes opened wide in a stare of ecstatic sensation. She bit her teeth together, clenched her fists and beat them against Randolph's covered belly, driving the breath out of him as he bucked under her and spent mightily.

When Randolph was finished he lay still and gazed up at her flushed face, trusting that his performance had been sufficient to improve matters between them. Henrietta sagged forward, for the moment satiated, and smiled down at him.

'That was a damned fine poke,' said Her Ladyship.

CHAPTER 15
The Path of True Love Never Did Run Smooth

Refreshed in spirit by the gratifications of his before-dinner escapade with Henrietta Fotherington, Randolph went to bed that night a happy man. Whatever malign influence had lain heavily upon him, he now believed it had been lifted, for his shaft had stood hard-on as readily as always and performed its pleasant duty with frantic enthusiasm.

Sometime during the night he woke in his bedroom in Cavendish Square in an exuberant state of mind, for he had dreamed about Dorothy Harker. In that dream he stood in her room to observe her morning toilet when she rose from bed. It was as Bella had described — darling Dorothy sat on a towel spread over a chair, a bowl of warm water on the floor between her feet, her night gown up round her waist. The maid knelt at her side to wash her lovely young pussy with teasing fingers.

When Bella told this to Randolph, she said that she brought off Dorothy every time she washed her, and sometimes twice or more. In the dream it happened otherwise — Dorothy glanced up from watching the maid's deft fingers stroking her soft young pussy and caught sight of Randolph standing with his back to the door. At once she smiled at him, and instructed Bella to stop what she did and dry her.

Bella looked at Randolph, disapproval on her face, but she obeyed her mistress and patted her pussy dry with the towel. Then Dorothy rose from the chair, her nightgown held up with one hand about her waist to expose all her belly and thighs, and she hurried on bare feet across the room to where Randolph stood. As is the curious way of it in dreams, where the normal considerations of the material world are suspended, he seemed to be wearing no trousers, only a frock coat and top hat.

Dorothy's dainty hands unbuttoned his coat and moved over his body, sending him into raptures of delight. She took firm hold of his hard-on shaft whilst she kissed him passionately, her bare thighs rubbing on his.

'You shall have me, my dearest,' she murmured.

Her hand brought his full-risen shaft to the entrance of her maidenly pussy and held it there, throbbing intensely. Randolph did nothing − she herself pushed her belly forward and sighed a long moan when she felt the swollen head pressed inside her.

It was a curious sort of poke − Dorothy's belly was squeezed against his, his strong shaft all the way up inside her. He did not tup her, nor she move on him, but they stood locked in that silent embrace, and he knew that the climax of sensation would be reached and his creamy flood would pump itself into her in two more seconds.

Instead, he woke up to find himself alone in bed, his shaft standing up like an iron bar in his nightshirt and throbbing powerfully. In his jubilation he clasped it in his hand whilst he spoke aloud into the dark, his words a hymn of praise to the female parts he loved the best:

'May God bless every pretty young pussy in the world!'

cried he. 'Bless every delicious one for the power it has to bring a man's shaft up hard-on in a trice! Bless each sweet warm pussy for the delight and sensations of bliss it can give to a man! Parsons and politicians may say what they like, but pussy is the source of all human happiness! How fortunate the man who finds one he can love between the soft swelling thighs of a lovely and amenable young female, who is as keen on poking as he! In the union of their parts lies the highest felicity that mankind may achieve! When they share a bed together, their joyful rogering is a foretaste of the divine happiness we are told shall be our portion in the Hereafter! Pish, let Heaven go hang – give me a lovely young pussy to poke every time!'

Whilst thus celebrating in words the pleasures of the sensual act, Randolph pulled his nightshirt up to his chest slid his legs wide apart. With the affection due to an old and valued friend, he rolled Mr Percival Proud up and down, whilst in his fervid imagination he thought he spied a vision of dear Dorothy as he had seen her on her sofa, her dress pulled up, the slit of her drawers open, to reveal her curly-haired pussy between smooth-skinned white thighs.

In sad reality this was the moment he had made the fearful discovery that his shaft was unready – but alone now in his bed Mr Percival was hard and thick, and bounding in his hand.

'Oh Dorothy, I shall have you!' Randolph gasped. I shall get this shaft of mine into your pussy, and flood you with my cream for the very first time! I'll bring you off, I swear it!'

His hand slid up and down his quivering shaft until the frenzy of sensation seized him. His legs jerked wildly and his essence came gushing out in rapid jets that soaked the sheets above him.

247

'Dottie, my dearest Dottie!' he gasped out to each wet throb of his shaft. 'This is how I shall poke you, again and again!'

Mr Percival, freed from whatever mental fetters had bound him, bucked and reared and spurted to full satisfaction, after which Randolph gave a sigh of content and fell asleep. He had no more dreams that night, but when Lizzie brought his morning tea his shaft was stiff once more.

He told her to leave the tea and sit on the bed beside him, and to pull up her clothes so that he might have a feel of her pussy. She had become extremely submissive since he had started on this course of handling her in the mornings and poking her, and obeyed him without a word. It was scarcely necessary to ask before she had thrown aside the bedclothes and pulled up his nightshirt to bare Mr Percival, pointing stiffly upwards.

'Take my shaft in your hand,' Randolph commanded, 'and play with him — you know what is required.'

Lizzie blushed bright pink, but all the same she clasped his hard and heavy shaft in the palm of her hand and bounced it up and down very pleasantly. Randolph lay at his ease, his eyes closed, indulging himself in a shameful fantasy.

'My darling Dorothy,' he murmured, not caring if the maid heard him or not, 'how nicely you handle my shaft! I dreamed I rogered you, my dear, and woke up in this state you find me in. The soft touch of your hand throws me into ecstasies of delight unequalled before!'

Whatever thoughts Lizzie may have had at hearing herself thus addressed as *Dorothy* she said nothing, but continued to rub firmly at the straining shaft she held, whilst, meanwhile, her thighs were spread to let Randolph's hand fumble at her pussy.

'How you raise my passions!' he sighed. 'But a moment yet and you will cause me to fetch off, Dorothy!'

Truth to tell, the make-believe that he was being manipulated by Miss Harker and not the under-maid, sent tremors of bliss through Randolph that made him gasp and pant, and his belly to twitch wildly. His nervous system had reached the limit of its toleration and was about to discharge his emotions in a spasm of climactic sensation. His fingers gripped Lizzie's bare pussy with cruel strength and thick white essence gushed like a tall fountain from his upright shaft.

When he became tranquil and Lizzie had wiped his belly dry, she ventured to ask timidly whether it had been to his liking.

'Very competent, Lizzie,' said he, 'you've a useful hand on a man's shaft now I've taught you.'

She flushed red at his arrogant tone, but when he ordered her to lie on the bed beside him and raise her dress to her waist, she did so without protest. Randolph propped himself up on his elbow and with inquisitive fingers pulled open her drawers. He felt her pussy to see if it had become moist with longing, but could detect nothing.

To be truthful, having been pleasured by, in his imagination, sweet and virginal Miss Dorothy Harker, he had little appetite for Lizzie's easily available cunny just then. Yet his natural urge to domineer would not let him send her away before he had again demonstrated his mastery over her.

'Put your fingers to your cunny and fetch yourself off,' was his order to her.

Lizzie's face blushed brick-red at the words, and her sense of outrage was great enough to refuse to obey him in this. He, not to be denied, took her wrist and forced her arm down, until her work-roughened hand lay across her belly.

'No, for shame!' she cried.

Randolph pushed her hand lower, till it was between her legs. Still she said him *nay* even when he moved her fingers over her bush and pressed them against her cunny.

'Do it for me!' he said masterfully, 'I insist!'

'Please don't make me, sir,' she pleaded. 'Poke me if you want, but don't humiliate me by asking me to do that.'

'The damned insolence of it!' said Randolph, enjoying to the full this show of resistance to be broken down. 'Do as I tell you, girl, or it will be the worse for you!'

Intimidated by his vague threat, her cheeks afire with shame and her eyes tight shut, Lizzie let her fingers trail over her pussy lips.

'Faster,' Randolph commanded. 'Faster, girl – open it and stick your finger inside! Do not pretend to me that you've not done it to yourself before – I'm sure you do it nightly.'

'Oh no, sir, no!' she exclaimed sincerely. 'How can you say such a thing!'

Whether she did it nightly, or weekly, was of no importance. She knew how to go about it, and there being no other way but to obey Randolph, she set herself to comply with his wishes.

His greedy eyes devoured her pussy. The sight of it drew him irresistibly to her, just as if it were a strong magnet and the hard shaft under his nightshirt a bar of iron to move towards it under the pull of its attraction.

'I am so ashamed, sir,' Lizzie whispered, 'to do this with you watching . . . it's not right.'

'Don't be a little ninny, girl,' he said forcefully, 'how can it be shameful for you to handle your own property and for me to observe it? Lascivious enjoyment resides not only in poking but in every amusing game the human mind can devise for the employment of shaft and pussy. If then it is permissible to handle each other's parts when a man and a female are together, then it cannot be shameful to handle their own privates by way of diversion when they rest between pokes.'

'I'm sure it must be wrong,' Lizzie protested.

'Fiddlesticks! There can be no objection to indulgence in these innocent sensual amusements, save the false prejudices of canting humbugs, whether of the cloth or the medical profession — for I have proved in my own person that even the greatest of them is mistaken — Dr William Acton's strictures on the heavy consequences of frequent indulgence in the sexual spasm are so much nonsense! I can do it again and again — and always will.'

Lizzie only sighed, not understanding of what it was he spoke so eloquently.

'Stop that miserable noise,' said Randolph. 'Pull the lips of your cunny open wider and let me see the button.'

Although the under-maid sighed and complained without cease at this gross abuse of her modesty, she continued to play with her pussy as ordered until she had progressed far along the pathway that leads to climactic bliss. Then her plaints ended at last, and she held wide the pink lips of her slit with one hand and with the joined fingers of the other rubbed at the slippery rose-pink bud that was exposed.

Randolph observed that she would shortly come off, and bring his fun to an early conclusion.

'Stop now!' he said. 'Move your fingers away from your pussy at once — at once, I say!'

Lizzie's eyes opened and she gaped open-mouthed and red-faced at him, not fully comprehending what he was at with her.

'You've given me a stand that needs to be taken care of,' he said. 'Leave your pussy alone, you slut, and take a hold of my shaft and give it a good feel.'

What he intended was to inflict the suffering of frustration on Lizzie, by causing her to stop when she was almost at the peak of her sensation. That was real mastery — to halt her when she was within moments of bringing herself off! He would have her stroke his new-risen shaft until he too was on the verge of spending, then disappoint her hopes of being rogered by putting her on her back and ravaging her rear entrance — for it was in his mind that he would feel easier about Dorothy if he took the pains to accustom himself to backstairs ingress.

In this he had reckoned without the vital force of Nature, if only the Nature of a downtrodden servant-girl. Lizzie was much too close to her culminating moment to be able to obey, even if she would, his cruel command. Her fingers rubbed furiously in her wet split, and her heels drummed on the bed.

'Oh, oh, oh!' she exclaimed, her back rising in an arch as she brought herself off in quick spasms.

'Damn you for a trollop!' Randolph gasped, astonished to see her coming off against his order. 'You've cheated me!'

Lizzie gave no sign that she heard his words or was aware of his anger. As for depriving Randolph of anything at all that was rightfully his, she was too far gone in sensual delight to hide anything from his sight. Her legs strained wide apart, her narrow loins bucked, and her hand flickered up and down at her wet pussy.

Randolph was undone by this display of female gratification — with a low moan of despair he threw himself between Lizzie's legs, his hand rubbing and pulling at his stiff shaft. His belly rested on hers and without a pause, he plunged six inches of hard gristle deep into her pussy, an rogered away for dear life.

'Oh sir, sir!' Lizzie gasped, her eyes bulging in her head, to feel herself being poked so fiercely. 'You'll kill me!'

'Yes,' he moaned back, 'I'll damned well kill you stone dead with poking, you slut! Shut up and keep coming off!'

Lizzie gurgled and gasped, kicking up her legs either side of him as he plunged in and out. In six more strokes he attained the very acme of sensation and spurted his hot lust deep into her quaking belly. She squealed and humped her body under him, while he spent in her to the very last drop.

After a sustaining breakfast of kedgeree and kippers, toast and best Oxford marmalade, Randolph took a turn about Cavendish Square, to settle his thoughts. He was in an exceptionally fine mood as he strolled round by the railings, even going so far as to throw a penny piece to an urchin in a peaked cap who was at work sweeping clean the road crossing.

The significance of his dream was clear – his heart was set on Miss Dorothy Harker. She came to him in visions of the night and asked him to have her, she stroked his belly and his stiff shaft and slipped it into her sweet little pussy. A fantasy of the night it may have been, but when he had tested the truth or otherwise of his nocturnal longing by having his shaft stroked in broad daylight by the under-maid, a veritable paroxysm of joy had been the outcome.

In this way, as he sauntered around the Square, tipping his hat to those other residents whom he encountered, Randolph at last persuaded himself that he was deeply in love with Dorothy. This conclusion was a bit of a facer for him, given as he was to playing the field and scattering his largesse with careless abandon. It threatened a change in his mode of daily life.

There had never been any doubt in Randolph's mind, not since he had first experienced the sensual spasm, that to be in love implied and required getting his shaft up the girl's pussy. Otherwise, it was merely sentimental rot. Therefore it followed that he must poke Dorothy Harker, soon and often. In spite of her apparent willingness to let him do so on the last occasion they had met, with curious results, he was tolerably certain that the moment he declared his undying love for her, she would close her legs tightly together and wait for a proper proposal of marriage.

'Confound it!' he said aloud, and hit the iron railings of the Square with his walking stick. 'If marriage is the price to be paid for rogering Dorothy at will, then so be it! I shall take a cab to Paddington after lunch and throw myself as her devoted suitor at her darling feet! She's of a decent family with land-holdings, and the pater will approve my choice.'

His mind made up, he returned home to change into his newest grey frock coat, and set off for his club, to lunch lightly and put the finishing touches to the elegant little speech he meant to deliver on his knees to his beloved. His liveliest hope was that, when Dorothy had accepted his proposal and given him her promise of betrothal, she would graciously allow him to set the seal on their agreement by giving her a jolly good poke.

Over lunch he chatted to a couple of his chums at the club — Billy Toothe-Tarkington, who knew something about proposing to a girl, he having been engaged to be married to the beautiful Miss Ella Blenkinsop for a twelvemonth or more; and Gussy Cranborough, who was in love with Charlotte, youngest daughter of Lord Fitchnewton, but could make no progress at all with his suit because the girl's father opposed it, thinking him of too restricted prospects.

After a bottle or two of wine, Gussy's advice was practical and useful. Win the lady's heart by taking her a large bouquet of red roses, he said, and some little trinket of a present to show her how thoughtful you are towards her. This had succeeded admirably with Charlotte, who worshipped him, but had no effect on her tyrannical pater. Billy had no advice to offer, but only smiled mysteriously when he spoke in the vaguest of terms about the bliss of being engaged to be married. From that Randolph deduced that he was rogering Miss Blenkinsop regularly.

Thus primed, he walked along Piccadilly after lunch to where he knew there to be a flower-seller on the corner with Regent Street, and there purchased for a couple of shillings every red rose the flower girl had to offer. For another shilling or two he could have had the girl as well, up against the wall in the mews, but his heart was set on Dorothy. To complete the advice he had been given, he strolled on into Shaftesbury Avenue, to the shop where Maria Peabody was employed.

His intention was to buy some small gift to take with him to Dorothy — a pair of gloves, perhaps, or a pretty fan, it being unseemly to take anything more personal. After they were truly engaged, he would make her secret presents of drawers, to have the pleasure of assisting her into them before rogering her on the sofa. Those were pleasures for the future, not for this important day of proposal.

When he entered the shop he was somewhat taken aback to find the proprietor present and behind the counter, though there was no good reason for surprise, for commonsense said that Mr Wyck would be more in than out. It was seeing him standing alongside pretty Maria that displeased Randolph. Mr Wyck was, as Randolph had thought, a man in his middle years, stout of body, with whiskers down his cheeks and a bald patch on the front of his head. He wore a vulgar turned-down collar and a tightly buttoned jacket, under which a paunch showed.

Maria concealed her embarrassment very well, and brought out fans and gloves to show Randolph while her employer looked on benignly and held forth on the high quality of the merchandise. If only the unwanted proprietor had been absent, Randolph would have slipped into the back room with Maria for a quick feel of her pussy, even though his mind was set on Dorothy. With a wink and a grin he conveyed this to Maria, and she blushed faintly.

Notwithstanding, it was disagreeable to contemplate that Wyck could at any time take Mara into the stock room and do as he pleased with her. The wretched shopkeeper had short and stubby fingers, Randolph noted — those fingers would toy with Maria's pussy later that day, after closing time. And horror of horrors — Wyck's wick would force itself into her and come off in that pretty slit Randolph had seen but been denied.

How monstrous it was, how infuriating! There stood the stout and cloddish shopkeeper, an ingratiating smile on his greedy face, and here stood, almost within arm's length of him, a most lovely and lascivious young female — a female Randolph had the most sudden urgent letch to poke, though it would postpone for a little while his visit to Dorothy.

Yet there was nothing to be done about it. The vile tradesman was in the saddle, so to speak, and there was no way to unseat him without bringing about Maria's dismissal. In the end, with gritted teeth behind his apparent indifference, Randolph bought a painted fan, had it wrapped, and left the shop in a far worse mood than when he entered it. He found a hansom cab to take him to Paddington Green, and sat fuming and calling down curses on the heads of shopkeepers who take advantage of pretty female employees and vent their low lust on their tender bodies. That activity should be reserved solely for gentlemen!

At the house in Paddington Green he plied the knocker briskly and the door was opened by Bella. She stared at him and at the bouquet of roses he carried, the strangest expression on her face. Randolph smiled at her and reached out to give a friendly squeeze to her vast round titties, but she drew back and told him that she could not let him enter.

'That be damned!' cried he, impatient of delays, and pushed past her into the entrance hall, and straight up the stairs to the apartment rented by the Harkers. Bella came scurrying after him, insisting that he was not to disturb Miss Dorothy, and in her haste forgetting her position and almost taking hold of his coat tails. As things were, he was nippier on his pins than she was, and gained the landing well ahead of her.

Not taking the time to tap at the sitting-room door, for fear Bella would overtake him and engage in insolent wrangling, he set his hand to the knob, turned it and pushed open the door. The scene that confronted him halted him dead in his tracks in the doorway. Lorimer Mawby was rogering Dorothy on the sofa!

The bodice of her dress was open to bare her plump titties, and the skirt was up round her waist to uncover her drawers — the very ones purchased from Wyck's shop, Randolph recognised. She had one stockinged leg stretched out along the sofa, and the other hanging over the edge, her foot on the floor — the posture requiring her legs to be widely apart.

The slit of her fine cambric drawers was also pulled apart by her position, the bare pink lips of her cunny and her neat tuft of curls on show to her companion. Lorimer had taken off his frock coat and his trousers were unbuttoned for his stiff shaft to stand forth in readiness — a shaft which, Randolph saw with distaste, was the equal of his own in length and thickness.

Neither of the lovers heard the sitting-room door open, being too engrossed in their sensual pleasures. Even as Randolph's eyes bulged astounded from his head, Lorimer treated himself to a feel of Dorothy's pussy, making her tremble and sigh. Then he kissed the fingers that had been privileged to touch her maiden charm and slipped them into her.

'This is so very indecent, Lorimer, my dearest,' Randolph caught her murmur, 'yet I would not have it otherwise . . .'

The blood drummed in Randolph's temples until he thought he would fall down in a swoon, to see Lorimer present the head of his shaft to the mark and sink it into Dorothy with a sharp push. She cried out a little, at losing her maidenhead, but her arms were about Lorimer, hugging him to her.

'Lorimer, Lorimer,' she gasped, as he thrust sturdily in and out of her pussy, and then, sooner than would be expected, her crisis of sensation arrived to the stab of his hard-on shaft.

'My darling!' Lorimer exclaimed, his voice choked by fierce emotions at the first throb of his spending. 'You are mine now, my dearest Dorothy, all mine!'

Randolph stood with a black scowl on his face to see darling Dorothy's stockinged legs kicking up in the air, and Lorimer's trousered bottom driving to and fro between her spread thighs as he spurted his desire into her.

To find himself forestalled in courtship of Dorothy by that fool of a Lorimer Mawby was more than could be borne! Randolph threw his bouquet of roses furiously across the sitting room, hoping he might score a hit on Lorimer's bouncing backside. The flowers fell short, landing harmlessly on the carpet, while the lovers continued to sigh and squirm in bliss, all unaware that they were observed.

Randolph turned on his heel and strode away, casting a look of detestation at the cowering Bella, and leaving the sitting-room door wide open.

CHAPTER 16
A Convenient Arrangement is Reached

Consumed by anger and jealousy at having seen Dorothy Harker being rogered by another man, Randolph flounced out of the house and hailed the first cab that passed by. Before long, he was back at his club in St James, where he found that Billy Toothe-Tarkington had left, but Gussy Cranborough was well into his second bottle of port wine.

Randolph joined him, sent for another bottle, and drank fast, being soon in a mood to confide in Gussy the failure that had been inflicted on him by a young woman he cherished, and the awful humiliation he had experienced to see her bestowing her priceless maidenhead on another. Unrequited love, said he, was the very devil, and he wondered how Gussy bore with fortitude Lord Fitchnewton's ban on an engagement to his daughter.

'It takes it out of a chap, keeping a stiff upper lip all the time,' said Gussy, who was by now a trifle glassy-eyed from the quantity of vintage Cockburn he had drunk since lunch. 'How I would bear up under the strain without the solace of dear Mrs Potter, I do not know.'

'Who might she be?' asked Randolph. 'A bawd who keeps you in young girls to bring down your cockstand?'

Gussy denied it indignantly, and claimed never to indulge his lust with doxies out of respect for Charlotte, the woman he loved and whom one day he hoped to make his wife, perhaps when Lord Fitchnewton was dead and gone and his eldest son, Hampton, succeeded to the title. Mrs Mavis Potter was, he explained, a dear and sympathetic female friend who lived in a villa he had rented for her by Wandsworth Common.

'By George, Gussy – you keep a woman for poking!' Randolph cried. 'Tell me about her – what class of person is she? Where did you meet her? Is she a good poke?'

Augustus Cranborough was far enough gone in his cups to have no objection to acquainting his good friend Randolph with some of the details of the case. He had met Mrs Potter on top of a horse-bus by Green Park, said he, on a rainy evening when there was not a cab to be had. She was a handsome well-fleshed woman of eight and twenty, in a dark coat and hat, with a fur wrapped round her neck. She was sheltering from the rain under her open umbrella and, there being no other place available, Gussy took a seat beside her on the bench.

He had left or lost his own umbrella somewhere that day, and sat exposed to the downpour as the bus rattled along, until the tender-hearted female next to him took pity and said he might share hers. Deeply grateful, he edged close to her and thought it no more than polite to introduce himself. She returned the favour, and they looked at each other with mutual liking. One thing followed from another, as the saying is, and instead of returning to their own homes, they found themselves becoming better acquainted in a rented room in Pimlico.

'By the Lord Harry!' cried Gussy. 'It was a damn fine poke, that first time with Mavis! There was a good fire burning in the grate, and we sat warm and snug, she on my lap, while I had a good feel of her titties. She has a good pair on her — not over-large, but nicely shaped and soft to handle. There we were together, chatting away, and she kissing my cheek now and then whilst I put a hand up her clothes. Her thighs moved apart to open the way to me, and we fell silent and joined our mouths in a long kiss when I fingered her cunny.'

'You've a talent for story-telling,' said Randolph, who was enthralled by his friend's frank account. 'What did her cunny feel like, Gussy?'

'There's no way to describe it — it was soft and hairy, with warm lips that parted easily to my touch. Damn it, Randolph, no words can capture the feel of a female article. We sat as if we were mesmerised, Mavis in the lascivious enjoyment of having her cunny fingered, I in the feeling of it. What more can I say of the moment?'

'Did she remain passive throughout?'

'Not she! When I'd made her cunny wet and slippery with my fingers, she exclaimed, *Let's have your trousers undone and see what you've got to offer me*, and an instant later she had out my shaft and dandled it between her fingers.'

'A sensible female who knows what she wants from a man,' was Randolph's comment. 'What then?'

'Before much time had passed we made our way across the room to the bed,' said Gussy. 'She took off her dress and drawers to lie on her back, the front of her chemise turned up to bare her thighs and belly. She has a great thick bush of reddish curls between her legs — a sight for sore eyes, believe me! I lay beside her and fluttered my fingers in her wet cunny, while she handled me until I was halfway coming off. *Oh, I must have you, Mavis!* I cried out, and at once she spread her legs wide for me. My frock coat was off and my trousers — I pulled my shirt up and laid my bare belly on hers.'

'A fine and comfortable poke,' said Randolph, 'no haste, no fuss — I prefer that myself, sometimes. At other times I would rather show off my mastery of the female slit. But go on, do.'

'What more is there to say?' asked Gussy. 'My aching shaft found the way easily enough into her cunny and I gripped hard the cheeks of her behind whilst I poked and she jerked her belly up to meet my thrusts. *That's marvellous*, Mavis cried, *I haven't had a poke for a week*! Her words threw me at once into a perfect frenzy of poking, my belly beating on hers in a rapid tattoo that stirred overpowering sensations in both of us. Her fingernails clawed down my flesh from shoulder-blades to rump, and I fetched off like the firing of a cannon.'

'Evidently it was a first-rate poke, for you continued your association with her,' said Randolph pensively. 'Why so, when so many pretty willing young females can be had for a sovereign or two anywhere in the West End?'

'I paid Mavis nothing for the poke,' said Gussy hotly, 'both of us did it for the pure pleasure of it. I arranged to see her again the next night, and then again the next, and after a week or so I came to realise that Mavis was filling an urgent need in my life.'

'Certainly,' said Randolph, 'the urgent need we all feel for a daily poke. What interests me most is why you continue so long with the same female.'

'I was — and I am — deeply in love with my darling Charlotte Fitchnewton,' said Gussy. 'I cannot look at another woman, so intense is the flame of my love and desire for Charlotte. The obduracy of her pater prevents the consummation of our love — I have for the past twelvemonth had no other consolation than my own hand on my shaft whilst I gaze fondly on a photograph of my dearest girl.'

'A twelvemonth without rogering – Good God!' Randolph cried, 'Fitchnewton should be made to sit with a bare bum on his own coronet, for putting you to such torment!'

'I have on more than one occasion, in deep distress, picked a young whore from the ranks along Haymarket and gone with her to her room,' said Gussy, 'only to find that, be she as pretty as a picture and hot for it as a bitch in season, my shaft refuses to stand, for in my mind I can think only of Charlotte watching me and I can do nothing.'

'Damme!' said Randolph. 'A pretty pickle to be in!'

'But you see,' said Gussy, 'with Mavis it is otherwise. When I first felt her pussy, no reproachful vision of dear Charlotte interposed between us. Then as now, when I lie upon her belly and roger her, I have no concern but the poke itself. Oh happy circumstance that I may fetch off without the least regret in Mavis's throbbing cunny! Do you wonder that I have continued with a woman who alone of her sex can afford me a fragment or two of pleasure to mitigate the pain of my separation from Charlotte?'

'All is clear to me now, Gussy. I find your arrangement to be admirable. How long is it since you installed her in lodgings at Wandsworth?'

'Nothing so mean as lodgings,' Gussy replied at once, 'I have rented a villa there, for which I pay a rent of twenty-five pounds a year. For the past five months or so, I have been there four times a week and rogered my fill.'

'It appears to me that what you have there are the conjugal pleasures without the inconvenience of marriage,' said Randolph in a thoughtful tone.

He remained at the club in conversation with Gussy until after six o'clock, then set out at an easy pace on foot, by way of St James's Square. His noddle was abuzz with lewd thought and speculation on the incessantly interesting topic of females and that most necessary item between their legs.

In retrospect, his escapade with Dorothy Harker had led him to nothing but trouble and unease, from the time he had found by chance an opportunity to knot-hole her, to this afternoon he had called to propose marriage to her, only to find her being poked on the sofa by another man!

Indeed, the very thought that he had been about to propose so serious a course as marriage to any woman at all, and thereby ruin his life of pleasure — the very memory made his blood run cold. As a wife, Dorothy would be a good poke for a half-year or so, young and frisky and apt for bedtime games — but motherhood and young children would put a stop to that, he suspected.

Her face would lose its youthful bloom under the endless care of parenthood, her titties would drop, her belly sag . . . how sad it was, how very sad, and yet that was Nature's great scheme of things for the female sex. He could recall some lines on it by Mr William Wordsworth:

> *When years ago, I Lucy loved*
> *and she was but thrice five,*
> *With eyes that flashed in amorous glow,*
> *The prettiest girl alive!*
>
> *Her lovely titties, round and fresh,*
> *My shaft stood when I felt;*
> *Her darling pussy, warm and soft,*
> *Beneath its silky pelt!*

> *But see her now — with children eight,*
> *Her bubbies swoll'n and coarse;*
> *Her burly shapeless dumpy frame,*
> *Hind-quarters like a horse!*

'No, the Devil take young virgins,' said Randolph to himself, 'for all such are a man-trap baited with honey, and the unwary enter this sweet trap between maiden's thighs, lured into it by a standing shaft. Unless they spend quick and pull out and run for their life, they perish in the embrace, perish by stages of boredom and sameness, perish slowly and most miserably when the first fine careless rapture of rogering turns at last stale and unexciting.'

Dr William Acton, whose doctrines Randolph held to be more or less true, although he despised the doctor's penny-pinching morality, had summed up the tragic lot of the married in a few well-chosen words:

As soon as the married female conceives, during the nine months that follow she experiences no sexual excitement, and therefore the consequence is that sexual desire in the husband is greatly diminished and the act of copulation takes place but rarely. After the birth, while she is suckling a child, the call made on her vital forces by the organs secreting milk annihilate all sexual emotions. As it is proved that a reciprocity of desire is necessary to a large extent to excite the male, we need feel no surprise to observe that, in the sanctity of married life, excessive indulgence is very rare, for the sensual feelings in the man become by degrees calmed down and extinguished.

That be damned for a Fate, thought Randolph, for if a

man has no letch for poking, he is well advanced towards old age and the tomb, though he be but thirty.

On the other hand, he had little regard, now he thought about it with care and logic, for titled ladies and all other society figures, pretty or not, such as Alice Hamilton and her friend, Lady Fotherington. These females and their ilk were fine for an evening's poking, but because of their elevated position in life they thought themselves able to demand at any time of day they chose an instant cockstand and a fast servicing.

They gave no heed to whether their companion of the moment had a letch to roger them or not. Their own female wishes were paramount, and this was a reversal of the proper roles of male and female. It was a gentleman's right to say when he wished to roger a woman, not the other way about.

Indeed, Alice Hamilton had all but worn him out with her keen relish for constant poking, so that he had given her up before long. Henrietta Fotherington had easier manners and conducted herself in a less Harpy-like manner in the bedroom, yet she too wanted her pound of flesh — or more precisely, her six inches of hard flesh, over and over, until it ceased to be interesting for a gentleman of quality.

Besides, confound it all, Henrietta was no longer young. She was not far off forty and, to Randolph, a gap of fifteen years between their ages put her in almost the same generation as his revered Mama. A gentleman of breeding made no impolite reference to a lady's age, whether he poked her or not, but it was impossible not to be aware that Henrietta Fotherington's titties were starting to droop and there were wrinkles appearing across her belly.

What then remained, if neither young gentlewomen or letching society ladies would meet the case? London was full of pretty young doxies, of course, costing only a few pounds for the best of them. Yet since he had passed his sixteenth birthday he had poked so many young whores that he was tired of their ways and wanted a change.

He enjoyed their skill in bringing a chap off, and the total willingness they exhibited to let a client do with them and to them whatever strange thing his fancy prompted. At a mere word a doxy picked up in Cremorne Gardens, or elsewhere, would get down on her knees and take a shaft into her mouth — and use her tongue on it until a chap spent fully.

Never in a lifetime would Miss Dorothy Harker be persuaded to lick a hard-on shaft, not even when she became Mrs Lorimer Mawby and the shaft was her lawful husband's, Randolph was sure about that. Nor would she ever permit Lorimer to make use of other orifices after they were wed — Randolph could take pride in having had the one and only use of her knot-hole.

Fortunately, of that she was still unaware, and would remain so forever, unless her maid Bella took it upon herself one day to reveal what had been done when Dorothy lay in a faint on the sofa. Then what of it? As Lorimer's wife, she would shy away from the least hint of scandal and keep her secret close. Poor Lorimer was welcome to her as wife, and to whatever he could get from her in the way of poking.

Meanwhile, what was to be done to satisfy Randolph's need for a sentimental attachment to a female as devoted to rogering as he was himself? A year before he had been head over heels in love with chestnut-haired Mrs Theodora Danty whose husband was away from their home in Camden Town very often, and for weeks at a time, attending to his employment of overseeing the laying of new permanent ways for the London and North Eastern Railway Company.

Being a full-blooded woman of five and twenty, Theodora

Danty had early succumbed to Randolph's dashing good looks and they indulged themselves very frequently in sensual delight. An age of blissfulness was compressed into less than a year, and never in their lives would he or she forget the delicious transports caused by the stiff insertion of his shaft into her pussy, time after time. However often they repeated their amatory exercises they were both thrown into voluptuous paroxysms at the stirring up of their Nature by his ravishing instrument and by the ready way in which Theodora received his assault, and returned it.

So lively and so repeated were the delicious enjoyments that together they participated in, that Theodora was brought into the family way, and to resolve her predicament she went north to lodge with her husband, declaring to him that she was alone too much. After a week or two of lawful rogering with him, she returned to London well able when the time came to persuade her spouse that the babe in her belly was his doing.

For another month or so, Randolph tried to revive the lively joy of their earlier days, but knowing her pussy to have been used by Mr Danty at his lodgings in Sunderland had lessened his appetite for it, though it was still freely at his disposal. When Theodora was four months gone, Randolph broke off with her altogether, declaring that she must lead a calmer life now that motherhood loomed near.

It disappointed her to lose him but she saw the good sense of his advice, and accepted by way of a parting gift a hundred guineas, with which to provide a layette when her child was born, and to be an endowment for its future. His child proved to be a girl, Theodora sent to inform him, when the happy event took place.

Even now, long afterwards, Randolph thought of dear Theodora with rueful lust, and as he continued his stroll from his club towards Haymarket, his shaft rose with his trousers in loving memory of the many days and nights of luxurious rogering he had of her. *Ah, Percival*, said he in his secret thoughts, *you were well provided for in those days, with a wet pussy awaiting your pleasure whenever you chose*!

In King Charles Street he overtook and passed by a man of his own age – not a gentleman, but a person poorly dressed in what must be described as a threadbare brown jacket and a billycock hat. The hat was brushed and the man's boots clean, from which Randolph deduced that he was a lowly but respectable employee in some nearby commercial enterprise, making his way home. A copying clerk, or something similar, paid thirty shillings a week.

Such creatures had not the easy access to soft young pussies that Randolph enjoyed, nor was there any reason why they should have. Even a two shilling poke in the dark standing against a wall was more than they could afford from their wages, and the first pussy they ever got their shaft into was on their wedding night. Their wives fell pregnant regularly, but that was the only pussy available, and they must get what pleasure from it they could.

In passing the fellow, who moved to the kerb to allow passage to his better, Randolph stared curiously into his face. He had a worried look about him, but that meant little – the working classes normally looked worried. How wide the abyss set between himself and this clerk of a man, Randolph thought – suppose he tapped the fellow on the shoulder and astonished him with the information that in the space of the last four weeks, the Hon Randolph Joynes had rogered no less than nine different females – maidservants, whores, society ladies? To say nothing of the time he had bung-holed a young gentlewoman in a fainting fit.

It was tempting to bowl an inferior over, but on reflection Randolph decided against the prank. Envy of the upper classes was a dangerous emotion in these days of Chartism and insolent workers demanding social reforms. Let the clerk go to his hovel and his squalling brats and console himself with his dismal wife if he could, happy in his ignorance that Randolph intended to make voluptuous use of a young cunny that evening, even if he had to pay a couple of guineas for it.

By the time Randolph reached the Haymarket and turned towards Piccadilly, he had lost the desire to choose a young doxy from the score or more waiting there for customers. Instead, he had come to the conclusion that he ought to take Gussy Cranborough as his example and provide himself with a fresh young female of middling class and education for a regular poke. A woman with no great prospects of marriage or advancement, was the ticket, a woman who would be honoured by a friendship with the son of an earl and give good value in return.

Not a whore, of course – it would be folly to become involved beyond a quick paid-for poke with a street woman. They lied and cheated when they could, they were unreliable and untrustworthy – in short, they were qualified for nothing more than a poke in a hired room. Nor did he want a servant, for having rogered the entire female staff of his Cavendish Square home, Lizzie being only the last of them, he could not bear their ingratiating way and their total ignorance of anything beyond cleaning, brushing and serving.

What he wanted, he saw clearly, was a young woman who had not lost all modesty, though she had had a lover before, a female with some refinement of manner, though not one of his own class hoping to be his equal. A pretty young female of the middling class, clean, cheerful, amusing, hot-blooded for a poke at any time. And who matched this description better than the shop girl in Shaftesbury Avenue – Maria Peabody?

It wanted ten minutes to seven o'clock when he stood outside Wyck's shop and, gazing through the window, he saw Maria alone, putting articles away in their boxes and tidying up prior to closing. Wyck might be in the back room, reckoning up the day's takings and waiting for Maria to close up and join him, to give her a poke before he departed for the bosom of his family.

Faint heart ne'er won fair lady, said Randolph aloud, though he could not recall which poet had penned the immortal line. He pushed open the shop door, setting the little bell to tinkling, and raised his hat to Maria. He asked softly, with a glance at the door behind the counter, if she was alone, and she told him that Mr Wyck had already left for the evening. Her manner was distinctly cold towards Randolph.

When he sought to find the reason for this, it soon became apparent that she had taken umbrage earlier, when he had called in with a bouquet of roses in his hand to buy a gift for a female friend, for thus she shrewdly assessed the situation.

'If you pass your afternoons with close female friends whose undergarments seem to be of such interest to you,' said Maria huffily, 'there is no reason for you to come here afterwards, for I have nothing for you, and seek nothing from you.'

'How your eyes flash when you are angry!' cried Randolph, in raptures at her heightened beauty. 'Before you send me away, hear me out, Maria! This afternoon I have felt no titties nor fingered any pussy.'

He spoke with perfect truth, though his failure to achieve a poke with Dorothy was by chance, not intent.

'Then who did you call upon?' Maria enquired, suspiciously.

'The flowers you saw and the fan I purchased here were for no female friend,' said he firmly, 'but for my Aunt Tabitha, from whom I have prospects. Today is her eighty-sixth birthday, and I called at her house in Hampstead village, to present my good wishes and compliments.'

'Is this true?' asked Maria.

'On my honour,' he replied, placing a hand on his heart.

'Then you are forgiven,' said she, smiling at him. 'Have you returned to make another purchase? Something of more interest to you than a fan?'

'I am here to make a certain proposal to you, Maria, one that I most sincerely hope you will give your diligent consideration before responding to it. But we cannot discuss it here where we may be overlooked by passers-by glancing in through the window. Close the shop, lock the door for the night, and let us adjourn to the back room, so that I may fully lay out my proposal.'

'It seems to me this proposal of yours may be concerned with the display or removal of undergarments not normally shown to a gentleman customer,' said she with a bewitching smile.

'There is an element of truth in what you say,' he told her, 'but what I wish to suggest to you is much more comprehensive.'

'Will you give me your word that it will in no way affect the loyalty and duty I owe to my employer, Mr Wyck?' she asked.

'You may trust me absolutely, Maria.'

With that assurance, she pulled down the blinds over the

door and the window of the shop, turned the key twice in the lock, then accompanied Randolph into the stock room. He gazed coldly for a moment at the desk, wondering if Wyck had poked Maria on it since last he was here. The irritating question passed and he handed Maria to the chair, taking his position close by, one cheek of his bottom resting nonchalantly on the fateful desk.

'I will not disguise from you, dear Maria, that in the short time we have been acquainted with each other, I have formed a high regard for you. This, coupled with affection and respect, emboldens me to hope you may accede to a plan of action I have devised that would enable me to offer you a far better mode of life than is at present your lot.'

'You mean to tempt me away from my duty,' said she, frowning slightly, 'that is unworthy of you after your promise not to!'

'By no means!' Randolph cried. 'For what I wish to propose to you is that you leave the employment of this mean-spirited shopkeeper and free yourself from his despicable abuse of your beautiful person.'

'What!' she exclaimed. 'Give Mr Wyck notice of leaving his employ? But how shall I live without my wage?'

Randolph took her trembling hand in his and pressed it gently while he explained that it would give him the very greatest of joy to acquire for her the lease of a villa in the pleasant suburb of St John's Wood, and to pay a wage to a maid to clean and cook for her. In addition to all that, he would put thirty gold sovereigns into Maria's hand on the first of each month, for her clothes and food and outings.

'Great Scott!' she exclaimed, amazed by the sums of money she was being offered in cash and in kind. 'I can scarcely believe it! How often would I receive you there?'

'Very often,' he said, 'for I have a warm nature and delight in giving it constant expression with a sympathetic female.'

Seeing that she was sorely tempted by his munificent offer in return for the use of her cunny, Randolph hastened to convince her fully of the advantages.

'First thing tomorrow morning,' he said, 'you must tell Wyck you are leaving his employment, being unable to tolerate for a day more his contemptible desire to take advantage of you. At half past nine o'clock, I will be outside in a hansom cab, to take you away from this awful place where innocence and female modesty are abused, and carry you to St John's Wood, to inspect unoccupied villas. You shall choose the one you please, and we will go at once to make the arrangement. Before the day is out, furnishings shall be ordered and delivered and you, dearest girl, shall be installed in your own household. What do you say to that, Maria?'

'Oh yes,' she cried, 'I accept!'

'Excellent!' Randolph said, very pleased by her enthusiasm. In her own establishment, she would be a damned lively rogering partner, he was convinced.

As if to seal the bargain, Maria rose from the chair and put her arms about his neck, to press her soft warm mouth to his in a tender kiss. He returned it willingly and holding her hips, he turned her round and himself with her, until her back was to the desk.

'Prove to me that you are mine, my dearest girl,' he said.

Without a moment of hesitation, she reached down to haul up her skirt and part her legs. Randolph eased her down until she lay on her back on the writing desk, her head hanging down over the far end and her legs off the end nearest him. He turned up her dress and petticoats to her

waist, and took down the white cambric drawers he had paid
for, to expose her nut-brown nest of curls and the delicious
pink lips of her pussy.

How ravishing a sight she was to his gaze, this pretty
Maria of the brunette locks and the wasp waist! How
enticing a cunny laid bare for him to pierce! He grasped her
ankles and raised her legs to the perpendicular, then parted
them a little, until her pussy jutted out from between, as
if pouting pertly at him.

Though her head hung over the far edge of the desk, he
could see the sweet smile on her lovely face as she awaited
the plunge of Mr Percival Proud into her cunny.

'Oh Maria, you make my shaft stand like a cast-iron rod,'
said he, and gazing fondly down at her charms, he recited
some lines penned by the celebrated poet Mr Samuel Taylor
Coleridge:

> *I gazed upon a lovely maid,*
> *Whose smile was warm and sunny,*
> *She'd full red lips and golden hair,*
> *A plump and open cunny.*
>
> *I laid her down upon a bed,*
> *To assuage my fiery lust,*
> *And brought her off, and me beside,*
> *With many a pleasing thrust!*

'How very charming are the lines!' said Maria. 'You may
put in your stiff part and bring me off as soon as you like!'

On hearing that, Randolph stood close in to her bottom,
and as if knowing his wish without the need to be told, Maria
took hold of his hard-on shaft and slipped the head between
the soft lips of her split.

'My darling!' cried he, and with a strong heave of his hips, he speared her as deep as he could go.

'Ah,' she sighed, 'you have more than I'm used to!' Randolph was not surprised to hear that his shaft was thicker and longer than a shopkeeper's, for that was the proper order of things. Wyck might have four flabby inches or so to slip up a girl and come off in a tepid dribble, but Maria was now about to learn that a titled gentleman's shaft was massive, noble and profuse in its spending.

He felt the warmth of her bottom against him, and held high her legs, close to his chest, while his belly touched against the backs of her thighs. She wore grey stockings, gartered with black watered-silk ribbons above the knee, and while he slid in and out of her pussy, he opened and closed her legs like a pair of dressmaker's scissors, by means of working her ankles. The lewd movement revealed and hid by turns her dear little split, in which he was preparing to unleash his hot lust.

'Maria – darling girl! What a marvellous pussy you have!' exclaimed he, an almost insane excitement gripping him whilst he closely observed how he was using her.

'I'm sure it's very ordinary, really,' she sighed modestly.

'No, it's a gem amongst pussies,' he insisted breathlessly, as he tupped into it with long sliding strokes, 'I don't think I ever liked one better!'

'Then do it as you will,' Maria moaned softly, 'for I am sure I have much to learn from you, and I shall be a willing pupil.'

Randolph's boisterous shaft leapt joyfully inside its lodging as he came to the short strokes and increased his pace. Only an instant later he fetched off in spurts of thick essence which shook him in rapturous spasm. Underneath him, Maria shuddered and gasped and jibbed her belly up to meet his out-pouring. The blissful throes diminishing at last, Randolph concluded that he had made a useful choice, and that Maria Peabody would do well for him for a year or two.

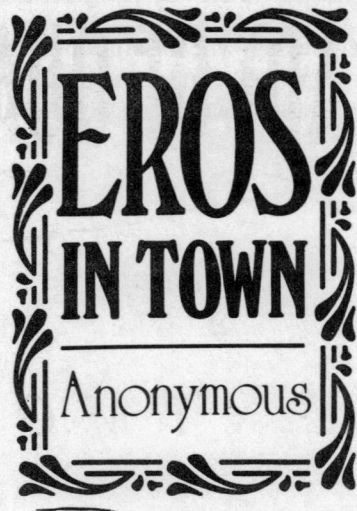

A LADY OF QUALITY

*A romance
of lust*

A N O N Y M O U S

Even on the boat to France, Madeleine experiences a taste of the pleasures that await her in the city of Paris. Seduced first by Mona, the luscious Italian opera singer, and then, more conventionally, by the ship's gallant British captain, Madeleine is more sure than ever of her ambition to become a lady of pleasure.

Once in Paris, Madeleine revels in a feast of forbidden delights, each course sweeter than the last. Fires are kindled in her blood by the attentions of worldly Frenchmen as, burning with passion, she embarks on a journey of erotic discovery . . .

FICTION/EROTICA   0 7472 3184 2

A selection of bestsellers from Headline

FICTION

STONE COLD	John Francome	£4.50	□
PRODIGAL SINS	Rosalind Miles	£4.99	□
MAGGIE OF MOSS STREET	Pamela Evans	£4.99	□
SHADOWFIRES	Dean R Koontz	£4.99	□
REASONABLE DOUBT	Philip Friedman	£4.99	□
THE OLD CONTEMPTIBLES	Martha Grimes	£4.99	□
THE ASSIZE OF THE DYING	Ellis Peters	£3.99	□
WATERSMEET	Philip Boast	£4.99	□
TREAD SOFTLY ON MY DREAMS	Gretta Curran Browne	£4.99	□
THE POWER	James Mills	£4.99	□
PURPOSE OF EVASION	Greg Dinallo	£4.99	□

NON-FICTION

THE ENTERPRISE YEARS A Businessman in the Cabinet	Lord Young	£5.99	□

SCIENCE FICTION AND FANTASY

SETI	Fred Fichman	£4.50	□
RITNYM'S DAUGHTER	Sheila Gilluly	£4.99	□
WOLFKING	Bridget Wood	£4.99	□
THE GOD KILLER	Simon R. Green	£3.99	□

All Headline books are available at your local bookshop or newsagent, or can be ordered direct from the publisher. Just tick the titles you want and fill in the form below. Prices and availability subject to change without notice.

Headline Book Publishing PLC, Cash Sales Department, PO Box 11, Falmouth, Cornwall, TR10 9EN, England.

Please enclose a cheque or postal order to the value of the cover price and allow the following for postage and packing:
UK: 80p for the first book and 20p for each additional book ordered up to a maximum charge of £2.00
BFPO: 80p for the first book and 20p for each additional book
OVERSEAS & EIRE: £1.50 for the first book, £1.00 for the second book and 30p for each subsequent book.

Name ....

Address ....

....

....